Sheer Madness

by

Laura Strickland

A Buffalo Steampunk Adventure

Sheer Madness

Cover Art by *Diana Carlile*

The Wild Rose Press, Inc.
PO Box 708
Adams Basin, NY 14410-0708
Visit us at www.thewildrosepress.com

Publishing History
First Fantasy Rose Edition, 2016
Print ISBN 978-1-5092-0753-4
Digital ISBN 978-1-5092-0754-1

A Buffalo Steampunk Adventure
Published in the United States of America

"The party's downstairs in the solarium, where my father's summoning the souls of the dearly departed. You must have taken a wrong turn at the stairs."

"No. I don't want him. I want you." Abruptly he realized it for truth: he wanted her as only a man possessed of flesh could—and surging flesh, at that. It made no sense, yet he couldn't deny it.

She shifted slightly on the balls of her feet the way she had just before she took on the two thugs who'd come through the window. Did she, then, think she needed to fight him off?

He said quickly, "I'm not here to harm you. Rather, I need your help."

She tipped her head. The black hair slid over one shoulder to caress a generous breast. His nonexistent fingers itched.

"I'm not able to help you." She waved a hand in the air. "Be gone, spirit, to the next realm."

"I can't."

"Of course you can." She leaned toward him, and her gaze moved over him with considerable interest. "Do not partake in my father's mischief. Spare yourself that. Move on and embrace peace. I dismiss—"

"No." He moved closer, and her eyes widened again. "Don't do that. Don't send me away."

She drew herself up to her considerable height, which had he possessed his body must nearly match his. "But, Mr. Marsh, it's where you belong."

"It isn't."

"Give me one good reason why," she challenged.

He could give her the very best of reasons. "I'm not dead."

Chapter One

Buffalo, the Niagara Frontier, January 1883

"A strapping sort of wench, ain't she?"

The voice issued from the direction of the bedroom window and made Topaz's eyelid twitch. She'd fallen asleep this night not only with the lamp still burning but with the window cracked, so the words came to her far more clearly than the speaker probably surmised, as did the hissed reply.

"Shut up, Sam!"

The first voice, male just like the second, ignored the directive. "I mean, Bert, she's not exactly a delicate little flower, is she? How are we supposed to abduct that?"

Topaz lay perfectly still except for that single eyelid which she opened enough to view the room. Her heartbeat accelerated and her fingers curled against the soft sheet that covered her.

An abduction attempt, was it? Yet another one. Did these fools never learn?

What a perilous place the criminal mind must be: From all she'd learned, it tended to be narrow as well as corrupt, impetuous, and lacking even a grain of common sense.

Take these two, for instance; they decided to abduct her on a cold January night with pellets of ice ticking like bullets against the window glass and a wind blowing straight off the Niagara River. They failed to study their potential victim, and they scaled the house to what had to be a dangerous perch on the ledge outside her window. They were, quite plainly, too stupid to continue drawing breath.

Weren't they aware of what had happened to the last idiots who attempted to abduct her?

"Shut up, I tell you!" said the second voice, which was deep, raspy, and unquestionably menacing. "She's one female, ain't she? How hard can it be?"

Topaz's lip curled, and she tensed in every limb. She knew she lay like a sacrificial lamb atop the bed, covered only by the sheet, a tableau to the eyes of these peeping Toms. Part of her wanted to shrink from their prying eyes; the other part ignited with rage.

"Get that window open."

"Damn, Bert, what kind of woman leaves the window cracked on a freezing night like this?"

"Lucky for us she did. Over the sill with you, and keep her from screaming."

"All right, all right. But you're carrying her down."

The window slid up. Topaz moved her hand just enough to ease the stiletto knife out from under her pillow. The silken feel of the hilt against her palm lent reassurance.

The first of the two men scrambled over the windowsill. His feet hit the bedroom floor at the same moment as Topaz's. She came up poised on the balls of her feet with the knife held in front of her, in a fighting stance.

Her potential abductor had landed not three feet from the foot of her bed. He wore a rough coat sprinkled with snow and a cloth cap pulled all the way down to his eyebrows, and stood no taller than she. No wonder he worried about manhandling her.

His startled gaze moved over Topaz, and his eyes bulged. "Sweet Jesus!" he breathed.

His companion came through the window and jostled him aside. A bigger man with wide shoulders and fists the size of hams, he had a face like an unpeeled potato, only twice as ugly.

Topaz smiled at him.

"She ain't screaming," said the shorter man. "Why ain't she screaming, Bert?"

"Because I have this." Topaz flexed the fingers that held the knife. "Gentlemen, you are trespassing. If I gut you, the law is on my side."

The little fellow shrank back to the window, proving himself marginally smarter than his companion. The wind blew the white lace curtains around him like a wedding veil.

"Come on, then," Topaz told the other fellow. "Try and abduct me."

His face creased in a ponderous scowl. He came at Topaz with his arms spread like the pincers of a crab, his big boots crushing the soft carpet.

Topaz narrowed her eyes, peering through black lashes, and tossed her head. She rose up on her toes and prepared to spring.

Her brother, Sapphire, had taught her how to fight some years ago, before he lost interest, as he did in most things. Topaz had kept up with it and now far outdistanced Sapphire in prowess. She figured if her father ever lost his great fortune, she could find work as an assassin.

She watched her opponent's eyes, set beneath filthy, scraggly eyebrows, and when he blinked she leaped, much in the manner of a striking cobra.

The sheet which had come up off the bed with her fell, leaving her naked as she always slept. Not a dainty miss, no—she was, as the men had already observed, no delicate flower. But her proportions, so she believed, must be enough to take any man's breath away.

The man standing at the window swore—or perhaps implored God. The bigger fellow balked, his eyes falling predictably to Topaz's chest, which provided just the distraction she needed.

She struck a blow of exquisite precision that laid his cheek open. Before he could blink, she struck again, her blade cutting through his coat at the shoulder.

He stopped like a bull hit between the eyes with a hammer.

The other fellow whimpered, but Topaz didn't spare him a glance. Instead she watched the blood well in the cut on her opponent's cheek and waited for him to make a decision. Had he had enough?

The wind streamed in through the open window and lifted gooseflesh all over Topaz's body.

"Frigging crazy bitch!" said her opponent and came after her again.

The next few moments proved vigorous and exciting. When they ended, Topaz was breathless, her black hair wrapped around her like the threads of a cyclone. Her opponent knelt on the floor clutching his arm, from which he bled heavily.

Topaz jerked her gaze to the little fellow who scrabbled at the frame of the window, as if he wanted to leap through it backwards, and never took his eyes from her.

"Get out," she told him softly. "Take your friend."

He nodded so violently his hat fell off his head, and he bent down to tug ineffectually at his companion. "Come on, Bert!"

"Yes, go on, Bert," Topaz repeated. She reached out a bare toe and nudged his chin. "Leave before I finish the job."

He glared up at her, big yellow teeth bared. "You cut me. You'll pay for that, bitch. I'll get you, understand?"

Topaz bent down and glared into his eyes, the now-stained stiletto still in her hand. "You are bleeding on my carpet. Remove yourself." She lifted her eyebrows. "Or do you want me to curse you, as well?"

"Witch! She's a Gypsy witch," the first man bleated. He seized his larger companion beneath the armpits and dragged him back to the window. "Come on, Bert. Let's get!"

Bert, seeping blood from half a dozen places, glared at Topaz. "You'll regret this night's work."

Topaz frowned at him. "If I ever see your repulsive face again, I'll castrate you. Understand?"

The smaller man made a sound very much like a sob. He dragged Bert over the windowsill and onto the ledge, from where they half fell, half climbed back down the rough stone exterior of her father's mansion.

Topaz tossed his cap out after him, shut the window, and thumbed the latch. She could see herself reflected in the glass, naked white skin, generous curves, and the long, black hair overlying all. Behind her, over her right shoulder, she caught the reflection of something else—an indistinct shape pale as smoke or

5

steam. She whirled so quickly her hair flared out around her and the breath caught in her throat. A chill chased down her spine, not caused by the fight just past or the cold air filling the room.

A voice sounded in her mind.

Impressive performance, lady.

A long shudder passed through Topaz's body. She shook her head. Three times in the last two days she'd thought she caught a glimpse of something from the corner of her eye.

One of her father's summoned spirits, perhaps, gone astray from the solarium where he did his work—and bled his clients for big money. Amazing what the bereaved would pay for a chance to regain some semblance of their loved ones.

But Topaz wanted no part of her father's business. And the spirits he summoned could stay well away from her.

The latch on her bedroom door rattled an instant before the panel swung open. Topaz snatched up a silk robe and drew it on just as her brother, Sapphire, stuck his head inside.

"Everything all right in here? I heard something…peculiar."

"Just another abduction attempt. I took care of it. Come on in."

Sapphire glided in, moving with his usual grace. An undeniably handsome man was Topaz's brother, with black hair that fitted his skull like the feathers on a raven and deep black eyes fringed with lashes even longer than Topaz's. The Hathor family showed quite clearly their Gypsy ancestry even if several generations' breeding with non-Magyars had paled their skin and bestowed upon Topaz eyes of amber gold to match her name.

Sapphire, with his slim height, flashing eyes, and slight widow's peak, had been known to more than once make proper ladies swoon.

Now he gave Topaz a comprehensive look and tipped his head. "Again? I hope you didn't get more blood on the carpet. Carlotta will be upset."

Topaz suspected Carlotta, one of the upstairs maids, had been sharing Sapphire's bed. She looked down at the plush cream-colored rug, now liberally splashed with red.

"Damn it," she said, and scrubbed at the stain with her foot. "I have to get a darker-colored carpet."

Sapphire laughed. One of the things that endeared Topaz's brother to her was his twisted sense of humor, which matched her own. One of the things that annoyed her was his inability to focus on anything for more than ten minutes at a time.

They were but two of their parents' brood, the youngest and the only ones left home. Two older brothers, Emerald and Diamond, had flown the coop early and now lived in other parts of the country. Two older sisters, Ruby and Opal, had wealthy husbands of their own. The matriarch of the family spent her time— and her husband's money—living the lavish life of a countess. Judging by her fragile beauty, no one would guess she'd borne so many children.

Sapphire scrutinized the trail of blood leading to the window and raised his eyebrows suggestively.

"What did you do with your would-be abductor? Toss him down two stories?"

"Abductors—there were two of them, and they

climbed back out."

"I'm impressed, little sister."

Impressive performance, lady. Topaz heard the words in her head again.

"You taught me well." Topaz planted her hand in the middle of her brother's chest and pushed him down onto the foot of her bed. "And now, dear brother, I need your help again."

Chapter Two

"Speak fast," Sapphire advised and raised his eyes to Topaz's. "I have an assignation in a little while."

"At this hour?" Topaz shot him a stern look. "And in this weather?"

He shrugged negligently. "It's not all that late. Mother's still up, and Father has a room full of clients downstairs. And who said I'm going out?"

Topaz bit the inside of her lip. So Sapphire *was* seducing Carlotta. A pity, because Sapphire's affairs only ever ended one way, and Topaz sincerely liked the little maid with the unlikely name.

"You should be ashamed of yourself, Brother."

"Me?" He widened his eyes in mock innocence. "Can I help it if I'm irresistible?"

Topaz supposed he couldn't. A blessing and a curse, she knew—but why couldn't she have inherited a few shreds of that deadly charm? Instead she got branded with descriptions like "strapping," "healthy," and even "hefty." Not that she carried much extra flesh, strictly speaking. Most of it was muscle. But she would have made a better Magyar warrior than Sapphire.

"I shall need to have a word with Carlotta."

"Yes, but not till morning, all right? It's a frigid night, and I do like a warm bed. Now you wouldn't want to keep me, dear sister, so what can I do for you?"

Topaz fixed him with a stare. She'd once been told

by a rare suitor that her gaze was too direct and impossible to endure. Sapphire met it without difficulty.

"Do you sense anything in this room? I think one of Father's spirits may have escaped him again."

"Ah." The expression on Sapphire's quick, clever face changed, stilled, and became intent as if he listened without using his ears.

As offspring of one of the greatest mediums of their time and certainly the most controversial in Western New York, they might well expect to have inherited a measure of the man's other-worldly talents. In truth the household made no fit place to grow up. Their four older siblings had fled as soon as practicable for good reason, and it might be said neither Topaz nor Sapphire fit the parameters of "normal."

Bad enough to have a father who possessed the ability to contact the spirits of the dead; Frederick Hathor, embracing the advances of his time, also experimented with the summoning, trapping, and "reassigning" of spirits, as he called it. A client with enough money and a sufficient weight of grief could seek to have the spirit of a departed loved one implanted in a custom-built steam unit, a specially constructed automaton, or even the body of an animal.

Adored by some, feared by many, and reviled by most, he'd been dubbed the Spirit Master. Buffalo's religious leaders denounced him and predicted he'd end up in hell. He'd survived two assassination attempts, and his family members had endured many attempted abductions by those who thought they could force either money or compliance from him. Last year someone had tried to burn his mansion down, but a sympathetic spirit had warned him in time.

Topaz and Sapphire, who both loathed their father's spiritual practices, did not like admitting they too could sense the presence of spirits. Sapphire treated his ability with a dismissiveness in line with his general attitude. Topaz never acknowledged—even to her brother or herself—how acute her own sense had become. She shrank instinctively from making contact with the lost spirits who haunted the place, flinched from their yearning, fear, and vulnerability—far more than she could bear.

Now she held her breath while Sapphire's dark eyes became opaque as onyx. She knew darned well there was a spirit in this room, but she wanted his confirmation.

"Well?" she prompted after a moment.

Sapphire's long, slender fingers tensed and then relaxed again. "I do sense something. Faint. Not like the spirits he usually attracts."

"Yes." Topaz drew the dressing gown more closely about her body and shivered. "It's been coming and going for the past two days. But it doesn't feel quite like the others."

From time to time spirits did escape the big room downstairs where Frederick Hathor did his work. As a child, long before she'd learned how a strayed spirit's grief could weigh her down, Topaz had spent weeks playing with the ghost of a dead pirate, and all the Hathor children had learned early *not* to look under their beds.

Sapphire shrugged. The mist cleared from his eyes. "So tell him. He'll clean up the vibrations and recall it."

Topaz nodded, but she still felt uneasy. "What's different about it, though? Can you tell?"

11

"No, sister dear." Sapphire gave her a significant look. "Maybe it escaped from the cellar."

Their father had a workshop in the cellar of the mansion on Humboldt Parkway, the door of which was always kept locked. Even Frederick's children weren't permitted to know what went on there, and only certain of the steam servants closest to him had leave to enter.

She leaned closer to her brother. "What do you think's down there?"

"I try not to think about those kinds of things, when Father is concerned. And I stopped wanting to know what he gets up to a long time ago. One thing you can bet—it will involve money. There are a lot of wealthy people in this city, and Father is out to fleece them all."

"He doesn't fleece them, though, exactly. In all fairness, he gives them what they want—the spirits of those they love returned to them in some form, even if it's mechanical."

Sapphire's gaze met hers once more with surprising frankness. "But there's no mercy in it, is there? I think that's what bothers me most. He's possessed of this very great ability he professes to use in order to alleviate the grief of the bereaved—which he will do only if they hand over great rafts of money." Sapphire frowned, his expression now completely serious. "I meet poor people every day who've lost someone, and their grief is as valid as that of the tycoons with whom Father deals."

Topaz knew her brother routinely haunted some of the lowest dives on Buffalo's waterfront. He'd learned his fighting skills—the same he'd taught Topaz—after being jumped there numerous times. She sometimes wondered if he might someday disappear into that dark underbelly and simply stop being Frederick Hathor's son.

She asked, "So why don't you help those people? Set up your own service for free."

Sapphire shuddered. "I'd rather off myself. Besides, I don't have the talent, only mere whispers of it. Too much of Mother's blood in my veins. But you"—his gaze moved over Topaz again—"you even look like him. I've often wondered how much ability you inherited."

Topaz shook her head in denial. Like her brother, she didn't want to know.

"And now, sister mine, I must leave you." Sapphire got to his feet and moved her aside gently. "I have a warm bed and even warmer kisses waiting for me."

He gave her a mischievous look. "You should try that sometime. One of the human footmen, perhaps— that Gerald might give you a tumble. Trust me, it burns off some of those troubling energies."

Topaz considered it. Gerald, six feet tall and with flaming red hair, might well make a fine choice. But she didn't need the complication.

She laid her hand on her brother's arm. "Just don't end up hurting Carlotta, all right?"

"Would I do that?"

"You always wind up hurting them."

"Well, I won't this time."

And why should this time be any different?

Sapphire moved to the door, where he paused to survey the room. "Oh, and Sister, about your trapped spirit?"

"Yes?"

"If you want to identify it, I can think of one way."

"Yes?" Topaz repeated, and he leaned toward her in a conspiratorial fashion.

"Ask it," he whispered.

Chapter Three

"Romney Marsh." He repeated the words over again as he had already a hundred times. His name. He had to hold on to it lest the last threads defying separation break and he forget who he was. How long could a spirit retain its identity after being banished from the flesh?

He didn't know; nor could he be sure how many other cases like his had occurred. Most spirits parted from their bodies only at the moment of death.

His body lived yet.

And, damn it, he needed to get back to it, but not where it lay now in a dim room at the asylum, nothing more than a drooling husk with a beating heart.

He couldn't—he wouldn't!—go back there.

Romney Marsh, Romney Marsh. The words echoed in the indistinct swirl of energy that now passed for his mind. He had become the *thought* rather than the thinker, the spark that endured all.

Cut adrift, he had fled the terrible place his body lay and followed a call, faint at first but increasing in power, that drew his spirit as a magnet pulled at iron filings. Two days ago that had been—two days and a night, for he'd drifted through the dark streets of this city, streets all limed in hard frost, the way an elusive tune twines through a memory. To his surprise, he could see—not the way a body sees but in misty color, like images viewed through droplets of water. He'd seen the large elaborate mansion from whence the calling issued. He'd hovered in the street, not feeling the cold, and observed other spirits flocking around the place and passing in.

So many spirits. He recognized them for what they were, being insubstantial as they. Incandescent clusters of light, they streamed and floated, clung to the outer walls and even the turret at the top of the house. Whatever called from within drew them powerfully and irresistibly.

He too had entered the mansion, seeping through the wall like blood through a bandage. Inside he could see it all—the lofty proportions and lush furnishings of the house, the humans and steam units inside, and all the spirits streaming to one of the larger downstairs rooms.

And he could feel everything, the steam servants' artificial intelligences and the calling which stemmed from not one but three places: the room into which most of his fellow spirits flowed, the cellar below it, and a single room upstairs.

When he concentrated, he could tell the sources differed in both degree and color: the call from the parlor sure and powerful—this had reached out into the city; that from the cellar dark and terrifying; that from upstairs fainter, but delicious.

The source in the parlor demanded, that in the cellar repelled, that from upstairs promised. Just like the three bears, he told himself ironically, and wondered from whence that thought had sprung. A bit surprising to discover a disembodied spirit kept its sense of humor.

He wished he could remember more of what must be contained in his mind. *Romney Marsh, Romney Marsh.*

Holding hard to what little he possessed, he parted from the other spirits, which seemed unaware of him, and floated upstairs. He had to see what—who—attracted him.

And it proved to be a woman. He gathered himself in the corner of the room she inhabited—her bedroom—and watched half dazed as she changed her clothes for dinner, stripped off rough blouse and skirt and donned the dress spread on the bed. The soft yellow lights of the room caressed her naked flesh, and he, coalesced much like the raindrops on the window glass, could only stare in appreciation.

No slender miss, this. She had a body of generous proportions, wide at the shoulders and hips and supple with muscle. She also had skin of pure milk-white, straight black hair that hung down her back all the way to her generous, tempting derriere, and, when she turned, a pair of breasts in which a man might lose himself. Her eyes, set slightly atilt in a heavily-boned face, were an unexpected and startling shade of tawny gold.

Shock sent him hurtling backward through the wall, unable to tell whether when she turned those eyes she caught a glimpse of him. He fought to recapture himself, to remember who he was—*Romney Marsh*—but after that he could return to no energy but hers.

He haunted her room. Of course, she did not spend all her time there. She sometimes went to a big chamber on the ground floor where she worked her body in a routine of fighting with her fists, a knife, or even a sword. He followed her helplessly and even watched her while she slept, the conviction forming that he must make her see him.

Could she help him resolve his dilemma? Or did he want her to see him for another reason, because she was quite simply the most fascinating woman he'd ever encountered?

After that he tried twice more to manifest himself within the confines of her room—once upon her rising and once after she put on an incredible display and chased two intruders from the place—no shrinking maiden, this. But concentrate his energy as he might, he couldn't quite materialize, though he felt sure she caught glimpses of him.

She had some affinity for spirits, he sensed. She definitely had some attraction for him. And he felt sure she'd heard him when he congratulated her following the fight late that night—undertaken in the nude on her part.

What man, corporeal or otherwise, could fail to admire that?

He observed as, clad only in a silken dressing gown, she spoke at length with a dark-haired man— discussing *him*.

And when the dark-haired man—her brother?— went out, leaving the two of them alone, seen and unseen, he knew it would be now or never.

Concentrating with unprecedented intensity, he hovered beside her bed, pictured himself as he knew he appeared when in his body, and did his best to make himself look solid.

She turned. Her unusual golden eyes widened, and she *saw him*.

About bloody time, he thought with a victorious rush. And now what? Could they communicate?

"Who are you?" she breathed in a low, husky voice that should have raised his pulse—did, for all he knew, back where his body lay.

"You can see me?" he asked, projecting the word-thoughts into her mind the way he had projected his image.

"Of course I can see you. Why else would I ask who you are?"

"Romney Marsh," he supplied the name to which he clung so hard.

Her eyebrows, like two black slashes above those incredible eyes, twitched. "Well, Mr. Romney Marsh, you've strayed to the wrong place."

"I don't think so."

"The party's downstairs in the solarium, where my father's summoning the souls of the dearly departed. You must have taken a wrong turn at the stairs."

"No. I don't want him. I want you." Abruptly he realized it for truth: he wanted her as only a man possessed of flesh could—and surging flesh, at that. It made no sense, yet he couldn't deny it.

She shifted slightly on the balls of her feet the way she had just before she took on the two thugs who'd come through the window. Did she, then, think she needed to fight him off?

He said quickly, "I'm not here to harm you. Rather, I need your help."

She tipped her head. The black hair slid over one shoulder to caress a generous breast. His nonexistent fingers itched.

"I'm not able to help you." She waved a hand in

the air. "Be gone, spirit, to the next realm."

"I can't."

"Of course you can." She leaned toward him, and her gaze moved over him with considerable interest. "Do not partake in my father's mischief. Spare yourself that. Move on and embrace peace. I dismiss—"

"No." He moved closer, and her eyes widened again. "Don't do that. Don't send me away."

She drew herself up to her considerable height, which had he possessed his body must nearly match his. "But, Mr. Marsh, it's where you belong."

"It isn't."

"Give me one good reason why," she challenged.

He could give her the very best of reasons. "I'm not dead."

Chapter Four

"Not dead?" Topaz sank onto the edge of her bed, never taking her gaze from the spirit that hovered just in front of her.

A good-looking spirit, she had to admit. And she'd seen her share from the time she reached an age to understand what the gossamer, semi-transparent entities were that flocked about her father like butterflies to nectar.

She'd never seen one to match Romney Marsh, who might have come straight out of some lurid dream. Indeed, had she imagined a man feature by feature for the sake of perfection, he'd look no different.

She blinked, trying to look *at* and not *through* him, for he was sheer as a fine net curtain.

He stood—or hovered—about five foot ten, with a build just the way she liked a man, broad shoulders and narrow hips, muscular but not bulky. Fair hair, well-mussed, tumbled over a noble brow, and he had a set of features at once expressive and handsome—a slightly hooked nose, lean cheeks, and the kind of lips she could only imagine pressed against hers.

Maybe this was a dream. She could have created it all—the fight, the conversation with Sapphire, and this, a fevered product of her brain. She shook her head in an effort to clear it of insanity. "Of course you're dead. You're a spirit."

He frowned. Curiously, that made him even more attractive. "I'm not, though. My body's still alive. I've just been booted out of it."

Topaz considered it. Possible, she supposed. People suffered accidents and fell into comas. Did their spirits then wander? Some spiritual practitioners could also project themselves from their corporeal bodies and travel the astral plane. Might he be a powerful spiritualist?

But he said *booted out*, which implied force. Despite herself she felt her curiosity stir. Not much piqued her interest anymore after twenty odd—very odd—years under her father's roof. But Romney Marsh did.

"Tell me," she bade him.

"I'm not sure I can." He writhed in the air as if seeking to control his image. "This takes a great deal of concentration and control. Can you help?"

"Me?" Topaz experienced a wave of reluctance. She'd never once employed the ability she knew lurked inside like a store of ammunition.

On the other hand, she quite suddenly didn't want Romney Marsh to depart. She wondered what color his eyes were when they weren't transparent. Fine eyes, level and intelligent. Devastating.

She shifted where she stood, unconsciously marshalling her forces. She didn't miss the way his attention slid to her breasts, tactile as a touch, before inspecting the rest of her body.

He'd seen her fighting her would-be abductors. That meant he'd seen all of her. Ruefully she wondered if he too considered her a "hefty lass."

Which had nothing to do with the matter at hand.

Reluctantly, she reached inside herself and captured the affinity that already stretched involuntarily to him. If she unfurled it and connected with his energy, would she be able to sever the bond later? She didn't know. Wisdom argued she shouldn't try—this was murky and dangerous ground.

But she often ignored the dictates of wisdom. She did so now. Tipping her chin up so her black hair slid down her back, she captured his eyes with hers.

"Concentrate on me."

She felt his attention focus the way one sometimes could feel another person staring from a crowd. Her spine tingled, and all at once emotion rose inside.

She beat it back. She knew enough to remember her father stayed always calm, even detached, during such encounters.

She felt anything but detached.

"I've never done this before."

She could no longer look away from him. Quite suddenly instinct took over, precisely the way it might during a sexual encounter. The untried ability within her rose of its own accord, reached for him, and connected in an unstoppable rush.

And it was...magnificent, strong, and yes, almost sexual in its energy. In fact, Topaz felt her body leap to arousal; her nipples tightened inside the soft, silk robe.

His image strengthened in the air. Still sheer enough for her to look through if she chose, he became more opaque, and Topaz could see details of his appearance like the slight wave in the fair hair that, over-long, tangled on his brow and spilled down his neck, and the clothes he wore.

He wore clothing—damn shame.

He smiled, and she wondered in alarm if he could hear her thoughts. She hoped not.

"Well," he said, "that was—phenomenal."

His lips moved, but his voice sounded only inside her head. It too had strengthened so she could better catch its timbre and tell that he had an accent.

"You're English."

"Indeed. I've been holding very hard to a few facts about myself since I was chased from my flesh. That, with my name, is one of them. And I'm on some sort of mission. Damned if I can remember what."

And damned if Topaz cared; she merely wanted the sound of his voice echoing through her—forever, if possible.

She knew quite well a lot of men inhabited this city, men from many different places in the world. A border town and a gateway of sorts, Buffalo welcomed traders and immigrants from Britain, French Canada, and various parts of Europe. Topaz had even had encounters with some of them during wild, rebellious nights when she visited the waterfront with her stiletto in her pocket.

None had ever made her feel like this.

"Yes," he said, more or less confirming her feeling, "phenomenal and *intimate*. Perhaps you'd better tell me your name."

She licked her lips and, though she rarely backed down from anything, retreated till her thighs hit the bed. She could feel him, his energy streaming across connections like spiritual threads that had formed between them. Desperately, she fought for control.

"My name's Topaz Hathor. What do you know of my father?"

"Only what you've told me, that he's a spiritualist."

"A very powerful one." She added deliberately, "Powerful and corrupt."

"Ah. Then I don't want anything to do with him, do I? I want you."

Yes, she thought, the desire ran rampant in the room. But he didn't mean that. He wanted her help.

Yet she knew had he possessed an actual body she'd have fallen on him like a ravenous woman at a feast, and devil take the consequences.

"How can I help you?"

"I'm not sure, only that I was called here—and not to that room downstairs. I think I need you to help reunite me with my body. But not where it lies. You need to get it out of the asylum."

"An asylum, is it? Not the new psychiatric facility Dr. Kirkbride designed on Forest Avenue? I've heard that's state of the art."

"I don't think so. Is that east of here? The place I escaped was a private building where I was held against my will."

"Because you're mad." He didn't feel insane. His energy seemed rational, if stirred. And anyway, what defined madness? People called her father—her whole family—mad. That didn't make it so.

Again he rippled in the air. Topaz realized it denoted distress. "I don't believe I'm mad. I think I was confined there for some other reason, though I can't grasp it now."

"Where is this asylum, besides east of here? Do you know the address?"

"No, but I think I could lead you there."

Topaz shivered. She didn't fear much, but the idea of following a disembodied spirit to an insane asylum failed to appeal, even if she went armed with ten stilettos.

He said, "I know you've no reason to help me, and I must be the last sort of complication you need in your life."

"I'm not sure I can help you, Mr. Marsh. You say you're more or less being held prisoner in this place?"

"Yes."

"Then how am I to get you out?"

"I don't know. But it's important. As I say, I believe I have a mission—"

He stopped speaking abruptly; Topaz sensed his helplessness and frustration. She fought back her corresponding emotions and crossed her arms on her breast.

"Look, Mr. Marsh, you'd be much better off searching out help elsewhere. I'm not the right person to assist you. For one thing, I'm not particularly sympathetic, and I'm certainly no do-good rescuer interested in saving strayed souls."

"Yet we've already bonded."

So he felt that too, did he? And did it mean she was doomed to have him following her around like a large, extremely attractive see-through puppy, continually stirring her libido?

Or would that last only till his body perished and his spirit moved on to where all good souls should go? She perched on the edge of her bed and thought about it.

"What shape is your body in? How was it when you left?"

26

He writhed and rippled in the air. "Not good. This place... The so-called doctors engage in experiments supposed to cure the patients. More like torture, really. I don't remember all of it, but..."

Topaz frowned. The pretense of healing might lend terrifying scope for abuse. Somebody must know the location of such a house in the city. But did she want to get involved?

"Mr. Marsh, while I grasp your plight—"

"Don't say no. You can't refuse."

She could. She should.

He moved closer. Topaz's awareness—and arousal—spiked. "You might make a report to the police, tell them someone is being held against his will."

"And they would believe this—why?"

"Because of who you are, the daughter of a spiritualist."

"Mr. Marsh, half the people in Buffalo despise my father and denounce him as a charlatan. The rest either worship him or call him a minion of Satan. It would scarcely further your cause to invoke his name."

"Well then, just report that I've been abducted."

"And how will I explain having this information? I can hardly tell Buffalo's finest you appeared in my room and introduced yourself."

"Then lie. Miss Hathor, this is of the utmost importance."

"Though you don't remember why."

"Not at the moment. It will come back to me, I'm sure of it."

"Mr. Marsh—"

Again he cut her off, his facility for communication

seeming to increase with his agitation. "Lie to them, Miss Hathor."

"To the police?"

"Have you never told a lie? Make something up if you have to, a fantasy."

"Such as?"

He moved closer. Caught somewhere between alarm and delight, Topaz stared into his eyes, wishing again she could tell their color. When he was near enough for her to count his eyelashes, he said, "There's only one thing to do. You will have to tell them we're lovers."

Chapter Five

"I'm looking for the Grayson Asylum. Do you know where it is?"

The man Topaz addressed looked like a respectable shopkeeper out sweeping his sidewalk of new-fallen snow, decided Romney, who floated at her shoulder. The fellow wore a jacket tossed on over trousers, shirt and apron, and sported large mutton-chop whiskers.

Romney had come up with the name—Grayson Asylum—after spending the remainder of the night hovering in the corner of Miss Hathor's chamber, something she had protested vociferously before falling asleep. She'd wanted him to leave, citing her right to privacy which, even in his view, had some legitimacy.

He'd left only to reappear as soon as she relaxed in slumber. Time held little meaning where he was, but he'd enjoyed watching her sleep for the next few hours, her black hair shining on the pillow and her breasts rising and falling with her breaths.

Funny, he could recall the name of the place where his body lay but not its exact location. He'd been able to lead Miss Hathor toward the general vicinity, eastward into the cold dawn. She'd taken a steamcab part way—he'd floated—before decamping to search on foot, the theory being that he, Romney, would be able to sense the place when they got close.

As well he might, though he found himself

distracted by his companion's appearance—distracted and a bit shocked and titillated. What woman went about clad in such a manner and armed with not only a stiletto but a tiny steam cannon sidearm as well?

He had watched her dress before they left her father's house, while pretending to be elsewhere—saw how the ruffled chemise caressed her creamy skin, followed by the bright patchwork skirt, peasant blouse, and corset. He was all too aware that beneath that chemise her generous breasts lay bare.

She'd donned a coat, as well, an incredible garment that looked like it should belong to a highwayman, with patch pockets, into one of which she fit the sidearm. On her glossy head she'd set a stylized top hat at a rakish angle, the hat and coat both a deep shade of rust that reflected color into her exotic eyes.

She looked like a gypsy on her way to a ball—a wealthy gypsy. And Romney found her utterly arousing. Wherever his body lay, he knew it must have wood between its legs.

The shopkeeper shook his head. "Never heard of it." His gaze moved over her, hat to boots, and he added doubtfully, "Miss."

Topaz Hathor raised her chin a notch, and her hair slid over her back. Nearly as tall as the shopkeeper, she possessed twice his poise.

"What do you sell here?" She switched her gaze to his shop. "I might patronize you."

No time for shopping, Romney whispered into her mind.

Shut up, she replied. *I'm working*.

"Books and German-language newspapers. Will you step in?" The shopkeeper abandoned his broom and opened the door for her. The shop, small but immaculately clean, felt considerably warmer than the chilly morning outside. Shelves occupied every conceivable space, meticulously organized.

Miss Hathor strutted between them, the heels of her boots clicking on the wooden floor. The shopkeeper, still wearing his jacket, watched her a bit nervously.

"Now then." She leaned on the counter and regarded him. "You, being a tradesman, must speak with a lot of people during the course of an ordinary day."

"Yes, miss."

"And people tend to gossip."

"Sometimes. Me, I do not listen to gossip."

"That's a shame." She drew a bill from the leather purse at her belt, the denomination of which caught even Romney's attention. She laid it on top of the counter as the shopkeeper stared. "Because I thought perhaps you may have heard of some place in this particular neighborhood where people ailing in their minds might be squirreled away—perhaps even against their will."

The shopkeeper's gaze flew to hers. "Oh," he said. "But it was not that name, what you said—"

"Grayson Asylum."

"There is a private house two blocks from here where such things might take place."

Topaz Hathor smiled. Romney felt that smile ripple through him, but it appeared to have a completely different effect on the shopkeeper, who took a careful step backward.

"Could you tell me the exact location of this house?"

"On Woodlawn, near the corner of Fillmore. Big gray building with a tower."

Romney rippled again as an image came to him. He whispered to his companion, *I remember.*

She gave a barely perceptible nod, straightened, and selected a book at random. "I will buy this. Keep the change."

The shopkeeper's eyes bulged. "Thank you, miss."

She laid her finger against her lips. "And not a word of this. You never spoke with me, should anyone come asking."

He shook his head. Miss Hathor went out, with Romney trailing her like invisible smoke.

"Well," she said when her boots hit the sidewalk. "That was interesting. Why did you call it Grayson Asylum?"

"Because that was the name that came to mind. Only I no longer have a mind, do I?" He rippled in distress. *"Or if I do, it's shut away in that place. Most perplexing."*

"Umm-hmm. Makes me wonder what else you've got wrong."

It made Romney wonder too, but he wasn't about to admit it. "Perhaps the name—like what goes on there—is kept private."

"Perhaps."

"Lets go get my body back."

"Mr. Marsh, there's nothing I'd like better. I am more than anxious to get you out of my head. But don't be too impetuous. This is but a reconnaissance mission."

"Best get moving," he advised. "People are beginning to stare."

"Are they?"

Truly, the people on the street going about their business—women and tradesmen, servants bent on errands—all turned curious looks on her. Romney supposed she would attract attention anywhere, tall as she was and clad as she was. She looked like an exotic bird touched down on the cold sidewalk.

"It's this way, I think," she murmured and started off. "Straight up Fillmore for several blocks."

"Since this is, as you put it, a reconnaissance mission, perhaps you might have dressed more inconspicuously."

"This is my inconspicuous coat."

"And the hat?"

"You think it draws too much attention?"

"I do. Not to say it doesn't enhance your beauty."

Her step faltered. "Careful, Mr. Marsh, or I will begin to believe you belong in this asylum. Surely you know I'm not beautiful."

"I know nothing of the kind, Miss Hathor."

"Ah, but Mr. Marsh, the fashion is for women to be dainty and delicate, with fragile faces and narrow waists. Whereas I have it on the very best authority I am a 'strapping wench.' "

"Damn the fashion. You must know how gorgeous you are."

He felt surprise ripple through her, accompanied by another emotion he couldn't identify. "I do believe that word has never before been applied to me." She quickened her steps and gestured as they reached a corner. "Ah—down that street, is that the place?"

Romney stopped as abruptly as if he'd been kicked in his nonexistent gut. All other thoughts dissolved as he writhed in extreme distress.

An immediate onslaught of images flooded him, none of which he wanted to recall. "Get me out of there."

"Easy, Mr. Marsh. That's the general idea."

"You have to get me out. Now."

She narrowed her eyes and regarded the building in question. Built of gray stone—was that why he'd called it Grayson Asylum?—it stood a full three stories high and had a turret at the northwest corner. Broad steps, flanked by stone lions, led up to a wide doorway. The building stood dark and quiet at this early hour, buttoned down tight.

"From the look of the place, that might not be so simple."

"I don't care. I want out."

"So I imagine. It's a grim edifice, isn't it? But what would you suggest? Should I ring the bell and request the return of your body?"

"Perhaps."

"I have no authority. No, this will require some thought. We've located the place; I suggest we retreat."

Romney wavered. Now that he was here, he felt a strong pull back to his flesh. He wanted very badly to stream inside, assure himself of his body's existence, and even reenter it. But if he did, would he be able to escape the torment again?

"You could inquire about me, let them know someone is aware I'm there. Make up some story."

"And tip our hand? No, Mr. Marsh, this has been a good morning's work. We need to retire and think."

"I disagree."

"If you want my help, you are going to have to

trust me."

"If I didn't trust you, I wouldn't have approached you in the first place." Only when he thought the words into her mind did he realize how true they were. Curious that; for he didn't suppose he trusted readily. And on the face of it this exotic bird didn't inspire confidence. Yet trust her he did, implicitly.

Her dark brows lifted. "I assure you, Mr. Marsh, I am more anxious to see your body in the flesh than you can imagine. But I think it behooves us to withdraw from the field now. And don't grumble in my mind— it's beginning to give me a headache."

Chapter Six

"You look pale, my dear. Are you unwell?"

Topaz looked up when her father spoke. He must be in one of his solicitous moods, almost harder to bear than his customary distraction.

"Just a bit of a headache, Father." Topaz loathed these family meals, yet Frederick Hathor insisted on attendance by every family member in residence, save himself, of course, when busy or consulting.

Today all four of them had gathered for luncheon—Topaz, her father, Sapphire, and Topaz's mother, who sat at the end of the table opposite her husband, dressed with elaborate perfection and, as usual, dithering.

A greater number of servants than actual family members filled the room—if one counted the steam units. One steamie stood as server at each of their elbows. Topaz's mother, Dahlia, waffled at hers, not sure whether or not she wanted her soup.

"Perhaps a ladleful, Doreen. But no, is that the beef compote? Made with marrow? I won't have any after all."

The poor steamie hesitated, ladle extended. The units, though created to be accommodating, didn't cope well with prevarication. Now Doreen began to leak steam from the joint at its neck.

"No soup for your mistress, Doreen," Frederick

told it. He had often, and in the units' hearing, declared them soulless husks, but he now ended Doreen's indecision before turning his attention back to his daughter.

"You should take a powder for the headache. I hope you have not been keeping too many late hours."

Sapphire, who sat opposite Topaz, made a rude sound but said nothing.

Topaz directed a glare at him before turning her eyes back to her father.

What an arresting man he was, she thought involuntarily, with his still-black hair sweeping back from his brow, his regal features, and dark, glittering eyes. Not for the first time she wondered how many of his female clients actually came to spend time with him rather than the spirits of their dearly departed.

"I do not like to take powders," she retorted, sounding surly to her own ears. Funny how frequently her father brought out the worst in her.

"You need to engage in something useful, Daughter," Frederick pressed, not for the first time. He wanted her to work with him, receiving his clients and conducting them into his presence. Topaz wondered if he sensed the latent ability inside her.

She would rather cut off her own toes than work with him.

"I do engage in something useful, Father." She conducted classes in self-defense in the back rooms of some of Buffalo's taverns, including the Eagle Club and Nellie's, both on Niagara Street, teaching women to protect themselves.

Frederick sniffed. "If you're talking about the instruction you give, I don't consider that a fit occupation for you, consorting with harlots and other low women."

"But they're the ones who are in jeopardy every day and every night, out on the streets alone. Patrick Kelly, from the Irish Squad, says crimes against women in that part of the city have actually declined since the women there have acquired a few self-defense skills."

"The Irish Squad." Frederick repeated it and gazed at Topaz intently. Sometimes she thought she could feel that dark gaze plumbing the depths of her mind. "You do realize automatons are nothing but soulless machines in disguise."

Topaz looked at Phillip, her father's personal steam unit, who did everything for him and now hovered solicitously at his side. Phillip had once taken a blast from a steam cannon, thereby saving Frederick from assassination by a religious fanatic. Topaz wondered if that kind of sacrifice required a soul.

But Phillip's expression didn't change. Of course, being molded from metal and implanted with glass eyes, it couldn't change.

"I like Patrick Kelly," she said with a shrug. "He has a wicked sense of humor."

Topaz had once danced half the night with the automaton police officer. He'd plied her with enough Irish whiskey to successfully seduce her, had he been capable of it.

Which he wasn't.

"I do not think—" Frederick began, only to be interrupted by his wife.

"Topaz, you cannot marry an automaton. Why waste your time with one? As for the streetwalkers"— Dahlia shivered delicately—"you must be careful not to catch something from them."

"Yes, Mother." Topaz glared at Sapphire who, no doubt glad her antics rather than his now received scrutiny, ate in silence. He returned her look with a derisive gleam.

Sheer stubborn defiance made her add, "Though you know, Mother, I'm not the marrying kind."

"Nonsense." Dahlia waved a dismissive hand. "You simply have not met the right man. I firmly believe there is someone for everyone. Frederick, my love, how about your new associate?"

Frederick froze with his spoon halfway to his mouth. So unusual was it for him to falter in anything, Topaz took notice.

Blithely, Dahlia went on, "He is unmarried and extremely wealthy, so you said."

When Frederick still did not answer, Topaz leaned her elbows on the table and asked, "What associate is this?" Not that she was interested but for the fact that she rarely saw her father discomfited.

"An investor," Frederick said shortly. "I hardly think, *mon petite*," he addressed his wife, "Danson Clifford is the sort of man with whom we would wish our daughter to form a lifelong bond." He frequently called his wife *mon petite*, an appellation he would never apply to Topaz.

Dahlia could be obtuse. "Why not, Frederick? You are already associating with him."

"That is business—not family." Frederick sounded so repressive, Topaz found her interest well and truly stirred.

"Just who is this Danson Clifford?" she asked.

"*Nouveau riche*," Sapphire supplied and wiggled

his eyebrows.

"We are *nouveau riche*," Topaz pointed out. "Father never ceases with telling us how our ancestors came here, fleeing ethnic cleansing, without a penny to their names."

Frederick had regained his composure; he smiled. "I have earned everything we enjoy, through my hard efforts." He looked at his wife. "And, *mon petite*, if Topaz is ready for marriage, I can find her a much better match than Danson Clifford."

"Why? What's wrong with him?" Topaz pressed.

"Nothing is wrong with him. But he would not be my first choice for son-in-law."

Dahlia took up the theme, and Topaz realized she'd landed on dangerous ground. "If you truly do wish to find a husband, Topaz, you could not hope for a better opportunity than Mrs. Rexinger's Valentine's Day ball next month. She's invited every eligible man in the city."

"I don't wish to find a husband."

"Well, you should think about it. You don't want to remain on the shelf too long. I hear that nice Mr. Fitzgerald will be there."

"Irish," Frederick denounced, not quite under his breath.

"But wealthy Irish," Dahlia persisted.

"He's a brainless idiot." Topaz had met carthorses with more wit and far more charm. "And Father, why should you object to the Irish, who for the most part, like us, came here with nothing?"

Sapphire gave her a look; they both knew the futility of baiting Frederick over his prejudices or any of his strongly held beliefs. One might argue with him but never win.

Frederick answered with deliberate patience, "Yet we have raised ourselves."

Yes, Topaz thought indignantly, by providing services that to many in the city smacked of the fortunetelling done in the old country, and fleecing people in what might be considered just a more elaborate version of their ancestors' activities.

She needed to get out of this house. The easiest route would be marriage, but she didn't see herself taking that path. She sighed. At least the conversation had distracted her father to the point where he didn't seem likely to sense Romney Marsh's presence in the house.

Romney Marsh. Just thinking of him made Topaz's pulse leap. She wanted to see him in the flesh so badly it hurt.

But first she needed answers to a number of questions: why had he been shut away in Grayson? Why was he, an Englishman, here in the city in the first place?

And why did just thinking about him elevate her pulse?

Her father glanced at her almost as if he sensed her rampant emotions.

"The time will come, Daughter, when you can no longer play at your life and will need to make a decision either for marriage or to take up some worthy occupation. I will tolerate nothing less under my roof."

"Then, Father, perhaps the time has come for me to leave."

Chapter Seven

"Where are you going?" Romney slid the question into Topaz's mind even as she set her hat on her head— a different hat this time but just as rakish as the top hat she'd worn this morning.

He'd watched her change her clothes—though he supposed any decent bloke, in spirit or in the flesh, would have looked away—and ached all the while to touch.

Outside the bedroom windows, dark had fallen; the panes of glass once more reflected the interior of the room, along with Miss Hathor's image. She wore a low-cut crimson gown with a golden corset, all worked with embroidered flowers, and a black velvet cloak. The hat, a jaunty little cap, dangled jet beads that rode on her forehead just above her eyes.

"Out," she replied shortly. She had been in a vile mood since luncheon; he could sense that much.

Now he protested, "It's a foul night." Snow had started falling some time ago, and a cold wind rattled the windows. Cold, dark, and dangerous. Why would she go out in that?

She adjusted the hat to a better angle and turned her gaze on the place he hovered. "I don't care; I'm not staying here all evening. I thought I might ask around, pose some questions relating to your plight." She hesitated before adding, very offhandedly, "Come with me, if you like."

"Where, precisely?"

"The waterfront."

Romney wavered quite literally in the air; he felt the separate sparks of energy from which he was made shiver and coalesce.

She said softly, "I'd like you to come."

She slid the stiletto into her pocket, but her eyes—those incredible amber eyes spiked with black lashes—never left him.

"Topaz," he began. "May I call you Topaz?"

"Since you've seen me naked—and more than once—I think you might as well."

He didn't need reminding. He wondered if those who tended his body back at Grayson marveled over his near-constant state of arousal.

"Topaz, while I appreciate your efforts on my behalf, I would not have you venture out on such a filthy night, and to such a redoubtable district, for my sake."

She faced him fully. "You may have seen me naked, Romney"—she paused and asked sarcastically—"May I call you Romney?"

"Of course."

"You may have seen me naked, but you obviously know little about me as yet. I'm stubborn. And headstrong."

And beautiful.

Her chin jerked up, and her eyes flashed as if she'd heard the thought. Christ, maybe she had. He consisted of nothing but thought, now.

"Flattery, my good Romney, will get you nowhere."

He moved closer, vibrating in the air. "But you are beautiful; you have to believe that."

"And you are in desperate need of my assistance. A word of warning, Romney: don't play me."

"You think I am?"

"False compliments always smack of manipulation. Now, are you coming with me or not?"

****

Snow swirled around them as Topaz stepped from the steamcab, the white flakes chased by a cold wind directly off the Niagara River. Among all the dives on the waterfront, this one had to be the worst. Clapped together from what looked like reclaimed planks, it jumped with the beat of live music. A crooked sign over the door declared it to be Nellie's.

Romney had to concentrate hard to keep from being scattered by the wind. "Here?" he objected.

"Here."

"I don't much like the look of the place."

"I don't much care what you like, Mr. Marsh."

She paid the cab driver, who took off in a flurry of snowflakes, and marched inside, not waiting to see if Romney meant to follow. He did, trailing her like a steamie's breath.

The interior pulsed with light, warmth, and energy Romney could feel. A bar built of packing crates dominated the wall on the left. Men—and a few women—stood there elbow to elbow. Directly ahead, on a small stage, a band consisting of a fiddler, a concertina player, and a mandolin man had set up; the music they turned out—traditional Irish—sounded like a heartbeat.

Small, round tables occupied the remaining floor

space along with patrons, some standing in groups and some dancing.

A big, redheaded man in an open-necked shirt turned when they came in and thrust his whiskey glass into the air.

"Miss Topaz! Come and dance with me."

Topaz smiled. Romney, who now consisted of pure emotion, didn't like the way that smile made him feel.

"Who is he?"

"Patrick Kelly, the king of this place." Topaz started forward and met Kelly in the middle of the floor. To Romney's intense consternation, they embraced.

"Welcome!" Kelly exclaimed. "Now we will have some fun."

"How are you this evening, Patrick?"

"Full of steam, as you see. May I buy you a drink?"

"You may. My usual, if you'd be so kind."

The patrons crowding the bar made way for Kelly the way the Red Sea had for Moses.

"Rum," Kelly ordered. He leaned close enough to touch Topaz's ear with his lips. Strangely, Romney sensed no lust from him.

Had he, Romney, been that close to Topaz's white neck he'd have been unable to resist a kiss.

"Your drinks are on me this evening, Miss Topaz. Consider yourself the queen of this place."

"How kind of you, Patrick."

"I am honored to have you here."

The bartender slid a glass of dark liquid across the bar to Topaz. She downed half of it in a gulp before Kelly seized her hand.

"Come. Let's dance."

Like an unstoppable force, the two of them moved to the center of the floor. Topaz removed her black cape with a flourish and deposited it at the nearest table, revealing the crimson gown with its golden corset.

The musicians, noticing the couple, struck up a wild tune. Topaz placed her hand in Kelly's, and they stepped out vigorously.

Romney, afire with consternation, hovered helplessly and watched. He had seen Topaz fight with her stiletto; he had seen her conversing with her brother and with the shopkeeper; he'd fancied he began to know the woman. Now, though, another Topaz Hathor emerged—an abandoned creature with flying hair and whirling skirts who could chug rum like a sailor.

He couldn't be the only man watching the flash of her ankles beneath her hem, or the movement of her breasts beneath the low-cut bodice, but he must be the only one who knew precisely what she wore under that gown—very little. Her feet in their ankle-high boots kept perfect time with Kelly's large feet, and a look of fierce joy possessed her face.

Wild and beautiful, Romney thought. But she'd clearly forgotten him. And when the dance ended to applause, she went and sat at a table with Patrick Kelly. The two of them put their heads close together and began an intimate conversation.

So was this, then, the man in her life? And if so, what could he, Romney, do about it? He wanted to sock the big Irishman in the jaw but lacked that capability; nothing more than a swirl of energy, pure emotion, he could only pour through the room to their table and hover like some frustrated, invisible eavesdropper.

Was Topaz aware of him? She gave no indication

other than a flicker in his direction from her incredible eyes. All her attention focused on Kelly.

And Kelly—his big hand rested on the table near her fingers. Romney struggled to overcome his reactions and find out something about this man who might well be a rival.

A handsome devil, and no mistake. Yet Romney still sensed something off about him. Or rather a lack of something.

He looked at Topaz as any man might, his gaze resting on her generous breasts as he called the bartender and ordered yet another rum. Did he hope to ply Topaz with liquor, get her tipsy, and take her upstairs to some sordid room such as usually existed at these sorts of places?

In agony, Romney hovered and watched while Topaz drank her rum and Kelly played with a glass of what looked like Irish whiskey, drinking very little of it, keeping himself sober for later, no doubt. And Romney began to burn with jealousy.

He didn't like the way it made him feel. He didn't often fall victim to his emotions; rather he had an orderly mind, one that kept both thoughts and feelings in line. He vaguely remembered he'd come to this city on a mission of some importance, one which required the application of logic; yet since arriving here he'd been subjected to the horrors inside Grayson, so drastic they had separated him from his flesh.

Now he consisted of nothing but emotion, a virtual cloud of it.

He needed a body—his or somebody else's—so he could impose himself between Topaz Hathor and Patrick Kelly. Maybe punch the big Irishman in the nose, though it looked a tall order.

The music started up again, and several couples took the floor. Would Topaz and Kelly join them? Part of Romney wished they would, just so he could watch her move once more. But they sat talking, now deep in an intense discussion. And Romney experienced a new kind of torment.

He looked around the room, his energy touching on patron after patron. The place had become still more crowded since Topaz and he had arrived; now there were no empty tables, and people stood in groups, talking and laughing. A few women danced—none of them could touch Topaz for beauty.

In the corner sat a man, head resting on his hand, gaze bleary, who watched the scene. A cadre of empty glasses on the table in front of him explained his half-conscious state. A mad idea blossomed through Romney's formlessness.

Could he? Should he? At the moment, fired by his jealousy, he felt powerful enough to do most any damn thing, including take over the body of another. Not a badly set-up bloke, either—looked like a dandy down on his luck, most likely some wealthy wastrel gone slumming on the waterfront.

Romney drifted toward him. The fellow had fair hair not unlike Romney's own, but there all resemblance ended. Romney knew his body lying back at Grayson might be considered reasonably good-looking. This bloke had heavy features now slack from the effects of the liquor.

But he looked up when Romney hovered over his table, as if he sensed his presence. Maybe he did; possibly the large amount of liquor he'd consumed had lowered his natural barriers to the supernatural.

Sheer madness, what Romney had in mind. Yet he needed physicality, and he needed it now.

"Excuse me, mate." He projected the words into the inebriated man's mind and saw him start. "But do you mind if I just snatch your body for a while?"

Chapter Eight

"May I have this dance?"

Topaz, in no mood to be interrupted, glanced up in annoyance when the fellow spoke. She and Patrick were deep in conversation; she had just begun telling him her suspicions concerning what might be taking place in her father's basement and intended to enlist his assistance with investigating Grayson.

Her eyes narrowed. She recognized the fellow as a rich boy who sometimes frequented Nellie's—young and too impetuous for his own good. His sort frequently came to grief on the waterfront. Topaz could hardly believe he hadn't already been robbed and dumped in an alley.

"I'm busy," she told him.

"But I like the way you dance."

"You and every man in the room," Kelly said. "Be off, lad. We're busy talking."

The idiot, failing to take warning, stepped closer and eyed Kelly as if measuring him up. Surely even a drunken dandy couldn't be so stupid.

"I won't take 'no' for an answer. Dance with me. You're the most beautiful woman I've ever seen."

Patrick started up, his chair scraping back across the wooden floor.

Topaz reached out and seized his arm. "Don't, Patrick. He's three sheets to the wind."

"Inebriated, you mean?" Patrick cocked his head in that endearing way he had and subsided into his seat. "Go away, little man."

The fellow bristled. "There's no reason she can't give me one dance."

"Listen, bud—I'm not in the mood."

"You will be."

The dandy reached out and touched Topaz's hand and she felt a rush of sensation that in only two days had become familiar. It vibrated through her from the place where the fellow's fingers met hers and arrested her where she sat.

"Oh," she said. "How did you—?"

"Never mind that now. Dance with me."

Topaz got up like a woman in a trance—which, perhaps, she was—and moved into his arms. Sensation flooded through her as his hands closed around her waist, and hunger flared, curiously mingled with pleasure.

From the instant she'd encountered him in her bedroom she'd longed to touch him. Now—in a way—she could.

Her head spun. This, of course, wasn't the way Romney Marsh truly looked—or smelled. But his essence now filled this flesh and assailed her senses, overriding the apparent. Strange and wonderful.

She leaned closer. The music—a half jig—didn't invite intimacy. She didn't care.

"You borrowed a body? I didn't know you could."

"Neither did I. Amazing what can happen under the impetus of jealousy."

A faint English accent colored his speech. Topaz's pulse picked up.

"Jealousy?" He swung her around, and she moved closer. "Jealous of what?"

"You've barely looked at anyone but that big Irishman since we came in."

"Patrick?" Topaz smiled. Didn't he know what Kelly was? She decided to enjoy the dance before she told him.

"What happened to the fellow who owns this body? Does he mind?"

"Lulled by alcohol. Seems to be nine parts asleep. Besides, why should he object to touching you?"

Romney slid his borrowed hands lower to cup her derriere and bring her still closer. His spirit enfolded her and set her tingling.

Madness.

Yet his emotions pulled at her, and she went with it, slid her hands up his shoulders and clasped them around his neck.

The song ended, but neither of them stopped swaying back and forth. They hadn't been dancing to the music anyway. After a moment, the band— observing them—struck up again, a slow rendition of "Give Me Your Hand."

Something inside Topaz melted, turned molten, and promptly caught fire. She pressed her body against her partner's and gazed into his eyes.

Not exactly handsome, this body he'd borrowed. Under ordinary circumstances Topaz wouldn't look at him twice: a florid, fleshy face, bulbous nose, and eyes the unfortunate hue of mud. Now, though, she could see Romney's spirit in those eyes, and the rest ceased to matter.

After a moment he murmured, "I wonder how you

taste? I've been longing to find out."

Her hands, at the back of his neck, were positioned perfectly to pull his mouth down. She met him with her lips parted, an open invitation.

He tasted her at length and then, proving who he was, spoke into her mind. "Umm. Delectable. I might never get enough of that."

She had to break the kiss to reply. "As good as you imagined?"

"Better." He dove for her again, and Topaz pressed closer. She couldn't imagine what Patrick or anyone else in the bar thought. She didn't care, because Romney's essence flowed through her and set her alight.

Suddenly she wanted to shed all her clothes, offer herself to him completely. She broke the kiss again. "How long can you hold onto this body?"

"I don't know. Not long, I fear."

"Then come outside with me." She wanted him in the cold and the dark, not in front of all these eyes.

"Won't your friend, Kelly, object?"

"Why should he?"

"Because it certainly looks as if the two of you have an intimate relationship."

"And that's why you're feeling jealous?"

"Yes." He admitted it readily, and Topaz smiled into his eyes.

"No need. We're just friends. I've never kissed him like this." She laid her mouth to his again, wooing his spirit into her, addictive as strong drink.

This time he broke the contact. "Why not? Good-looking bloke."

Her smile widened. "Don't you know what Patrick

is? An automaton. That's a member of the famed Buffalo Irish Squad."

"What?" Romney's borrowed head jerked round so he could face Patrick, who watched them lazily.

Topaz laughed. "No matter, because it seems to have spurred you to a wonderful breakthrough. I've wanted you, Romney Marsh, since you first appeared in my room. And borrowed flesh is better than none."

"Are you suggesting what I think?"

"What do you suppose, Englishman?"

"That I bring this borrowed body back to your house, where you'll welcome me."

"Not sure I can wait that long." She caught him by the hand and towed him off the dance floor. At the back of the barroom, a door led to the bog and to an alley where the cold air met them. Snowflakes swirled lazily here, but the narrow confines shut out the wind.

Romney backed Topaz against the brick wall and kissed her again. She shivered in delight.

"Cold?" he asked into her mind.

Reluctantly, she dragged her mouth from his. "No."

"I could give you this fellow's jacket."

"I want fewer clothes, not more. Touch me."

"I wish I had my own body."

"So do I, but this is better than nothing. Touch me," she begged again. "See if you can read my mind and tell where I want you to put his hands."

She almost felt the energy inside him shift and quest for her. He unerringly moved one hand to her breast. She leaned in and claimed his lips again; while their mouths fused his fingers caressed her through the thin fabric of her bodice, and she peaked with cold and arousal.

"I want to taste you everywhere, Topaz Hathor."

She wished she could reply in kind without removing her mouth from his. She also wished she could sample the real Romney Marsh. This body tasted of the gin its owner had consumed, and for all her desire, she detested gin.

Still, the potency of Romney's presence made her want him regardless.

"You have the most beautiful body, the most luscious breasts."

In answer to her unspoken prayers he moved his borrowed lips downward across her chin to her throat and lower still. Topaz's heart began to hammer in her ears like a drum.

He bent his head and, hot and wet, his mouth found her through the fabric of her bodice. She twined her hands around his neck and drew him closer.

Damn that fabric, anyway. She wanted him fused to her, flesh on flesh.

Maybe he could hear her thoughts, her desires, after all, for one borrowed hand came up to cup her breast and tug the fabric down. With tantalizing deliberation he latched on, and Topaz nearly climbed the wall with the rush of sensation.

This went beyond—far beyond—any kiss and cuddle she'd ever experienced. For she could feel his spirit; it tingled and intertwined with hers, augmenting the sensation.

"God, Topaz, how I want you!"

He didn't lie. His borrowed body, pressed to hers, had become flagrantly hard. She had forgotten now the acquiescent resident spirit who owned the body and any last shreds of her own propriety. She would gladly—eagerly—accommodate him here against the wall.

"Not half so much as I want you, Romney," she returned.

He freed her other breast from the bodice. Cold rushed at her, and it felt marvelous; when he found the second nipple with that hot mouth, pleasure spiked sharp as pain.

"Here?" he asked.

"Here. Anywhere."

"With this body?"

"With any body."

"I want it to be mine."

Well, Topaz wanted that too, but she was now so aroused she couldn't imagine delaying. If they coupled, it would be on a spiritual as well as physical level. And she wasn't about to wait till they freed him from Grayson.

She reached down and hitched up her skirt, captured his hand, and placed it against her leg. She wore stockings and nothing else. They ended with garters at the thigh. Above that was only flesh and heat.

"Oh, Mr. Marsh—please."

"Mr. Marsh?" Laughter rippled through him and caused the most curious sensation, mingling warmth with the passion. His tongue still caressed her breast and that felt fine, but she wanted it lower.

At the thought, her desire elevated impossibly.

His fingers traced her stocking upward, encountered the ruffled garter, and skittered above it to meet her flesh. Things got hotter as he continued upward.

"You feel like heaven."

This was heaven. She couldn't live if he stopped now. Snowflakes landed on his shoulders and her eyelashes, where they swiftly melted. She felt at once cold and unbearably hot.

His hand continued to slide upward to the core of heat between her thighs, and brushed her curls.

"Please," she implored.

"Well, now, Topaz Hathor—I don't imagine you're a woman in the habit of begging men for anything."

"I'm not. So I'll ask you nicely—touch me."

"That's not an order, is it?"

She whimpered.

He laughed again, and it rippled through her. She felt wild to have him—his true body—in her bed, all warmth and laughter, to love him all night or possibly even for days on end.

Slowly and tantalizingly, he thrust one finger inside her. She very nearly came apart there against the wall.

"Damn," he said.

"What? If you stop now I'll murder you."

"He's waking up."

For an instant, Topaz didn't understand what he meant. Her dazed mind, on overload, knew only sensation. "Eh?"

"My host. He wants into this. Coming out of his stupor. Topaz, touching you would raise the dead."

"I don't want him. I want you."

Yet she could feel him slipping away, the spirit and essence of him draining from the flesh that held her like water from a basin. All at once a stranger had his hand up her skirt—a randy stranger, at that.

"How dare you?" she cried. A twitch dislodged his

hand from the intimate place Romney had placed it. "Get off me!"

"Umm." His only reply came in a tipsy murmur. His mouth dove for her breast. Without conscience she kneed him in the groin.

He stiffened and began to fall; before he reached the ground, she had her stiletto out and at his throat.

"Touch me again, and I'll bleed you, understand?"

"What happened?" he asked piteously.

Topaz relented. "A misunderstanding." Stepping away, she fitted herself back into her bodice. Kelly would be waiting, no doubt wondering what had happened to her.

What *had* happened to her?

"Nothing," she said, addressing the dark as well as herself. "Nothing but a touch of madness."

Chapter Nine

"We need to get your body out of that place," Topaz declared. She lounged on her back atop her bed with only one lamp lit, deep in the night. Romney Marsh hovered beside her, his presence spurring her frustration.

The fumble in the alley had failed to satisfy her in any way.

"I agree. But how?" he demanded. "From what I can remember—and it's damned little—the rooms in the asylum are more like cells than berths in a hospital ward. I'm locked in."

"Well I need to get that door unlocked. But once I do, you'll have to make love to me, understand? Rampant, earth-shattering love."

"I can manage that." She felt his energy move over her and dance across her skin, which only further augmented the problem.

"Don't tease me," she warned.

"Me? Tease you? With you lying there dressed like that?"

Upon returning from Nellie's, Topaz had shed her clothes and donned a semi-sheer nightdress of emerald green. With him near, her body now strained against the fabric, everything on alert.

"Who's tempting whom?"

"We need to do something about this," Topaz

growled. "Go borrow another body."

"I've just said, Topaz Hathor, when I enter you I want to be wearing my own."

"I want that too. But meanwhile—"

"Where am I to get a body at this hour? Especially one that won't insist on participating."

"We want no outside participation." She desired him, only him.

"Precisely. I'd need a corpse."

"I'm not sure how I feel about that." Topaz opened her eyes wide, contemplating it. Dead flesh between her thighs? Yet if he inhabited that flesh... "Where would you get a corpse?"

"There are a number of them in the cellar of this house."

Topaz sat up abruptly and stared at him. Semi-transparent, he hovered an inch or so above her mattress, his head resting on one bent arm. "How do you know that?" She thought furiously. "Have you been down there?" The cellar was kept locked at all times.

"No, but I can sense things."

So could Topaz, and she'd long harbored suspicions about her father's activities in the nether regions of the house. But they hadn't involved corpses.

No way to get down there and investigate now. Meanwhile, she supposed she'd just have to live with her double frustration.

****

Night lay deep around the mansion, so thick and quiet Rom could feel the spirits rustling all about him as he had that first night when he'd streamed here, drawn to Topaz. They floated near the ceilings of the big rooms downstairs and congregated near the chamber

Frederick Hathor inhabited.

But he, Romney, was the only spirit here in Topaz's bedroom. He alone had the privilege of watching her sleep.

As usual, she'd left the window open a crack; what need had she to fear cold or would-be abductors? A trickle of light came through the window. But what need had he—in spirit—for illumination? He could see her in the dark, and feel her also.

He knew very well he'd left her unsatisfied in the alley. He'd been able to feel her frustration and her desire. His own level of desire had surprised him—he'd always believed it to be a hormonal matter, dependent on the flesh, but his want for this woman clearly surpassed that.

He wanted to be inside her, the craving intensified by the knowledge she wanted him there as well. They'd almost succeeded, out behind the tavern. But what about now?

He moved toward her, shifting like a current of air. She sprawled with her hair spread on the pillow in a black fan. He ached to bury his face there, the better to inhale her beguiling scent.

He had no face to bury, but might he still manage to touch her?

She lay with one arm outside the velvet coverlet, revealing the swell of a breast. Rom hovered above her and concentrated all his being as he had when he filled the dandy at Nellie's. If the dandy, why not Topaz also?

It took his full concentration to brush her breast. Delight danced through him in separate, distinct particles; he felt himself change color and intensify, his very existence altering to match hers.

He slid beneath the sheer gown she wore, caressed the full, heavy globe of one breast, and felt her heartbeat quicken even though she still slept.

Ah, so this thing was possible. He could feel her and she could feel him.

He shifted his substance, slid over the satin skin of her belly, brushed both legs beneath the blankets, and returned to her breast. His ghostly lips closed on her nipple, and he became one with her—shockingly, gloriously.

She stirred and came awake—aware—in a bound. Both inside and outside of her simultaneously, Rom felt her desire, previously unsated, reignite. Her lips parted even as he continued his spiritual dance at her breast, and she whispered, "I'm dreaming."

"No dream, love." His own desire increased his powers of concentration; somewhere his body— battered and singed—achieved a state of arousal, but his spirit existed with her here.

"Oh, God," she moaned. "Oh, my God, I can feel you. How?"

"Desire is a force of its own. I want you, Topaz Hathor." He spoke into her mind.

"Touch me. You can touch me." Yearning filled her voice, along with exultation. "Please, please, I want you so."

"I can tell. I can feel everything you feel. Let me in."

She parted her legs instinctively, and he fluttered downward, a wave of pure sensation. What a way for him to enter her for the first time. For a brief instant regret touched him—then her desire, pounding through her with each heartbeat, engulfed him; he had room to regret nothing.

Like a breath of air he slipped through the curls between her legs and began another dance, one that fondled and caressed. Instead of his hands—trapped with his body back at Grayson—his very being parted her, stroked, and drove her instantly higher.

She bucked on the bed and moaned, a sound he felt rather than heard. She dug her heels into the mattress and opened herself still further to him in a gesture of total surrender—she, a woman who surrendered to no one easily if at all.

When he'd taken over the body of the drunk at Nellie's, it had been relatively easy—he'd been aroused then as well by Topaz's dance and costume. And on some level he'd been familiar with the male body. This proved far different; the feelings racing through her felt wild, tumultuous, and very feminine—desire and demand, supremacy and sacrifice. He could feel parts of her, from inside, he'd never possessed. For an instant he convulsed inside her, overwhelmed by the strong, beautiful being she was.

Then her desire and his twined together, an unstoppable force that robbed him of all hesitation.

Her spirit spoke to his, an intimate caress.

Rom, I can feel you. Here, inside me.

Yes, love.

Oh, God. Too good to be true. Too good for words. Can you feel?

Everything. Give yourself to me.

She'd already done a lot of giving for a woman who always kept herself strictly under control, guarding against the spirits that thronged this place and against her father's influence. Now he felt the last threads break as she yielded herself up to him.

Use me. Love me.

He flowed through her like warm honey. Her delight intensified, flared from her lips all the way down. He felt the pure want that roused in his wake, danced between her legs, and ripened her breasts.

Her body, his. Her being, his—if only for a few moments.

Please, Rom, I can't stand...

He smoothed one of her hands up her belly and cupped a breast. Ah—the delightful weight and softness of it, tipped with that bud of aching sensation. He used her fingers to do what his could not and experienced the staggering dual pleasure, his and hers combined.

She gasped and arched her strong, glorious body, whispering to him soundlessly of what she wanted, what she needed. He commanded control of her other hand and the fire inside her became a conflagration.

Ah, God, why didn't this flesh of hers set the sheets aflame? Her spirit already consumed his as even the torture had not. When this finished, he'd surely be ashes.

But worth it. Worth it all.

In command now, her spirit totally in his ghostly hands, he abandoned one breast and moved her hand downward. As if they were his own, he used her fingers to plunder her wet heat, delighting as much as she in every stroke and every plunge.

Mine. You're mine, he told her, and she gasped in helpless agreement—and erupted into wave upon wave of pleasure.

He went with her, his spirit almost entirely indistinguishable from hers. He shuddered with her, broke apart into separate, dancing particles, and came together again, unwilling to separate from her any more than had they been joined in the flesh.

The pleasure ebbed slowly, bringing languorous contentment in its wake.

That, she still spoke in her own mind, *is the most intimate act I've ever experienced.*

And me.

Don't leave me. Please, Rom. Don't go yet. Can we do that again?

Greedy woman. I think that was born of my extreme longing and your extreme desperation.

I can get desperate again. Rom?

Yes, love.

She drew a breath, pondered long before she spoke the next words. *I'm not sure I can live without you now.* She gave a hard laugh. *I—who swore to maintain my independence above all things. So swiftly, look what you've done to me.*

He stirred, left her body, and spread out like a spectral blanket, caressing her skin.

I would stay with you if I could. Believe that. But I'm not sure how I escaped my body. How can I guarantee I won't be called back again?

"We absolutely have to get you out of there." She spoke it aloud into the silent room, a vow. "Whatever it takes."

Chapter Ten

"Rom, I've been thinking about what you said. Are you sure there are corpses in the cellar? Could you go look and make certain?"

"Do you think that's a good idea?" he asked, his voice a caress in her mind.

"Probably not. But I'm intrigued by the idea of you appropriating a body that won't interfere with us. Even though I don't like to think what my father could be getting up to that would require the presence of dead flesh."

"Well, I'm fairly sure I can go most anywhere. But I'd rather not leave you."

The energy of which he was made flickered and broke apart into separate particles like muted light. These shifted and moved to touch her, arousing her all over again. He brushed her throat, caressed her cheek, and slid inside her bodice.

"Oh," she breathed.

Nice—titillating, in fact—but she couldn't let him distract her again. Wanting this man who wasn't a man could drive her out of her head.

"You're a goddess, Topaz Hathor."

His energy still danced across her breasts, and she narrowed her eyes before she answered, "I look like an overgrown gypsy." She might believe that, but she'd take any compliments he cared to dish out.

"You're the most arousing, fascinating woman I've ever known."

She pushed herself up in the bed, and he returned to the pillow beside her, a dim form through which she could see the bedspread. "If you're going to look in the cellar, we'd better do it now, while everyone else is asleep. Do you fancy acting the part of investigator?"

He contemplated it and replied thoughtfully, "No acting required there, love. I suspect in truth that's what I am."

****

The big house felt eerie with the lights muted, all the human inhabitants sleeping and most of the steamies shut down.

Romney trailed Topaz down the corridor like smoke, past closed doors through which he could sense life, or emptiness. She paused momentarily outside the door one down from her own and mouthed, "My brother."

Sapphire, that would be, with whom Romney had observed her speaking. Two energies occupied the room. Sapphire did not lie alone.

Lucky bastard, Romney thought bitterly, watching the twitch of Topaz's robe across her rounded bottom as she moved on.

At the head of the stairs, she paused again outside another door and mouthed, "My father."

Did her parents not sleep together, then? Rom sensed only one soul within. But what a soul! Even at rest and acquiescent it shimmered with power, and the spirits who, like Romney, had been drawn to this house teemed around it.

The man possessed genuine ability, like Topaz's

only a hundred times stronger, and well developed.

Romney skittered away, half afraid the man might sense him. What then? Would Hathor emerge and banish him? He didn't want that to happen for more than one reason: he wanted Topaz's help, and he wanted her.

Would Hathor be able to isolate his—Romney's—spirit among the many that flocked to this place?

He descended the wide, curved staircase ahead of Topaz and waited for her at the bottom.

"What's the matter?" she hissed.

"I didn't want your father to sense me."

"Right. Mind the steamies, now."

A unit on standby waited beside the grand front door. Romney knew it would switch on if anyone drew near enough. Topaz led him along the side of the staircase to the back of the house.

"The cellar door opens off this hallway outside the kitchen. Don't look in there." She indicated that room. "It always gives me the shivers."

The kitchen, lit by one muted lamp, looked like a forest of steam units, all shut off and staring with blank, sculpted eyes. It took many mechanical hands to feed a household this luxurious.

He examined the cellar door even as Topaz whispered, "It's locked."

"No barrier to me. But I'll have to go alone."

"Yes." She looked at him with concern. "I'm not sure what you'll find down there, but it might be dangerous. Are you sure you can get back out when you want to?"

"If I can move in, presumably I can move out." But if he did find a usable body, it wouldn't be much good to him unless the door could be unlocked from the inside and he could force that body's fingers to work the latch.

"Presumably," she echoed. He could feel her emotions, a mix of excitement, worry, and desire. A woman of flagrant courage on her own behalf, she nevertheless feared for him.

"Don't do anything stupid. Just see what's down there. And look for a body. We don't want to attract my father's attention."

But who knew what might do that? Romney could still feel Hathor's power one floor down. What might Hathor feel?

Moving softly, he shifted through the door. Immediately sensation rushed at him, nearly too much to handle in his disembodied state: the typical scent of a cellar overlaid by a myriad of other things. Chemicals, new wood, burning, decomposition, and blood. The energy of which he consisted twitched in response; whatever took place down here, he didn't like it.

He forced himself to move on anyway. A series of dim lights illuminated the stairs and a hallway that led from their foot straight onward. Doors—all closed—lined the hallway. The things he could smell lay behind them.

He drifted down the stairs and halted, sudden memory, like déjà vu, flooding over him. Abruptly he transported, via memory, to another place.

A corridor not unlike this one but above ground, lined with closed doors, each secured by a lock. Hard hands hustled him along even though he was trussed like a goose in the market stall, arms bound tight to his body in a cloth shirt. His emotions nearly choked him and made it hard to breathe: anger, intense frustration, and a healthy wallop of fear.

"You can't do this to me," he told the two men leading him along—orderlies wearing gray coats. Gray. Just like that, he knew where he was; he remembered. "Someone will come looking for me, and once it's discovered I've been held against my will—"

One of his minders struck him, a blow that took him in the mouth and rocked him on his feet.

"Keep quiet unless you want your feet in a bucket and a wire down your back."

Quiet? The place was anything but. He could hear moans, cries, and screams coming from behind the locked doors. They had paused before a room, and his keeper swung that door open. Romney balked, knowing if he went in he'd never get out under his own power and would soon be screaming just like the rest.

He fought as hard as he could with his hands secured, kicked out with his feet and shoved with his shoulders and head. He knew himself to be a doughty—and dirty—fighter when in possession of all his limbs.

Now, though, the two keepers subdued him summarily, and brutally, using fists and a rubber cosh. They thrust him into the cell, and he fell to the floor, where he lay bleeding, still convulsed by rage.

He came to himself in Hathor's cellar, the images now bright in the field of energy that passed for his mind. As if a sluice had opened, he recalled scene after scene: the days of being locked away that brought him to the edge of madness, the frustration and helplessness that beat at him ceaselessly, and the long, repeated sessions that had finally separated spirit from flesh.

He had been driven to madness inside Grayson

Asylum. And his body—would it be any good to Topaz if he got it out of there?

They wanted to break him because—he groped for it—he knew too much. They dared not kill him outright, but destroying him mentally proved an effective tool for assuring his silence.

Only he had escaped. Into Topaz Hathor's bedroom.

He hovered in the dank air of the cellar hallway, reluctant to go on and unable to turn back. He thought of the woman waiting outside the cellar door, and even now desire flared. He had never felt for any woman what he felt for Topaz Hathor. For her sake he needed to move on.

He drifted through the nearest door. No light illuminated the space, but it seemed spirit didn't require light. He could see it was an office equipped with chairs and a desk stacked with papers. Those would no doubt warrant perusal at a later date.

He moved through the wall into the next room, a larger space that felt cold and contained several bodies stretched out on slabs.

Jackpot, he thought, and drifted over to look.

Three corpses, two male and one female, all completely devoid of spirit. They must be fresh, for they smelled of death but not much decay. He examined both the male bodies closely, considering appropriating one of them. Both were middle-aged, one with graying hair and a neat beard, the other black-haired and with a livid steam blast through the center of his head.

Murdered? He couldn't tell. But if so, why?

Why would Topaz's father have freshly-killed corpses in his basement?

He hovered above the corpse with the beard, wishing he could communicate with its occupant and obtain some answers, but its spirit had definitely flown.

Frederick Hathor might be able to call the fellow's soul back; Romney could not.

Could that be what all this was about? Did Hathor's wealthy clients pay the man to recall the souls of their dearly departed, reanimate them somehow? But how? Dead flesh remained dead, right?

He abandoned the three corpses and drifted on through the rest of the huge cellar. One room contained high quality steam units, nothing as sophisticated as Patrick Kelly but finer mechanicals than Romney had ever seen. Still another room, farther back, looked like a torture chamber rigged with metal tables, a large steam plant, and what he recognized as electrodes.

Memory nearly drove him against the wall. Quite suddenly he recalled his bare feet drenched with water and an identical electrode thrust against him. And pain that shattered him into a thousand pieces.

He came apart now in response, the separate bits of energy of which he was composed flying from one another in his distress, scattered into the gloom of the cellar beyond his recall.

Chapter Eleven

"Romney?" Leaning against the locked cellar door, Topaz whispered his name. Part of her awareness—seemingly bonded to him—had accompanied him through that door and down the stairs. She'd half sensed his progress as he moved steadily away from her, and now she sensed something that made her heart leap in her chest.

He had vanished.

Alarm widened her eyes and made her press her palms against the panel. How could he just disappear from her awareness that way?

Panic flooded her, swift and hot. She couldn't have lost him...no. For in only three short days his spirit had become part of hers; the sudden loss now stunned her.

Could she reach for him? Would the latent ability inside her stretch so far? Leaning against the panel, she considered the question. She had never wanted to utilize the talent she knew lay within. Fear and a certain level of decency prohibited it. Yet dealing with Romney Marsh had limbered it, freed it, and she would risk far more to assist him, were he in trouble.

To reach him.

She closed her eyes and for the first time in her life opened all her senses. She quested for him.

Beyond the doorway, down the stairs. She knew how the cellar looked; she had been there in the past, though not recently. A hallway led straight from the stairs, lined with doors. Tiny sparks of light led her along like breadcrumbs, shed as it seemed by Romney's spirit. But beyond that—nothing.

Desperation caused sweat to break out all over her body. Where was he? She needed to find him. She unfurled all her power and tried again.

"Topaz?" Her father's voice, close beside her.

She started violently; she hadn't heard him approach, far too distracted to notice even his ever-present cortege of spirits.

Yet he now stood at her elbow, clad in his dressing gown of golden silk, a curious look in his eyes.

"Daughter, what are you doing?"

Hastily she withdrew her questing senses, wondering how much her father could feel. He watched her steadily, awaiting an answer, so she said, "I thought I heard something."

His black brows lifted. Never a man to speak in haste, he pondered before replying, "You heard something all the way upstairs?"

"No, I—came down for a bite to eat after being out."

His dark gaze never wavered from her face even though he nodded at the kitchen beyond. "And why would you not request something from one of the units?"

"They're all on shut down at this hour."

"And they exist for our convenience, only that."

"Of course. But I'd just as soon prepare a sandwich for myself. I'm sure I heard something behind this door."

And was that a tactical error? Would her father

send his acute senses there and, being much better refined than hers would they detect Romney's presence?

Something flickered in his dark eyes. Topaz felt his energy—always so focused—shift momentarily. But he said nothing.

Did that mean Romney was truly gone? But where? How? And how would she bear it?

"Father," she said, "what is down there?"

He placed his warm hand on her shoulder. "Nothing to worry you, Topaz."

"Then why do you keep it locked?" She wanted to break through that door so badly she nearly foamed at the mouth.

But he shook his head. "You know the kind of work I pursue. No sense letting the servants stumble on our projects."

"Projects? But you—"

Calmly he said, "I coax willing spirits into manufactured bodies at the requests of their loved ones. You are already aware of that."

"And—into animals."

"Yes, sometimes."

"Perhaps that's what I heard, an animal in distress. We should go down and see." Anything to get her nearer Romney.

Her father frowned. "Is that how it sounded? Like an animal?"

"Perhaps. Yes."

"But there are no animals on the premises at this time."

"Just mechanical units? Nothing alive?"

Frederick Hathor smiled. "Nothing alive, I assure

you."

Dead bodies, Romney had said. So her father did not lie. But why would he have corpses in the house? What possible reason could there be?

"Father, I wish you would tell me more about your work."

"Really? Why now? For years I have been trying without success to get you interested in my work. 'The work of the Devil,' I think you called it. Let souls go where destined at death, you said—yes, I am sure that's what you told me."

"Yes, but..." Agonized, Topaz turned her eyes back to the cellar door. Still she sensed no hint from Romney. Nothing...

She fought back her panic and struggled to master her thoughts. "I remembered you saying you had some intriguing experiments ongoing in conjunction with your new colleague, Danson Clifford. Tell me about those."

Frederick put his arm around her and turned her firmly away from the cellar door.

"If you're truly interested in my work, Topaz, you should agree to become my assistant. I have been asking you this last year or more."

"You asked me to act as receptionist for those who come to you for spiritual guidance, not—not be involved in your experiments. I think I would find that much more interesting."

"Yes?" Still steering her toward the grand staircase, he cocked his head. "That would require you to work with young Danson."

"I've not met him." Topaz remembered how Sapphire had described the man: nouveau riche. But this city was filled with the newly prosperous—and the devastatingly poor. For her part, Topaz knew which she preferred.

But such thoughts wouldn't get her into the cellar.

Her father went on, with some emphasis. "It would also require absolute confidentiality on your part." He laid his finger against the side of his nose. "You couldn't breathe a word of what Danson and I share to anyone—including your mother or brother."

That distracted Topaz for an instant. What could her father possibly be about that he wouldn't share with his wife? And which required corpses...

"You can certainly rely on my discretion." Her father didn't know half of what she got up to and never would. And she would readily sell her conscience for Romney Marsh's sake.

She paused at the foot of the stairs and considered that fact. She loved her brother and the other members of her family—even this man at her side in a way too complex for her to unravel. She also cared deeply for certain members of her community—Patrick Kelly included. But she couldn't say she would abandon her principles for any one of them.

So how could she in just a few short days bond with Romney Marsh to such a deeper extent? A man she had never actually met, had never seen more clearly than as a hazy, transparent image hanging in the air. But what an image! And what a spirit he had that whispered to her, claimed her, set up a level of need she fully realized only now that he was gone.

She looked her father in the eye. "I would very much like to be part of this new project."

"Then I will introduce you to Danson. He will, of

course, have to agree about including you."

"Of course."

Frederick smiled. "He will be here this afternoon, Daughter. You can meet him then."

****

Romney. Romney Marsh.

The call came like lightning arcing through water, spearing the black void into which Romney had dispersed. Very like droplets of water in a vast sea, the particles of energy from which he was composed had nearly been assimilated by the darkness.

But now desire pulled at them, aroused and drew them together. Someone called him. He had a reason to be.

Separate pricks of light, well-scattered, moved in the blackness of oblivion, and the nothingness abruptly became the cellar of Frederick Hathor's mansion. One bit of energy joined another, gathering strength as they combined. Not destroyed, he existed yet.

He existed for her.

A bright picture flooded his consciousness: a woman armed with a stiletto fighting naked in the cold breeze from an open window. Long black hair swirled about her and brushed against her generous white curves; strength commanded her every line and danger glittered in amber eyes, set aslant in her face.

Topaz.

Recalling her, longing consumed him. He remembered little of his identity or how he'd come here, scattered. Dead. Not dead.

But he knew he needed to be with her, drawn as irresistibly as iron to a lodestone.

He became aware suddenly that other spirits

accompanied him here—a horde of them. He could feel their emotions: grief and fear, anxiety, eagerness and longing that matched his own. They all wanted something, had all—like him—been drawn to this place. Now some could not get away again.

Could he? Where was "away"? Where did he belong, save with Topaz? How could he escape and return to her?

Determined for it, he gathered himself, strove to answer her call. But he had barely condensed before a greater call descended upon him. With a rush of horror and dismay he recognized it.

Not dead, no: and that being so, he had still a connection to his body. That drew him now with irresistible force. He had no power to resist and, gathered into a glowing net of energy, his spirit flew abruptly backward, like water down a chute, until he found himself sailing, sailing, sailing to a place he did not want to be.

With a perceptible *pop* he reentered his body, and pain descended on him like a hammer.

He opened his eyes and began to scream.

Chapter Twelve

"I need to get into the cellar."

Topaz burst into her brother's room soon after first light and delivered the words without preamble. Outside, a combination of sleet and snow hissed down. She saw that Sapphire had drawn his drapes against the weather and the room lay steeped in gloom.

She located Sapphire still abed, snuggled beneath his velvet coverlet, his dark hair mussed on the pillow.

"Do you never knock?" he greeted her in complaint.

"I have no time for niceties—this is important."

"Well, for God's sake come in and shut the door."

Topaz frowned and complied. As she stepped in, her eye caught movement on the pillow beside her brother's: a small, fair head as mussed as his. His companion ducked down quickly, pulling the cover over her head, but Topaz didn't need to see her in order to guess her identity.

Carlotta, the little maid to whom Sapphire had taken such an unfortunate fancy.

Her mission momentarily forgotten, Topaz gestured wildly. "Are you mad? Do you want to get her in trouble? You know Mother will dismiss her at once if she finds out."

"She won't find out. I trust you."

"What if somebody other than I had come walking

in, say another servant?"

"Everyone else knocks, including the servants." Sapphire stretched luxuriantly, displaying absolutely no concern. "The servants probably know anyway; they know everything. Isn't that right, my dove?"

Carlotta's tumbled head reappeared, cheeks flushed with either embarrassment or the warmth beneath the covers. She gave Topaz an uncertain look.

"Sorry, miss. I'd get up, miss, but I haven't any clothes."

"Never mind, stay where you are." A sudden thought made Topaz ask, "Is it true what he says? Do the servants here know everything? Do you know how to get into the cellar?"

"Can't be done." Sapphire answered before Carlotta could. "So far as I know, Father has the only key."

"I am aware of that. Where does he keep it?"

Sapphire shrugged. "Close to him, I should imagine. On his person during the day."

"And at night?"

"I'd guess in his study. Carly, do you know?"

Carlotta shook her head. She truly was a pretty little thing, Topaz thought—especially out of her maid's uniform. Delicately boned, she proved that Sapphire ascribed to his father's taste in beauty. Carlotta looked much as their mother had when young—Topaz had seen her portrait—only Dahlia had rich brown hair instead of blonde.

"We are not allowed to clean the master's study. Only the steam units go in there—just one or two of them."

"And the cellar? Who cleans there?"

"No one, miss. At least none of us does. Those same two steamies are allowed."

Topaz wondered if she might successfully question steamies. Any in which her father placed trust would be sanctioned against speaking.

"What's so important about the cellar?" Sapphire inquired.

Topaz bent and picked up Carlotta's gray uniform from the floor. "Here, put this on and go about your duties before you get in trouble."

They waited while the girl dressed, Topaz with her gaze firmly turned away, Sapphire watching lazily, his eyes half narrowed.

As soon as the maid slipped out of the room, Topaz hissed, "Are you really that selfish, Sapphire?"

"Yes, entirely. You should know that about me by now."

Annoyed, Topaz perched on the foot of his bed. "Can you spare no thought for her?"

"I assure you I spare her plenty of thought, sister— near round the clock."

"Are you determined to ruin her?"

"That had not—for all your protestations—crossed my mind."

"Well, it should. Mother will go all proper if she discovers this and toss the girl out on her ear. You know and I know what often happens to young girls dismissed from service."

"They go astray. But as you seem to see it, Carly's already gone astray here in my bed."

"That won't save her on the streets." All too many of the streetwalkers whom Topaz schooled in self-defense had started out in service. A maid dismissed without a reference stood little chance of getting taken on elsewhere; situations weren't plentiful, with all the steamies about. Mechanicals didn't demand so much as a pittance in salary and never needed sleep. Indeed, those in Frederick Hathor's house shut down merely to conserve energy.

"Do you truly think I'd see her come to harm?" Sapphire's dark eyes flashed.

"I don't know, do I? What if she comes up carrying your child?"

"Do you suppose I'd abandon her even then?"

"It happens, even when men say they care."

Sapphire pushed himself up in the bed, revealing a well-muscled, naked torso. "And you want me to sit here discussing my deepest feelings?"

"No, I want you to give Carlotta up before she pays the price for this liaison."

Sapphire froze for a moment, a curious look coming to his face. Then he said, "You know, Topaz, I don't think I can. I've been with a lot of women. They're something of a habit with me."

"Yes?"

"Yes. But Carlotta puts them all in the shade and relegates the habit to oblivion. If they were a habit— well, she's an addiction. I simply can't resist the taste of her on my tongue. I don't suppose you'd understand."

"I might." Topaz suspected if she ever once tasted Romney Marsh—the real Romney Marsh—she would never free herself from wanting him.

She wanted him now, damn it.

"Why Carlotta, of all women?"

"Cursed if I know."

"Are you in love with her?"

Sapphire twitched beneath his blankets. "What's love? I doubt if you, I, or any of the Hathors know."

"Father loves Mother."

Sapphire gave a dark laugh. "Is that what you call it? He wraps her in cotton wool and treats her as if she's brainless. The woman hasn't made a decision in years. A fine example to set before us. And effective. Ruby's marriage is a farce, and as for Pearl—she's in love with her husband's money, nothing more."

"So what do you feel for Carlotta?"

"Desire, as I've said. A surprising amount of tenderness. If she—as you so delicately put it—came up carrying my child, I'd stand by her."

"Marriage, you mean?"

He shrugged again. "Why not?"

"If you want Mother to flip her wig. To say nothing of Father."

"Yes well, sister, I care little for what they think. And if you're talking about the class difference—"

"I'm not, but they will."

"I care nothing for that either."

"Father will cut you off."

"Money, you mean? Let him. It's dirty money; you know that, don't you?"

Topaz pointed out with a touch of irony, "It allows you to live comfortably, sleep till noon, and dabble in all your special interests. Marry your little Carlotta and you'll have to find—and keep—a job."

Sapphire sat up in one swift movement, his expression suddenly serious. "You have no idea of what I'm capable. I'm *this* close to leaving here already, losing myself somewhere on the west side, and never resurfacing."

"You wouldn't do that. You won't leave me here alone."

"Come with me. There's enough gypsy in our blood to let us survive anywhere. And the smell of corruption is starting to taint my soul."

Topaz leaned closer. "Do you have any idea what Father and Danson Clifford are up to in the cellar?" Sometimes Sapphire just knew things as if he had some occult sense.

"Why are you so interested in the cellar all of a sudden?"

Topaz lowered her voice. "You remember that spirit I thought was in my room?"

"The stray? Yes."

"He wasn't a stray. And I—" Topaz hesitated. "I connected with him on a significant level. But last night he went into the cellar and...I've lost him."

Sapphire began to laugh, low and wicked. "Regular men not good enough for you, sister? You have to choose those like Kelly and disembodied spirits?"

"This is serious. I want him back, Sapphire. I need him."

"Ah. The way I need Carly?"

"I don't know, do I? Maybe. Will you help me?"

"Get into the cellar? Pointless. If he were there, he'd be able to come out again."

"Unless Father and Clifford have some contraption there, some device for trapping spirits. What if they're experimenting with capturing the spirits of the departed at the moment of death or something? Sapphire, there are corpses down there."

Sapphire did not appear as surprised as Topaz felt he should. "Yes? How do you know?"

"Romney told me."

"Romney! Your spirit?" Sapphire considered it. "Can you communicate with him?"

"Not now. I have to find him, Sapph—free him, get him back."

"I have to say I've never known you to act like this. Have you actually seen him?"

"Well, yes."

"Clearly?"

"I can see him and see *through* him—I know it sounds crazy."

"Good-looking fellow, is he? Your usual type?"

"I don't have a type."

"You most certainly have: fair-haired, not overly tall, blue eyes, and classic features."

Topaz squirmed uncomfortably. "I can't tell what color his eyes are." She knew there was nothing typical about her attraction to Romney. "None of that matters. Will you or will you not help me?"

"How can I possibly help?"

"Make an excuse to get into Father's study. Say you're looking for a book or something, and while you're there you can search for the key."

"A book? Me?"

"I know you read. Why do you insist on playing the dilettante?"

"We all play at something, Topaz—even you with your stiletto and your highly honed fighting skills." He sat back and examined her coolly. "What will you give me if I help you?"

"My undying love?"

He wrinkled his nose. "We've already established the love of a Hathor isn't worth much."

"What do you want?"

"Your silence where Carly's concerned, for a start. And a little less criticism of our relationship."

"That's two things."

"Your silence, then."

"Agreed. You'll search for the key tonight?"

"I will. But let me know if your straying spirit comes back to you. I wouldn't like to be caught in the act."

"Good. And meanwhile I've told Father I'm interested in working with him on his latest project."

Sapphire's brows soared. "The one that involves the corpses? He's been trying to get you on side for years. You truly must be enamored, to agree now."

"I'm supposed to meet his partner this afternoon." Topaz laid her hand on Sapphire's arm. "Sapph, you really don't know what they're up to?"

"Sister, I wouldn't even like to guess."

Chapter Thirteen

"Danson, I would like you to meet my daughter, Topaz. Topaz, this is Danson Clifford."

Topaz lifted her gaze to the face of the man opposite and froze in surprise. She didn't know what she'd expected of her father's new associate: not this.

Unmarried, her mother had said of him, and extremely wealthy. She'd mentioned nothing about his appearance, and Topaz could see why. If she had to choose a word to describe Danson Clifford, it would be "nondescript."

Neither tall nor short, neither particularly well nor poorly dressed; he didn't look like a man with money, though she knew her father wouldn't associate with him if he weren't.

Mousy brown hair lay limp around a dome-shaped skull. A pale complexion argued he might well spend a lot of time in cellars. Eyes of a watery gray peered through wire-rimmed spectacles that perched on a thin, sharp nose. What nature had added to the nose she'd subtracted from the chin, the weakness of which contrasted with a prominent Adam's apple.

"Pleased to make your acquaintance, Miss Hathor."

A second shock passed through Topaz; this one tingled. His voice, very soft and cultured, bore a now-familiar accent.

"You're from England," she said in surprise. The

second time in mere days she'd encountered such an accent. What were the odds?

"Yes. Like so many others, I've decided to avail myself of the opportunities offered by this brave, new world."

"From what part of England do you hail, Mr. Clifford?"

"East Anglia—the Fens. Most people on this side of the pond have not heard of it."

He spoke in a tone so hushed Topaz had to lean close to hear. When she did she caught a hint of his scent, an odd combination of mustiness and decay. A slow shiver traveled up her spine, and she drew back again.

Her father spoke. "Topaz has expressed an interest in assisting us with our new project, Danson. She has suitable talents—admittedly undeveloped as yet—and might prove useful, if you have no objections."

"To your daughter? How could I object?" Danson smiled, revealing slightly pointed teeth.

He looks like a rabid animal, Topaz thought. Or a hare beset by some other strange disease.

"Keep it in the family, eh?" Danson went on. "Family members never betray secrets."

"Secrets?" Topaz echoed. "I wish you would tell me, Mr. Clifford, just what this new project entails. My father has hinted at just enough to keep me intrigued."

"My daughter, like all my children, becomes bored easily."

"Oh, I am quite certain we can find something to hold her interest. Miss Hathor, do you often help your father in his work?"

"Never. But he rarely ceases reminding me we

have a duty to those who come to us for solace." I should be struck dead for hypocrisy, Topaz thought even as she spoke the words. But she'd say anything she must for Romney's sake. Desperation still gnawed at her. All night long she'd found no rest and caught no hint of him, not so much as a whisper.

Frederick turned away and filled three snifters with brandy. They had met in his study—the very place Topaz wanted to search for the key—and she struggled to keep her gaze focused on Clifford rather than speculate about her father's possible hiding places.

Frederick placed a snifter in her hand. Feigning interest she asked, "And, Mr. Clifford, precisely what is your occupation?"

"Undertaker."

"I beg your pardon?" What had he said in that soft voice of his?

"For many generations, Miss Hathor, my people have cared for the dead even as yours have listened for departing spirits and aided them. An ancestor of mine used to travel around the Fens with a horse and cart, tending the newly deceased. Today we are much more…organized."

Undertaker. A second chill followed the first up Topaz's spine, this one so violent she barely kept still. And there were corpses in the cellar.

Suddenly she didn't want to know what went on there. She looked from her father's dark eyes, which could hide any number of secrets, to those of Clifford, so oddly difficult to read behind his lenses, and horror touched her.

Run from this, her every instinct told her—the same that guarded her when she went abroad in the dangerous parts of the city, and that kept her safe.

She fixed her gaze on Clifford, and the sense spoke again: *Get away from him.*

But she had to discover what had happened to Romney—help him if she could. And she prided herself on being fearless, the kind of woman who chased away would-be abductors. Why should she be so disturbed by this mere drip of a man?

She sat on the leather settee, assuming a mild interest. "And, Mr. Clifford, how did you meet my father?"

The two men exchanged glances before Clifford lowered himself into a chair, holding his brandy snifter as if not quite sure what to do with it. "I sought him out. Your father, Miss Hathor, is one of the foremost spiritualists of our day. Even in England we have heard of him. Does it not make sense that one such as I, who deals with the dead, should wish to make his acquaintance?"

"I don't know. Does it?"

"Oh, I think so."

Frederick took the other end of the settee. "Danson brings knowledge that, combined with mine, may change how we perceive death and could ultimately negate bereavement."

"Really?" Topaz's thoughts flew. She leaned toward Danson, even though her every instinct still bade otherwise, and asked confidingly, "What are you attempting? Do tell."

"All in good time, Topaz," Frederick said almost jovially. "First you must prove your sincere desire to be part of this great undertaking."

Undertaking? The undertakings of an undertaker…

surely her father made a joke. But no, Frederick Hathor rarely displayed a sense of humor. "How am I to do that, Father?"

"Apply yourself. Leave off wasting your time and frittering away your energies in the seamier parts of the city."

"I do not waste my energies."

To Clifford, Frederick said, "My daughter insists on visiting waterfront dives, teaching self-defense to prostitutes, and consorting with automatons. Oh, yes, Topaz—you're aware I know every detail of what you get up to at Nellie's and the Eagle Bar. Do you think I don't have sources whispering to me? They whisper constantly."

Anger and frustration twisted together to turn Topaz's stomach. Did her father have to flaunt his knowledge? What else did he know? Was he aware of her connection with Romney? Had he somehow got rid of him? Did he guess what she was about even now?

Or was that just what he wanted her to think?

Frederick Hathor might be a talented spirit master; he was also a consummate confidence man. He did, in truth, contact spirits at the request of those who came to him. He also prolonged their reasons for coming and procured from them large amounts of money—enough to keep this grand house with all its comforts.

Solace for the bereaved—at a price. But where did an undertaker from East Anglia fit in? Especially one who raised Topaz's hackles to such a degree.

"Well, then, Father," she said solemnly, "I guess I'll just have to prove myself to you." She pierced Clifford with a glance. "To both of you."

Frederick smiled. "Welcome home, Daughter.

Welcome home at last."

Topaz drained her snifter in a single gulp.

Chapter Fourteen

"He's coming around."

Moist, dense air beat at Romney's face, pressed against his mouth, and funneled down his throat, making it difficult to breathe. The chamber where he lay felt very warm—steamy—and his flesh had become slick with moisture. Condensation? Sweat? Blood?

He couldn't tell. Strange to be once more housed in flesh, especially this flesh that lay strapped to a table, kept immobile by force, which would drive a man to...

Madness, madness, madness.

Surely he'd been mad for a while, had been out of his body, as well. And who wouldn't flee this? Here was nothing but pain.

He wanted Topaz. Gypsy dancer, beautiful woman, all strength and fire. He held to the idea of her as to a flare of light in darkness.

A shadow materialized above him; a face peered down at him, backlit so he could not see the features.

"Welcome back, friend. I thought we had lost you."

"Not your friend." His lips barely moved; he had lost some of the ability for controlling the flesh and now felt doubly confined. He could not tell whether or not he actually produced the words.

"You were gone several days," the shadow informed him.

Gone with Topaz, where he wanted to be again.

But the demands of the flesh had called him home and now tethered him.

He must be in the asylum. At the thought, he felt his heart thump hard in his chest. A strange sensation after its absence. He didn't want to be here, had successfully fled once before. Could he escape again?

But no; his spirit had settled back into this flesh as into a prison. He gathered himself and tested his bonds; right wrist strapped down tight. Left wrist. Right and left ankle. Chest and thighs. At least he did not sit in the chair with wet feet and the electrode coming at him.

The figure looming above demanded, "Tell me your name."

He struggled to recall. Only one name came to his mind: Topaz Hathor. But he could not utter that, would not endanger her at any cost. He had a sudden vision of her here in his place, strapped down with her black hair fanning out, her breasts rising and falling with her distress, agony possessing her body.

No, no, no—not that. He would suffer anything before betraying her.

"Your name." The demand came again, absolute as death. His mind raged and screamed and produced the only other appellation within its reach.

"Romney Marsh."

Calmly the voice asserted, "Romney Marsh is a place. I want your name."

His thoughts flailed wildly: he possessed nothing else. He tried to shake his head but a strap pinned his skull to the table.

"He's forgotten. You've shocked it from him," said a second voice from beyond his line of sight.

"Perhaps."

"I did warn you."

"He'll remember with the right persuasion. If it's in his head, I'll obtain it. Tell me, friend, why did you come to Buffalo? What is your mission?"

Helpless, he remained silent.

"Tell me." Soft yet utterly relentless, the voice pressed on. "Or shall we employ the electrodes?"

"No. No, no—"

"If he doesn't remember…"

"My good man." The form hanging above him half turned to address the other man, and he caught a glimpse of a profile: sharp nose, receding chin, and a pair of spectacles. "This man is devious beyond your comprehension. He could be playing us even now. He would not have been sent were he not among the very best."

"Then kill him," the other urged. "End it. What will reducing him to quivering jelly accomplish?"

"Killing him will not tell me what he knows."

"Perhaps he knows nothing."

The man who leaned over the table snorted. "So he would have us think. This is a top agent of the Crown. Only think how many days it took for us to induce him to scream."

Agent of the Crown? He echoed the words in his mind. Her majesty's Crown—Victoria? Surely not. Yes, he had come from England. Home.

But no—Topaz Hathor was his home.

The spectacled man said, not raising his voice, "I have told you repeatedly I dare not kill him outright. He has influential connections and will eventually be traced. But if those who come find only a babbling, drooling husk—that's not murder, is it?"

"Worse than murder, some might say."

"Not according to the law. I have no wish to be hauled back to England for a neck-stretching. Bring the orderlies, Cecil, and prepare the electrodes. We shall try once again to discover just what he recalls."

****

"What do you think of Father's new associate?"

Topaz, who had encountered her brother in the front hall, paused and shivered involuntarily. She glanced over her shoulder, half expecting Danson Clifford to hover in a corner, like one of the spirits that plagued this place.

"An appalling creature," she told Sapphire. "You've seen him?"

"Indeed I have." Sapphire's eyes gleamed. "Seems an unprepossessing specimen to me, if thoroughly wet and unpleasant."

"Don't you believe it." Topaz leaned close to her brother. "Did you know he's an undertaker?"

Sapphire lifted his brows. "I did not. Father said only that he had brought vital innovations from England and was engaged in some fascinating experiments."

"Clifford told me his family had been undertakers for generations in some place called The Fens."

"You mean Romney Marsh?"

Topaz froze where she stood. "What did you just say?"

"It's a place in the southeast of England—Godforsaken, by all accounts—and from whence I'm sure Father said Clifford hails. Sister, at times your ignorance shocks me."

"You must be mistaken," Topaz said through suddenly stiff lips.

"Why do you say that?"

"Because Romney Marsh—well, that's *his* name—the name of my missing spirit, that is."

A gleam appeared in Sapphire's dark eyes. "He told you that?"

"Yes."

"A curious thing. Because it's a place, as I say. Sure you're not mistaken?"

Topaz shook her head. "Don't you think it's odd, brother, they're both from England, my spirit and Father's new associate?"

Sapphire gave a lithe shrug. "Life is all too full of coincidences. Have you convinced Father to let you assist him?"

Topaz wrinkled her nose. "For that privilege he requires many sacrifices. I must apply myself to his above-stairs endeavors, strive to develop my affinity for spiritual communication, and forego my activities on the waterfront."

"Ah. So where are you bound now?"

"To the waterfront," Topaz admitted. "I have a class scheduled this evening and would not like to disappoint the girls who come. They rely on the skills I teach them."

"And if Father finds out?"

She shrugged. "He claims to know everything we get up to, right? That means you and Carlotta, as well."

"He claims. Father claims many things. Some percentage of it is truth."

"Well, I'll take a chance this once. Come with me?" she added hopefully.

"I am otherwise engaged."

"Not Carlotta again?"

"I've told you, she's an addiction—an awfully sweet one. But I promise, sister, once she falls asleep, I intend to go creeping into Father's study in search of your key. I take it you've still had no contact from your spirit."

She shook her head. "Go safely."

"You as well."

"No fear—I'm armed. And Patrick Kelly may be there, too."

"Your mechanical watchdog?"

"Not mechanical. He's far more than that."

****

"Well done!" Topaz praised the girls and women arranged in rows before her in various states of dress and undress, all of it ragged. She herself wore only her chemise and a fine sheen of sweat.

The storeroom of Nellie's Bar, where they gathered, was barely heated, but she'd worked hard. They all had. The boxes of gin and vodka and the barrels of Irish whiskey had been pushed to the walls to afford them room.

In one corner lounged Patrick Kelly, keeping an eye on things, his ever-present glass of whiskey in his hand. He never drank from it, but when he was off duty it had become an appendage.

And an identity? Topaz shot a thoughtful look at him. What must it be like to be human but quite possibly not human enough? And what constituted human enough? Patrick had more than once told her he doubted he possessed a soul.

She, Topaz, didn't doubt it. He was one of the finest men she knew, and she trusted him implicitly.

She turned her gaze back to her students, who, all

but one, breathed heavily. She'd put them through their paces this evening, but hopefully they'd react as needed the next time they faced a threat of any kind.

She looked at Suzie, who sat on a crate at the edge of the cleared space. Suzie had shown up tonight willing to take part in the lesson, but Topaz had forbidden it.

She asked, "Any questions?"

"Yes, miss." One of the older women, with a riddled, pockmarked face, spoke up. "You say in a pinch it's smart to go for the fellow's vitals, if you know what I mean—his man bits. Ain't that right?"

"Better than getting cut or beaten up," Topaz returned, determinedly looking away from Suzie.

"But won't that put a damper on future trade?"

An outbreak of sniggering ensued. These women, as Topaz had learned, possessed a crude sense of humor, dark as the lives they led.

"Chance you'll have to take. There are plenty other johns on the prowl, right? And you want paying for your services—not grief."

"Friend of mine got raped the other night," said a younger girl. "The bastard left her lying in an alley, bleeding."

"Precisely. You ladies lead a perilous existence. Some of the tricks I've shared with you just might save your skin someday."

More gently she added, "That will be enough for this session. Dry off well before you go out into the cold."

"A dram in the bar for any who wants it," Kelly said jovially, getting to his feet.

"Miss Topaz?" It was the only appellation by

which she was known here. The name "Hathor" had never been uttered, so far as she knew.

"Yes, Peg?"

"When will we meet for another session?"

Topaz hesitated. If she continued to defy her father outright, could she expect to win his confidence? She dared not risk doing anything to jeopardize reconnecting with the man she still thought of as Romney.

But she looked into the worn, worried faces before her and couldn't find it in her heart to refuse them.

"Same time next week and—same place?" She glanced at Kelly, who nodded. "And," she added, "bring your friends, all who will come."

Chapter Fifteen

The women dressed and filed from the storeroom quickly, eager for their promised drinks. When Suzie moved to follow, Topaz held up her hand.

"Wait, Suzie, if you will. Can we have a word?"

The girl paused at the end of the line and dropped her gaze. A tiny thing and surely no older than fifteen or sixteen, she barely reached Topaz's ear.

"Yes, miss?"

"What happened to you?" As if Topaz didn't know. She examined the girl's face: skin split above one cheekbone, two black eyes, and lips swollen so she could barely speak.

Suzie shrugged. "He wouldn't pay up front and didn't want to pay when we were done. When I tried to insist, he did this."

"How bad's the rest of it, under your clothes?"

Suzie shifted uncomfortably. "Not too bad. I won't be turning any tricks for a while, though." She winced and admitted, "My face hurts the worst."

Topaz turned as Patrick Kelly strolled up. "What do you think? Broken cheekbone?"

His green eyes examined the girl's countenance. "Quite possibly."

"Suzie, you need to see a doctor."

"Oh, miss." Suzie shrank. "I can't."

"Why not? You have to get proper care or your

face might not heal right."

"I can't afford it, miss. Don't know where I'll get money to eat till I can take paying customers again."

Topaz turned and searched among her clothes, which she'd shed at the beginning of the session, and came up with her clutch purse.

"Here. Find a doctor—and not one of those quacks who operate around here. Pat, do you know anyone?"

"Dr. Fleming on Jefferson will see her."

"Go there, then. Here's money for his fee and enough for another visit if he tells you to go back. If he does, you must comply, understand?"

"Miss Topaz, I can't take your money."

"You can and you will. What are friends for? There's enough to buy some hot meals and pay for a room. You're skin and bone." She stuffed the money into Suzie's hand and looked at her sternly.

"Is there no way you can get out of this life?"

The girl shook her head.

"No family?"

A more violent shake.

Helplessness flooded Topaz. Why should she have so much and this girl so little? "Well," she said, struggling to conceal her emotion, "we can't let this happen to you again. What you need is a weapon—a knife such as I carry, or perhaps a very small pistol. Patrick, surely you could procure one."

"I could," Patrick replied, expressionless. Well, he usually was more or less expressionless, though Topaz could often gauge his feelings.

"But miss," Suzie protested, "if I used a weapon on a john—or worse, shot him—I'd be arrested, and no excuses."

"But it would be self-defense."

"Not for the likes of me," she asserted. "Ask him."

Topaz lifted her brows at Kelly.

"I am afraid she is right. The law tends to go hard on women in her position."

"That's not right. What is she supposed to do?"

"I did not say it is *right*, merely that it *is*."

"Thank you for the money, miss. This will see me through till I'm on my feet again."

"Pat, will you see her safely home? To a room, if she needs one?"

"I will. And, Suzie, I am off duty tomorrow. I will accompany you to see Dr. Fleming, if you wish." He added gently, "Go get your drink now, against the cold. I will be right out."

The girl went, and Kelly eyed Topaz. "You are a kind woman, Miss Topaz."

"I only wish I could do more for them."

"We do what we can. I wanted to mention while we are alone: I have news for you."

"News?"

"I have made inquiries, unofficial ones, about the place you call Grayson."

Topaz's heart leaped. She lowered her voice. "Tell me."

"It is not an asylum proper but a private house owned by one Cecil Crittenden. I discovered they do in fact house and apparently treat patients there on a basis most discreet, and for an exorbitant fee."

"So it wouldn't be out of the question for someone who had been confined there—say against his will—to refer to it as an asylum."

"It would not." Again Kelly's expression remained

bland, though Topaz felt his interest quicken. "Confinement against one's will—as we discussed before—would be a police matter."

"Yes. But as we also discussed, I have no proof." Not even the testimony of a spirit, at the moment.

"A pity," Kelly remarked.

"It is."

"I do not like men who use other men for their own ends. Is there a way for you to get evidence? If so I will act upon it."

"I'm working on that. Tell me, Pat, do you believe in an afterlife?"

"I should, Miss Topaz, since I'm living it."

"I speak of the continuation of the spirit after death."

"So do I. If I did not believe in the continuation of spirit, I would possess no humanity other than this skin I wear."

Topaz nodded.

"But," Kelly went on, "is the spirit the same as the soul? Having researched my past, I know I was raised in the Catholic Church. I would not like to risk perdition."

"You have researched your past?"

"Indeed. I had a life before this one—as a full-fledged man. I had a wife. I have met her."

"What?"

"She wanted nothing to do with me in this guise and has left the city to live elsewhere with relations. She took our children—two small lasses."

"Oh, Patrick, I'm sorry. She's a fool."

"She is not. She married a man. I am not him. But I can still do some good in the world. Come to me if you find your evidence. Meanwhile, I will make sure Suzie has her drink before I see her home."

"Thank you, Patrick."

"You take care, Miss Topaz." And he left her to don her clothing and make her way back to the mansion on Humboldt Parkway—the last place she wanted to be.

Chapter Sixteen

Topaz walked swiftly through a night made cold with a breath of air straight off the Niagara River. It penetrated her clothes and made her wish for a cab, but she had no chance of catching one in this neighborhood. The only cabbies to be found in the area would be off duty and looking for a quick tumble.

At least, she thought wryly, she had good boots and a warm coat. Pity the poor girls like those she'd just left who had to make do in their shabby dresses, needing to show a bit of leg in order to attract customers.

She wished with sudden passion she could free them all from the life. How dared her father criticize her for trying to assist these women? They hadn't been born to the luxuries she enjoyed.

Not that she'd wish life in the mansion, with its secrets, on anyone.

She rounded a corner and the wind drove pellets of ice into her eyes, half obscuring the dark street. But she heard a woman's cry, followed by a man's raised voice, just ahead.

One of the girls struggling with a john? Fearing the worst, Topaz hurried forward and saw a couple just ahead on the sidewalk. But they weren't alone.

The woman cried out again, and Topaz heard the sound of a slap; the woman fell back onto the bricks of the street.

Topaz's boots made barely a whisper of sound as she darted forward. When she drew near enough, she saw the girl was indeed a streetwalker, one she knew but who hadn't attended tonight's meeting. She now sat on the ground with her soiled petticoat showing and fear in her eyes.

Her companion looked like a gentleman, no doubt out looking for a quick fumble. He wore a fine coat and scarf and stood with his back to Topaz.

Two men faced him, and with a shock Topaz realized she knew them also. One, tall and bulky, wore a shabby coat and had a filthy bandage on one leg. The other, shorter, wore a soiled dressing on his head and another wrapped around one hand. This didn't prevent either of them from holding weapons, one an ancient pistol and the other a knife.

She'd interrupted a holdup.

One of the bandits—the shorter—caught sight of Topaz over his victim's shoulder and stared. His eyes widened in horror.

"Look! Look, Bert, it's *her*."

"Eh? What's that, Sam?" The bigger fellow hadn't taken his eyes off the gentleman. "Who?"

"The strapping wench. With the knife."

Bert jerked his gaze from his intended victim, who also looked around, and fixed it on Topaz. A snarl contorted the villain's face when he recognized her.

A smile came to hers. "Gentlemen—and I use the term most loosely—we meet again." She let her gaze move over them, inspecting the damages she'd inflicted, before she looked at the man in the fine coat, a dandy who at the present moment appeared both shocked and embarrassed.

"Sir," she flung at him with a gesture toward the girl in the street, "please see your companion to safety. I'll take care of things here."

Instead of complying or making any display of relief, he flung a glance at the streetwalker, another at his assailants, and took off down the street as fast as his well-shod feet could take him.

Bert, who held the pistol, visibly thought about firing on him; Topaz saw the weapon waver before it turned back toward her.

"Now you've done it, missy. Took us a long time to find that mark."

"Injured as we are," his fellow put in. "You think it's easy to do business, given the shape you left us in?"

"I did nothing but turn away a couple of trespassers. Not my fault if you were stupid enough to fall off a building."

"Looks like you're gonna have to pay for it." Bert grunted. "I did warn you."

"Bert—we could nab her after all, here and now."

The streetwalker—Topaz recalled her name as Tillie—scrambled to her feet.

"Off with you," Topaz told her. "Go somewhere safe, mind."

"I'll not leave you here with the likes of them," Tillie declared, proving herself far more honorable than her former companion.

"Go to Nellie's. Pat Kelly might still be there."

Tillie nodded, hiked up her skirts, and ran, leaving Topaz alone with the two thugs and the cold darkness.

She drew the stiletto from the sleeve of her coat. "Remember this?" she asked Bert.

"Not likely to forget, is he?" asked Sam. "You cut

him bad. On second thought, Bert, let's not take a chance nabbing her. Shoot her, quick."

"Yes, Bert." Topaz went tight and still. "Shoot me."

He grunted again. "Not sure I want to damage the goods. There are customers will pay a high price for that—on the black market."

"What are you talking about, Bert? You promised revenge, if we ever saw her again."

Topaz shifted on the balls of her feet. Given Bert's injured leg, she knew she could out-maneuver him, and she had time to waste in conversation. "Tell me more, Bert. What black market is this?"

He bared his teeth at her. "You should know. Rumor has it the end products've been makin' their way into that mansion of your father's. Be a funny thing to sell him his own daughter's corpse, wouldn't it?"

"Corpse?" Topaz's mind flailed over the implications.

"Maybe you should just nab her after all, Bert." Sam virtually jumped up and down, the knife in his hand. "Now, while we have the chance. You can decide later what to do with her—sell her or"—he licked his lips—"enjoy her ourselves."

"Stupid bitch needs to suffer for what she did to me."

Bert, his decision apparently made, raised the pistol. Before he could squeeze the trigger, Topaz leaped, her muscles quick and supple from the workout at Nellie's. Her right foot knocked the pistol from Bert's hand. Her left fist followed and took him in the jaw, snapping his head around.

Sam swore and exclaimed.

Topaz, with no attention to spare for him, delivered a blow to Bert's gut that doubled him over. A final smack to his nose sent blood streaming into the street.

The big man went down with a groan. Topaz turned on Sam.

"Now tell me." She fixed him with an unblinking stare. "What's all this about my father's house and bodies?"

"I don't know. Honest, miss." He gestured at the unmoving lump that was Bert. "You'd have to ask him."

"Were you trying to rob that gentleman, or abduct him?"

"Bert just said to grab the fellow while he was distracted with the whore. I'm not sure what he meant to do with him after."

"I don't believe you."

"It's the truth. I'm not the brains, just the brawn." He eyed the thin blade in Topaz's hand and seemed to reconsider. "Though I did hear Bert say they were paying up to a thousand dollars each."

"For what?"

"Corpses. In good condition. Let me go, miss, please."

"Give me your knife."

Sam tossed it on the ground.

"Now tell me you'll consider going into a different line of work. This isn't healthy for you, as you can plainly see."

The sound of pounding footsteps came from behind Topaz just then; Sam took off running.

Topaz let him go and turned to see Patrick Kelly

appear, with two other automatons, all puffing steam like breath. Tillie trailed them, gasping.

"Miss Topaz, are you all right?" Pat called.

"Didn't even break a sweat. Caught this one trying to rob Tillie's companion, or so I thought." She gestured at the now-stirring Bert with one boot. "I'm wondering, though, if it wasn't an abduction attempt."

"We'll haul him in and try to learn what he was doing." Pat nodded to his fellow members of the Irish Squad, who dragged Bert up, still bleeding.

Topaz turned to Tillie. "Thank you for bringing help. It was most valiant. Pat, will you send one of your men to see Tillie home safely?"

"Of course. I'd like to see you home, as well, Miss Topaz."

"Do I look like I need assistance?"

Laughter ground from between Pat's lips. "No."

Topaz stepped up closer to him. "Pat, you keep your ear to the ground. Have you heard anything about an increased number of abductions in the city?"

His green eyes searched her face. "There have been one or two. But there always are."

"A thousand dollars is what that fellow said someone is paying for corpses."

"A huge sum of money. Are you quite certain you're well? You appear shaken."

If she was, she could blame more than kicking down one thug in the street.

"I'm fine, Pat," she replied, and wondered if he could tell she lied.

****

Hours later, Topaz gave up chasing her thoughts around her mind and lay staring up at her ceiling. Night ticked over to the accompaniment of sleet on her bedroom window, and she turned from pondering the inexplicable activities of her father to the whereabouts of Romney Marsh. Drawing on the powers she allowed herself to use so seldom, she marshaled her thoughts and sent them out like a beam of light through the darkness.

It felt strange to search not with her eyes or her ears, or any of her more familiar senses, but that which she usually kept so fiercely battened down. Only when she had tried to follow Romney into the cellar had she unfurled it, and then her father had come in response. Dragged from his sleep by her psychic ability that spoke to his own?

And did Frederick Hathor sleep now? Did he ever sleep? Topaz knew only that he had retired to his chamber, the one next to her mother's; they no longer shared a room. The house had become quiet, with most if not all the steam units on shutdown.

She twitched where she lay and sent her consciousness out into the ether again. Instincts she'd never guessed she possessed came into play. She could virtually see with her mind.

Doing so distressed her, and her heart accelerated, but she pushed on. She could sense her father's consciousness—a knot of power that seemed to glow like golden fire. She sensed her mother's, as well, far more acquiescent. Sapphire's room lay empty. On the third floor, the human servants slept.

If she let herself—if she didn't shut them out—she could also sense all the spirits that crowded around the house, both inside and out. Many clustered near her father's room, others lingered in the chamber where he did his readings; some clung to the outer walls of the mansion. She could virtually see them when she used her inner eye.

None inhabited the cellar. Romney—or whatever his true name might be—no longer lingered there.

Where could he be? Destroyed? Chased into the outer darkness?

A sudden thought struck her with such impact her entire body twitched again. Could he have fled back to his imprisoned form? To Grayson, the place he'd regarded with such horror?

If so, could she reach him? Had she the ability, the strength?

She curled her fingers into fists so tightly the nails bit into her palms.

"Let's see what you're made of, Topaz Hathor," she growled to herself, and sent her consciousness forth again.

Chapter Seventeen

He lay in absolute darkness. Not so much as a glimmer existed to tell left from right, up from down. He knew very well part of his captors' strategy lay in disorienting him. He had suffered this before between the sessions that dealt pain.

Now once more he began to worry about his mind.

He did not suffer disorientation easily. A man of somewhat orderly patterns of thought, he enjoyed a reasonable measure of control. Now all control had been stolen from him, just like the light.

His body hurt, and his heart struggled in his chest. He wanted to escape this flesh, wanted once more to stream away from this place even as he had before. He longed to return to Topaz.

The prospect of being with her might be the only thing keeping him from going insane. He squeezed his eyes against the terrible, suffocating darkness and imagined her as she had looked when she arose from her bed with the stiletto in her hand. Eyes flashing, black hair swirling around her strong body, balanced lightly on bare feet, grace in every line.

A strong woman was Topaz Hathor. The kind a man could admire, follow for a lifetime…love.

A rush of pain surged over him, more intense than that dealt by the electrodes. He would never know what it meant to love her, to answer this need that lay inside.

He would end here for certain—broken, if not dead.

Surely he had broken already, back when he fled his body. They had revived him sufficiently that his body had called him back.

To more pain. But now loss accompanied that hurt and made him want to scream into the darkness.

Topaz. His mind shouted it, as did his spirit. He fought the bond of his body even as his limbs might fight the straps that pinned him. True madness nibbled at the edges of his sanity.

He caught his breath and desperately tried to master himself. He had overheard his captors talking. When they broke him for good—rendered him a dribbling remnant of a man—they meant to cart him back to England for those who cared about him to find.

He had connections, the man said. Connections high up. They dared not murder him outright—but destroy him? Oh, yes.

An agent, they claimed.

He frowned, eyes still shut, and sought to remember. What sort of agent? Working for the Queen? Why did that seem likely to him? If only he could remember why he had come to this country, on what assignment.

Hopeless—he could not recall. Topaz possessed his mind. If only his longing might let him reach her.

He sent out all his desire, reaching through the darkness.

Romney.

Surely he had become unhinged, for now he imagined he heard her voice: low, slightly husky, and unimaginably erotic in the darkness, an answer to his call.

Where are you?

By God, he did hear her, and felt her also, reaching for him with tiny tendrils of energy like wisps of light—or life—that came curling through his terrible void. Light and life. All at once they had become one, and he drew a breath of pure sustenance.

Here, he told her.

Where is here?

Grayson.

Come with me. She wrapped around him, her bright consciousness caressing his. *Come away with me now.*

I can't. He wanted to, wanted it with all his being. He felt her strength lift him, and he gasped, torn between bliss and agony. *I can't get free of my body.*

You did before.

They had broken me, then.

Her spirit danced around him, appalled and agitated, seeking a means to free him.

Go, he told her, even though every separate particle of his being wanted her to stay. *Save yourself.*

Who has done this to you?

Don't know their names. They say I'm an agent of the Crown, the British monarch—

Listen to me. Are you being held against your will? Tell me.

You know I am.

You must say it.

I'm being held against my will.

I can notify the police. Patrick Kelly will act on this.

Can't. No proof.

Damn it. Her frustration, just like her warmth, flooded him. *I can't bear to leave you here.*

117

He couldn't bear it if she left him in the darkness, but better—better than her becoming trapped here with him.

"Go," he groaned aloud into the darkness of his cell.

Perhaps I can drag you with me.

Try.

She did. He felt her spirit seize hold of his and tug mightily. Before she finished—and failed—she wept for him.

I refuse to leave you.

You have to, he bade while still he could.

I will free you. I swear it. I swear!

Abruptly she left, the departure of all hope, and he fought back despair deeper and darker than any that had come before.

****

"I regret to say, sister, you look like hell. You're rarely ill, so I can only assume you spent a rough night."

Rough did not adequately describe the hours just past. Topaz eyed her brother, who leaned against her doorway, and smiled bitterly. "You have no idea. Come in."

Sapphire strolled in and shut the door behind him. Early as it was, he had dressed in a fine suit and wore his overcoat.

"Where are you bound?" Topaz asked.

He eyed her bed, a mess of rumpled blankets and crumpled pillows, before he replied. "I, sister dear, am bound to look for a new residence."

She stared. "Are you in earnest?"

"Do you see any humor in these eyes? Your wise

words when last we spoke have penetrated. I'm getting out, and I intend to take Carlotta with me."

"What!" Topaz sank onto the edge of her bed. "To live in sin?"

"What's sinful about it?" He shrugged. "And who knows, I may marry her."

"My God! The philanderer redeemed! But how will you make a living? You know Father will cut you off without a cent when he finds out."

Sapphire drew himself up. "You insult me. I have myriad talents with which I can make my way."

"Such as?"

"You just let me worry about that."

"Father will be furious."

"Yes, and I'm sorry to leave you here with the ramifications and the current craziness. But I took what you said about Carly to heart. She has no one to rely upon but me. I need to consider that."

"I see."

He smiled his slightly acerbic smile. "I thought you might like this before I go."

Reaching into the pocket of his overcoat, he produced a key. Topaz's amazement deepened.

"You found it! Where was it hidden?"

"Inside a book entitled *Shades of the Dead*. You have to think the way Father thinks. The fact that I can terrifies me and makes up one of the reasons I want out."

"What happens when he discovers it's gone?"

"He already has. Can't you feel the dark energy building?" Sapphire blinked. "Come with me, Topaz. Make the break."

"I want to. I can't, now that I have this." She

plucked the key from his hand. She knew Romney had escaped the cellar—she also knew that whatever he had encountered down there had affected him terribly. "Father's new partner gives me the willies, and I can just sense he's engaged in something unsavory. Don't you want to know what it is?"

"As I said before, Topaz, I don't. I can barely stand to think about what Father gets up to. Now I just want a life of my own. Be careful." To Topaz's surprise, Sapphire leaned forward and embraced her. He rarely showed affection, at least not with family.

"But surely I'll see you again."

"Of course. Look after Carlotta for me, if you can, till I'm able to collect her. And hide *that* somewhere Father or his minions won't find it."

"Minions?"

"Those steamies of his. You know they'll search your room; he's bound to suspect you."

"He won't find this unless he has them strip me."

"Keep your stiletto close at hand at all times." Sapphire turned to go, and in sudden panic she seized his arm.

"You promise you'll remain in the city?"

"For now. Stay on your toes, sister."

Soundlessly he slipped through the door and left Topaz struggling not to feel bereft.

****

"Topaz, I don't like being forced to cross-examine my own children. I hoped we would share a degree of mutual trust."

"We do, Father." Topaz lifted what she hoped were guileless eyes to meet her father's gaze. They'd encountered one another in the solarium, where

Frederick waited to receive the first of his afternoon appointments, whom he wished Topaz to greet and escort into his presence. His exalted presence, she thought ironically. Her job used to be performed by a particularly efficient steamie, but Frederick believed his clients would benefit from a more human touch.

"It will give you an opportunity to read them," he had told her when they discussed it earlier. "Exercise the ability that lies within you. Flex your spiritual muscles."

Had he any idea how she had flexed them only last night? Like a tiger, she'd torn through the distance between her and Romney.

Did her father know? Did he bait her? Staring into the bottomless darkness of his eyes, she couldn't tell.

His cross-examination of her now was made more uncomfortable by Danson Clifford's presence. Why was the man in the room? He had nothing to do with Father's readings.

A bit more aggressively she asked, "What makes you think I know anything about the missing key? You quite likely dropped it somewhere."

"I most certainly did not. And you, Topaz, showed great interest in the cellar just the other night."

She shrugged. "Well I'm certainly not interested enough to defy you, Father. Shall I show in your first client?"

Frederick raked her with his gaze as if searching her mentally. She strove to give no reaction, even though the key in question nestled beneath her left breast.

Danson spoke, making her start. He had come up close behind her, though she hadn't heard him.

"Fortunately, Miss Hathor, I possess a duplicate key, so I shall be able to continue our work today. I believe your father is merely concerned that the key should fall into the wrong hands."

"Well," she held up her hands, palms upward, "it's not in mine."

Clifford went out, and Topaz gave an involuntary shiver. She caught her father's gaze once more upon her.

"You do not like my new associate," he observed. "I wonder why."

Topaz hurried from the room without answering.

Chapter Eighteen

"So, Mr. Clifford, tell me about your work."

Danson Clifford turned in surprise when Topaz spoke. Finished for the day at last, she'd come upon him in the solarium where Frederick usually met with his clients, all of whom had now gone. At least, so much could be said for those living—the spirits of the dead, as she could feel quite clearly, still congregated in the room, some floating near the ceiling, some milling about looking for Frederick, the way they often did.

Clifford too waited for a meeting, or so Frederick had mentioned before hurrying off to handle one of Dahlia's crises in the kitchen.

Topaz looked on it as an opportunity, albeit one that made her skin crawl. She didn't like being near this man, but needs must.

"My work," he repeated in that soft voice of his, and narrowed his curiously lifeless eyes at her. She wondered suddenly just what those eyes had seen to make them look so like a reflection of death.

Some of the spirits in the room shied from him when he spoke. They fluttered to the windows as if seeking escape. Disconcerting.

Topaz worked to keep what she felt from her face. "It must be fascinating if you've won my father's interest. I must tell you he's notoriously difficult to impress."

Clifford smiled, revealing those slightly pointed teeth. The smile did not reach his eyes.

"Actually, Miss Hathor, you and I have a lot in common."

"Have we?" Topaz didn't like that assertion at all.

"Oh, yes. Like me, you harbor a very ancient ability. We carry the wisdom of the ages into what will be a brave new world."

"Will it?"

"Yes." He leaned toward her, and she caught that scent which always lingered around him, the faintest whiff of corruption. "If, Miss Hathor, you are sincere about taking up your father's work, you will be part of something that will revolutionize life—and death—as we know it."

"Of course I'm sincere." What did he suspect?

Clifford gazed at her for a moment. "From the time I met him, your father has stated his desire to bring one of his children into this endeavor. To be frank, I imagined it would be your brother."

"Sapphire?"

"But he shows no interest. And your father assures me your latent power is impressive."

"Power." Topaz began to feel like a damned parrot. Her father, yes, was all about power.

"Raw and undeveloped as it might be. However"—Clifford sucked in a breath—"it's not your ability that concerns me so much as your state of mind, your devotion to our exalted cause, and your level of ruthlessness."

Exalted cause? The man truly was mad.

"I assure you, Mr. Clifford, I can be utterly ruthless."

"Can you? As ruthless as death itself? Through the ages, Miss Hathor, my people have become intimate with death." He smiled again. "We understand its demands, its requirements. Its secrets."

"My father knows something about that, too."

"He does, which makes him the perfect partner for me, though he—like you, ultimately—deals with death and the release of the spirit." He lowered his voice still further from its half-whisper. "I speak of the secrets of the flesh."

"I see." Topaz fought her creeping horror.

"Miss Topaz, what do you think of marriage?"

An interesting question, if one she found inappropriate at this moment. She had mingled feelings about the state, having watched what her parents shared, as well as her older siblings.

"It can be an important bond, in the best of circumstances."

"The best circumstances, yes. And what are those?"

"Commitment on both sides. And willingness, along with devotion."

"Ah, but you and I both know there are many marriages wherein willingness does not exist. Yet the bond endures."

Topaz frowned. "I'm afraid I don't see—"

"This work in which we are engaged, Miss Hathor, is like the arrangement of marriages."

"Is it?"

"Marriages between the spirit and the flesh."

That Topaz could understand. Spirit and flesh shared the most intimate of bonds, so close that for most of life they considered themselves one.

But as she'd learned from Romney, and from existing all her life in her father's shadow, they were not in fact one.

Clifford gazed at her intently. "I see you comprehend my meaning. To pursue the marriage analogy, some such unions are sundered due to the death of one spouse or"—he leaned still closer—"to the scandal of divorce. Often the widowed or divorced parties remarry, do they not? That, my dear Miss Hathor, is what we are about."

Topaz's instincts leaped to it ahead of her conscious mind. "You're arranging new unions between spirit and flesh? But yes, I knew my father had been experimenting a long time with that, anchoring departed consciousness in steamies."

"Not steamies, Miss Hathor."

"And—and animals."

"Not animals. Before my arrival in this country, your father had made great leaps, yes, with resettling consciousness. But he lacked the other vital half of the equation: the perfect host."

"Which is?"

"Surely, Miss Hathor, a woman of your perception and intelligence can guess."

"Another living body." But what had that to do with corpses in the cellar?

"I—through my ancestors—possess the knowledge, the piece of the puzzle your father lacked. Together we shall create that new world of which I speak. Are you strong enough to join us?"

Topaz's eyes narrowed. She made no reply.

"I would be certain, Miss Hathor, before I share my deepest secrets with you. I trust your father. You, if you will forgive me saying, have not been tested."

"If you trust my father, you must rely on the trust he in turn places in me."

"Your father's motivation is strong. He is with me completely in this endeavor."

"Is he?"

"Any important act of creation requires a considerable amount of destruction. I need to know, Miss Hathor, you will undertake that aspect of our enterprise as ruthlessly as we do."

"Destruction?"

Those dead eyes of his met hers. "The price of success is first failure. The price of daring is first fear. The price of life is first death."

Topaz went suddenly breathless. Gazing into his eyes felt like staring into an abyss while poised on a precipice. What would happen if she fell in? What to her body and her spirit? Her every instinct bade her back away.

Yet how could she give up now? How think of herself when horror might well lie beneath her very feet?

"Do you fear destruction, Miss Hathor? Will you pay the cost of greatness? Of earning the gratitude of the multitudes?"

He's quite mad, she thought clearly before she hauled up all her courage, tossed her head, and said, "As you may well imagine, having been raised in my father's company I fear very little. And I assure you, Mr. Clifford, I am willing to pay nearly any cost on behalf of those I love."

His gaze released hers at last, moved over her face as he examined her minutely, hovered too long on her bosom. He suddenly gave a high-pitched giggle so at variance with his usual half-whisper it startled her.

"I shall have to thank your father. Working with you will be a pleasure. An unexpected treat. I will enjoy sharing my secrets with you, thrilling you, and perhaps impressing you. What impresses you, Topaz Hathor?"

Another good question. She'd seen far too much and built too thick a wall around herself to be impressed easily. Like Sapphire, she often affected a mien of indifference meant to deflect her own fear and uncertainty.

Now, though, horror penetrated that armor. She thought about the things she valued. Kindness. Courage in the face of want. Warmth and connection, humor and the spark of humanity in an automaton's eyes.

Nothing this man had to offer.

But she needed to play along, to play him in order to gather whatever information she could. So even though it turned her stomach and overthrew every instinct she possessed, she leaned into him and said, "I'm sure it will impress me when I learn all your wise ancestors' secrets. I can't wait." She allowed a gleam of seduction to show in her eyes. "You, Mr. Clifford, are like no one I've ever known."

In that, at least, she spoke the truth.

Chapter Nineteen

"Patrick, I need your help."

Topaz had come to Nellie's after another interminable afternoon spent greeting her father's clients, which she found unexpectedly taxing. Not only did Frederick wish her to conduct them into his presence but also to offer tea and conversation to those awaiting their sessions. Hardly the woman to provide tea and sympathy, she found the assignment awkward and uncomfortable.

Besides, her psychic senses, apparently freed when she unleashed them to search for Romney, refused to go back into the mental box she had long ago constructed for them. She could all too clearly feel the emotions of those who waited to see the great man, from anxiety to wracking grief. The grueling experience drained her emotionally.

A terrible price to pay for her attachment to Romney, she thought as she moved through the dark streets to Nellie's Bar, her dark cape rendering her very nearly invisible. But this seemed a time of reckoning.

Kelly, sitting at his favorite table with the inevitable whiskey in his hand, looked up at her, expressionless. Or was he? Curiously, her newly-sharpened acuity seemed to extend even to him. She could sense something—surely not emotions as such, but consciousness.

She sank into the chair opposite him. How did Father deal with the awareness, all the feelings coming at him—and the spirits battering at him, demanding to be heard? How could he open himself to just the ones he sought to assist for filthy lucre or any other reason?

"What is it, Miss Topaz?"

Topaz leaned across the scarred table. To her horror, tears filled her eyes. "Pat, I'm in a most desperate situation."

His hand came out and cradled her elbow gently. "You are upset. We cannot speak here."

"No? Where, then?"

"If you will do me the honor of accompanying me to my room, it is not far."

And wouldn't that just turn some heads—the big automaton leaving with the scandalous gypsy, melting into the night. Imaginations would run wild.

Did she care? Her life had been ripped from its moorings. True, Topaz had let herself experience the dark side in the past, but only when she deemed fit, as if playing the part Sapphire described. Now, aspects of herself she barely recognized—and dreaded—had roused to life.

She nodded. Kelly got up and, keeping hold of her elbow, escorted her back out into the inky night.

"This way."

And how curious it felt moving with him through the streets. Leaning into him as might any woman into her escort, she could feel his warmth, finding it difficult to remember it came from the coal-fired boiler situated in his chest and that he exhaled only steam. For an instant reality threatened to slip away from her, and she stumbled on the pavement.

Kelly's strong arm caught her up. "Careful. It's just here."

His room proved to be a spacious accommodation on the ground floor of a tall house that stood dark when they arrived. Topaz sensed no other consciousnesses in the building.

"Who else lives here?"

"Other members of the Irish Squad, men like me. Either out now or...resting."

He lit the steam lamps as they went in. Did he also rest here? Sleep? Shut down like an ordinary steamie? He was her friend, and she felt ashamed to admit she didn't know.

A bed occupied one corner of the high-ceilinged space, but it looked as if it had never been slept in. A cavernous armchair appeared more well-worn; Topaz could picture Kelly sitting there like some ancient lord. A narrow settee lined one wall, and a table with two chairs stood by the windows, but there was no food—Kelly did not eat, as such. She wondered where he got the nutrition to keep alive his skin and the one or two organs he retained.

His uniform hung neatly from a peg on one wall, and on a shelf Topaz saw a collection of what looked like antique firearms. Besides those, she saw books—books everywhere, in stacks and piles and crowding the rest of the shelf space.

"You read?" she asked, surprised.

"I do. I must have a way to pass the time, and reading is edifying. Through the written word I am able to experience things I never actually will." He emitted the grinding sound that, for him, denoted laughter. "I have traveled the world, Miss Topaz, and studied the human condition."

What must it be like, having once been human and being human no more? He had attained a state other than but not necessarily inferior to humanity.

"Was the ability to read something you retained from your past life?"

"No. I taught myself. It is a facility that increases with use. Now it might be said I worship the written word. Sit down, Miss Topaz. Would you like a drink?"

"Yes, thanks." She needed one. She chose the settee; sitting in the armchair would be tantamount to stealing a throne.

"I have whiskey."

He would. "Whiskey's fine."

He poured her a glass, took a second for himself, and appropriated the armchair.

Did the other automatons congregate here? Did they sit about not drinking their whiskey?

"Tell me what has upset you."

Topaz did. It helped that he already knew part of it—they had speculated together about what went on in her father's cellar, and he had investigated Grayson. Now she strove to explain how she had contacted Romney on a spiritual level and discovered he was being held against his will.

"It would be difficult," she concluded, "for me to go to the police. So I've come to you instead."

Patrick did not move; he sat with his glass of whiskey resting on the arm of the chair, face blank. But she could feel him thinking.

"Do you come to me in an official capacity?"

"Well, I—I'm not certain. Could the police raid the asylum? Pull my friend out? There may be others there also held against their will for all I know."

"There may. But it might be argued that all mental patients are held against their will, with very few exceptions. Who would choose to reside in an asylum?"

"True."

"In order for me to approach my superiors and suggest a raid, I would need to present proof—significant proof—something beyond a psychic connection established by the daughter of one of the most notorious men in this city."

"I see." Topaz's heart fell. "I was afraid you'd say that."

"You must understand, Miss Topaz, many consider your father a charlatan. I know, because you have told me, that his abilities are genuine no matter how he may barter them. Those who denounce him are not likely to lend credence to any ability you might have inherited, either. I believe you in all that you say because you are my Friend." He capitalized the word by virtue of the way he spoke it.

Topaz nodded wretchedly. "I appreciate that, Patrick, and I do understand. But I can't leave him there. He's suffering both mentally and physically. Whatever tortures they subjected him to have once separated his body and spirit. What if that happens again and he is lost to me? I would do anything—*anything* to prevent that."

"You love him."

Topaz stared at Patrick Kelly while she weighed the assertion. Impossible. Preposterous. She was not the kind of silly woman who fell in love precipitously—it had never happened yet. Unlike much of the female population, Carlotta apparently included, she did not need a male to make her complete. She could fight better than most men and prided herself on her fearlessness.

Patrick raised an eyebrow at her.

"I can't be in love with him," she objected. "Technically, I've never even seen him—at least not in the flesh." Had never touched him, never kissed him if she didn't count that quick fumble in the alley through the poor medium of the young sot's body and that wondrous interval in her bed, after.

Yet she could not deny Romney Marsh—by whatever name—had taken hold of her spirit.

Spirit versus body: Which demanded love? Ideally, she supposed, it should be a combination of both, raising the connection to the sublime. But as Sapphire had pointed out, that all too often failed to happen. Sapphire had chosen the flesh and his self-professed addiction to little Carlotta.

To Patrick she said, "What is love?"

"You ask me? I am ill-equipped to answer."

"As am I. My brother likes to say we Hathors may be gifted in some areas but we are maimed when it comes to that singular emotion."

"You think so? I know only what I have read." He nodded toward the bookshelves. "There is a wide range of opinion."

"Do you read romance?"

"I read everything I can. It adds up to human experience."

How sad, Topaz thought with a sudden rush of compassion—and how immeasurably admirable. Should her heart bleed for an automaton? Why not? He was her Friend.

She asked simply, "Can I love a man I've never met?"

"In my view, you have encountered him, exchanged thought and emotion. Therein, I would venture to suggest, lies love."

Topaz got to her feet, suddenly restless. "All I know, Pat, is I barely recognize myself since I, as you put it, 'encountered' him. You know me. I have little time for foolishness or sentiment. I've worked hard at relying on no one. Now I feel vulnerable, as if I'm the one being held hostage."

"As I understand it, love makes one vulnerable, since the object of one's concern is suddenly outside oneself."

"Well, I don't like it. At the same time, it's the most marvelous feeling I've ever known. Marvelous, terrible, powerful, and frightening."

"I can only envy you. I believe I have achieved loyalty—not love."

She spun on her heel and looked at him. "Loyalty is a form of love, Pat. Never underestimate yourself."

He sat there, his big form far too motionless, all but his green eyes, in which Topaz saw…what?

Abruptly he said, "You are far too kind, Topaz Hathor."

"Me?" She laughed incredulously. She who bled would-be abductors and suspected her own father of terrible misdeeds?

He nodded.

"Listen, Pat." She hunkered down beside his chair. "There must be a way to get Romney out of Grayson."

"Tell me about your father's new partner."

She blinked at the sudden change of subject but

answered readily, "Danson Clifford." Even speaking his name sent an involuntary shiver down her spine. "Do you think there's a connection? Because he's from England, just like Romney. I haven't been able to reconcile the fact that the place from whence he says he comes is the same as the name Romney gave me. Romney Marsh."

Patrick tipped his head, which meant he consulted his artificial intelligence. "That is, indeed, an actual place in the southeast of England."

"Clifford refers to himself as an undertaker."

"And the Egyptian goddess Hathor was known for escorting the souls of the dead to the afterlife. An intriguing combination. You say your brother gave you the key to the cellar?"

"Yes."

"If you could get a look at what is down there, it might prove most enlightening. I would not wish you to take any chances with your safety, Miss Topaz. But I cannot help believing there must be a correlation between the cellar and your lover's return to Grayson."

My lover.

Topaz nodded. "I can try, but my father's already missing his key and may change the locks. He might also set some units as guards. It will be difficult."

"As I say, do not take any chances. But if you could find sufficient cause for a raid, I will act upon it."

"And Romney? What of him?"

"Give me the best description you can."

"He's fair-haired, about five foot ten or eleven and with light-colored eyes, very handsome, and has an English accent. I know it's not much to go on—"

"Held against his will, you say?"

"Very much so." Topaz swallowed hard. "And very nearly broken."

The green gaze met hers. "Leave it with me, Miss Topaz."

"But you've said you can't go to your superiors—"

He gave her a solemn wink. "Leave it to me."

Chapter Twenty

When they dragged him from his cell and hung him once again in the steel room, he knew what must then come. Suspended by his wrists from the high bar, clad in nothing but his smalls, he could already taste the pain. Next would come the water wetting down his feet, the hiss and throb of the steam plant, and pain.

The steel chamber, brightly lit, blinded him after so many hours in absolute darkness. He squeezed his eyes tight shut and willed himself elsewhere. Anywhere.

With Topaz.

Why couldn't he flee this flesh, fly from here and stream to her like an arrow to its mark? Would he die here in this terrible place and never reach her again?

Ah, but perhaps after death...

Upon the thought his tormentors entered the chamber—the man with the black beard and the other who wore his weak rabbit's face like a mask.

The evil rabbit—a name floated in his mind, just out of reach—approached and peered into his face. Reluctantly he kept his eyes open against the light.

"Let us begin our session with a simple question," the rabbit hissed in his soft voice. "Answer truthfully, and we will not need to apply the persuasion we have used in the past: What is your name?"

Damned if he could remember. The only name that came to mind was Topaz's, and he would not utter that, not if they flayed him alive.

"I don't know."

The rabbit's expression changed, sharpened with something akin to anticipation. Strange thing, anticipation. It could be as intense awaiting enjoyment as pain.

This man, filled with cold, detached hate, enjoyed what happened in this room.

Another question, one he'd also heard before: "Why did you come to this city?"

"I don't remember."

The evil rabbit leaned closer. "You may not consciously remember, but you do know—deep within the recesses of your mind. I believe we can reach those recesses with the right persuasion."

The bearded man shifted uneasily. "Perhaps the memories are truly gone; we have pressed him hard. In my opinion—"

"Did I ask for your opinion?"

"As a matter of fact, you did, when we began all this. If he doesn't remember, you are safe. We can drop him somewhere—"

His heart leaped with treacherous hope. Hope, the seducer. Hope, so often false.

"What is your position with the British government?"

"I don't fricking know!" He shouted the words so they echoed off the walls, just like his screams—the ones he had promised himself not to utter.

"Fire the generator," the evil rabbit said.

****

Topaz!

The word burst into Topaz's awareness the way a

comet streaks across a night sky and caught her in midsentence. She stood in the small parlor where her father's clients waited until she ushered them into the solarium and his presence. A pleasant place, so her father claimed, with its soft sofas and tall, narrow windows.

Today those windows admitted no sunshine—only gray light and the sound of the icy sleet that pelted down and ticked against the glass.

She'd been making conversation with Mrs. Randolph after serving her tea, all while clad in a gown that, to Topaz, seemed outlandishly sedate.

"He was such a good man, you see, and we were together so very long. I wed him when I was seventeen and"—Mrs. Randolph leaned forward confidingly—"I am almost sixty-seven now. A very fortunate match on my part, even though arranged by my parents. But I fell in love with him, truly I did." The woman's eyes filled with ready tears, and she raised a lacy handkerchief to her face. "And stayed in love. That's what makes it so difficult now."

Love, Topaz thought. In the past she might have dismissed it out of hand, even sneered at this woman with her wealth and comforts. How compare her loss with that of a woman living in one of the poorer areas of the city, who when she lost her husband lost everything along with him, including her livelihood?

But now, with her senses so recently opened, she could feel Mrs. Randolph's genuine hurt and bewilderment, and her heart softened. She knew how it felt to long for someone to the exclusion of all else, to ache as with a hollow wound.

"I am so sorry for your loss, madame."

"I only hope your father can help me. I've heard such good things about him, my dear—but can you tell me? Does he truly contact those who have gone from us?"

"Quite often, yes, madame."

Mrs. Randolph wept harder. "I only want to know my Arthur is all right. Just to reassure myself."

At that instant the cry tore across Topaz's mind, dislodging every other coherent thought.

She froze where she stood as alarm flooded her, swift as reflex. The connection between her and Romney flared brighter than lightning and held tight, unfurling the ability within her, and she followed it back, back...

To its source.

A hot room that echoed with the throb of a generator and reeked of agony, sweat, and scorched flesh. She caught only a dim, cloud-enshrouded glimpse: a man suspended from a metal bar, twisting in pain.

Her man.

And she saw another, one whose face she knew all too well—he stood with a set of electrodes in his hands and an avid expression on his narrow, rabbity face. *Danson Clifford.*

"My dear! My dear, are you all right? Are you ill?"

Mrs. Randolph's well-intentioned query interrupted the spell and broke the connection. Topaz swayed where she stood.

Mrs. Randolph, her face full of concern, got to her feet and cried, "Here, my dear, you sit down. Shall I call one of the servants?"

"I'm sorry?" Topaz, stretched by horror, stared.

The diminutive woman barely reached her nose.

"You've taken a turn."

Topaz!

He called her again, and the power of it nearly split her in two. Her knees wobbled beneath her.

"Here, Miss Hathor, sit down." Mrs. Randolph guided Topaz to a chair. "I shall summon your father."

"No. God, no—don't interrupt his session." A cardinal sin, as they had all been taught from an early age. Topaz strove mightily for control. "I'm all right."

Where was he? Was the terrible room she'd seen somewhere inside Grayson or right here in this house? Because his tormentor—his torturer—was her father's new associate. Topaz drew a painful breath. She would not leave him so a moment longer. She would find him, gather her weapons, including the steam-cannon she kept in her closet, and storm that room. Break him free. Smash down the walls if she had to; claim him for her own.

For all time.

The thought shocked her. She pressed her fingers to her temples and tried desperately to separate all the voices clamoring for her attention—thick on the ground here, so near her father's presence—and hear only his.

But after the second cry she heard no more.

Hold on, she thought at him. *Keep strong. I will be with you.*

"Daughter, are you unwell?"

Impossibly, her father stood before her, dressed in the rich black frockcoat in which he received his clients. But how? He never interrupted his sessions; as Sapphire sometimes said, the house could burn down around him and Father would stay in communion.

Now he frowned at her, an unreadable look in his dark eyes. She gazed back at him, wondering what he knew about Clifford's activities. Her father couldn't be involved in Rom's torture; he simply couldn't.

"Oh, Mr. Hathor, your daughter has been taken unwell," Mrs. Randolph gushed. "I truly think she should be relieved."

"Certainly, madame, I agree with you. Spiritual overload perhaps, Daughter? I could feel your…distress."

Ah! Danger. He knew far too much. But had he heard the call, also? Surely not with so many others clamoring for his attention.

"Your session—" she began.

"It has ended. I wondered why you did not escort Mrs. Randolph in." Frederick snapped his fingers and a steam unit appeared and hovered solicitously.

Frederick told it, "See Miss Topaz to her room. Daughter, do you require a doctor?"

"No."

His dark gaze probed hers. "Are you quite certain?"

"Yes, Father."

"We shall speak shortly. Mrs. Randolph, I apologize for the delay. Please come right in."

"Not at all, Mr. Hathor. The poor girl—I thought she would faint."

"Topaz, faint?" Frederick gave a curious laugh even as the steam unit—named Edward—placed its cool, metal arm beneath Topaz's fingers and helped her up.

"Miss Topaz?" It clicked at her.

She stared into its empty glass eyes. Her father

143

purchased only the finest steam units, but they couldn't rival the comfort lent by Patrick Kelly.

She allowed it to lead her from the conservatory and to the foot of the staircase.

"Leave me, Edward. I will go up on my own."

"Your father has instructed me to escort you."

"I am well now. I'm fine."

She felt anything but well, she acknowledged as she hauled herself up the stairs. The contact with Romney had affected her like a blast from a steam cannon, had scorched all her senses. And her father had been able to tell.

In the upstairs hallway she encountered Carlotta in her gray uniform with the ruffled white cap and apron. The girl stared in dismay.

"Miss Topaz, are you unwell?"

"Come into my room with me."

Carlotta obeyed, looking uncertain. Topaz wondered if the girl called her brother "Master Sapphire" when she lay beneath him, and dismissed the thought as irreverent.

"Listen to me, Carlotta—do you know how to reach Sapphire?"

Carlotta shook her head. "He didn't say where he was going, miss." She lowered her voice. "But I do know he's out looking for a place for us to live."

Damn. She'd hoped he might have returned. For if Topaz knew her father, he would make sure she didn't leave this house until he spoke with her. And she needed to send a message at once—to Patrick Kelly.

****

He floated in oblivion, nearly disconnected from flesh. Once before he had achieved this state, freed himself from the agony and escaped this prison of blood and bone. But he wasn't sure how. Some connection in his mind had, perhaps, snapped and tumbled him into madness which in turn translated to freedom.

But now the tenuous ties held, anchoring him to his suffering body. He had been returned to the darkness that served to disorient him, abolishing his perception of up and down, left and right. His mind teetered so close to breaking he could barely breathe.

If he stopped breathing he would die. Would he go to Topaz then? Stream to her like a gust of air? But then he would never be able to touch her, kiss her, and lie with her as, even now, he so longed to do.

He concentrated on her, fastening all his will on the promise of physical togetherness as to the memory of sunlight.

He caught a whisper of her voice in his mind. *I hear you. Just hold on. Keep strong.*

Chapter Twenty-One

"Carlotta, I need you to deliver a message for me. Do you think you can get away without being seen?"

"I'm not sure. Where do you want me to go?"

Topaz, already seated at her desk with a sheet of notepaper in front of her, paused. A good question: Where might Patrick Kelly be at this time of day? On duty? In his book-filled quarters? At Nellie's? Topaz could not send Carlotta there.

Yet urgency—and Romney's pain—still tore at her, throbbing like a livid wound.

She glanced at the window, where sleet continued to tick against the glass. Neither could she send the little maid out in this—not even if she gave Carlotta cab fare. Sapphire would never forgive her.

She got to her feet and began to pace the bloodstained rug while Carlotta stared. All the while her senses stretched for the least hint of communication from Romney, but none came.

Had he perished? Would she be able to tell?

She said, "You must have some idea where Sapphire has gone."

Carlotta folded her hands and shook her head. "He said he meant to speak to a few acquaintances, seek lodging for us, even if temporary—and procure a job."

That made Topaz stare. "He told you that, did he?"

"He promised, miss."

"He's never held down a job for more than three weeks at a time. You do understand his character, don't you? You're aware of the nature of this star to which you've hitched your wagon?"

Carlotta returned her stare with calm eyes. Not for the first time, Topaz wondered about the girl, so quiet and unassuming and yet so ready to jump into Sapphire's bed.

"Yes, miss."

"He's a ne'er-do-well, a philanderer. A brilliant one, perhaps, but a philanderer all the same."

"No, miss."

"You think not?" Topaz's frantic edginess made her brutal. "Then you're a fool."

"No, miss. I believe we present one face to the world and another—truer—to those who love us."

That made Topaz stare harder. Was it so? Did Carlotta see the real Sapphire beneath all the layers of careless dispassion? Even Topaz couldn't be sure she knew her brother through and through.

"Love," she grunted. Patrick Kelly had one view of it, Carlotta obviously had another. "An indefinable prospect."

"Say what you will, Miss Topaz. I believe that your brother loves me and that he will keep his promises."

"And why," Topaz asked, not unkindly, "should Sapphire fall in love with you, a servant in his father's house—convenient to his bed? You do know he has been introduced to most of the heiresses in this city?"

"Yes, miss." Carlotta raised her chin a notch. "I did ask him the same thing. I am aware that I come from humble beginnings. But he is educating me."

Topaz just bet he was.

147

"And he says we knew one another before, in a past life."

That halted Topaz's wild pacing. "Eh?"

"He knows such things, miss. Surely you are aware your brother has unusual talents?"

"Yes." Topaz also imagined he could spin quite a tale in order to get a girl—a good girl—into his bed. "Indeed." And Topaz would have words for the rascal when she next saw him. She eyed the young woman standing in front of her. Why couldn't Carlotta fall for a fellow servant, or a steamcab driver?

Then again, how could she when she had Sapphire Hathor whispering in her ear?

Very gently she said, "Just be careful, and look before you leap any further. I would like to say my brother is trustworthy. But you have a good place here, and you would not be wise to jeopardize it, perhaps end up alone and carrying his child."

Carlotta searched Topaz's eyes. "Miss, can I rely on your discretion?"

Dread stirred in Topaz's heart. "Yes."

"I am already carrying your brother's child, which is what's prompted him to move us out." Her hands moved to her apron. "I'm not very far along yet."

Topaz could think of nothing to say. She sagged where she stood.

Carlotta nodded at the paper on the desk. "Do you wish for me to take a message?"

"I cannot send you out in this weather. Go about your business. And let me know at once if you hear from my brother."

****

"Are you feeling better, Daughter? I must say, you

still do not appear your usual robust self."

Topaz looked up and met her father's dark gaze across the dining table. Just three of them had met for dinner this evening, along with the customary host of mechanicals.

She felt as jittery as a cat treading on hot coals. After speaking with Carlotta she'd tried unsuccessfully to make contact with Romney again and had striven to formulate a plan. She knew what she had to do but needed to keep her thoughts shielded from this man with his all-too-acute perception.

She pushed her food around on her plate. "I'm not sure what came over me, Father."

"What is this?" Dahlia looked up from her food. "Topaz ill? But you are never ill, child."

Frederick smiled. "She has inherited a gypsy's constitution—among other things. But, *mon petite*, our daughter took quite a turn this afternoon and frightened one of my clients."

"Psychic overload," Dahlia pronounced, quite astutely for her. Her husband and daughter stared. "Do not look at me that way. Am I not married to one of the foremost mediums of this—or, indeed, any—time? Remember how it was with you, my love, when first we wed."

Frederick said nothing, and Dahlia leaned toward Topaz. "He used to come over all strange, what with trying to keep the voices in his head sorted."

"Some of them can be very demanding," Frederick agreed. "You will have to learn how to exercise control." His gaze flicked over Topaz's face. "You may be more sensitive than I suspected."

"Yes, Father." Topaz added truthfully, "I can't

imagine how you do it."

"The ability will come in time. You, Topaz, have always been so focused on the physical, what with your lessons in fighting and tending toward earthly matters—it may take you a while longer. But an ability such as you possess should not be neglected."

Topaz laid her fork aside. "How can you tell how much ability I possess?"

His gaze met hers again. "I can feel it, Daughter. But it is wild and undisciplined. Even now I can tell your energies are all scattered. I don't doubt that has made you ill."

"I bow to your superior wisdom in this, Father."

"Well!" Dahlia exclaimed. "That's a first, Topaz bowing to anything. And speaking of rebellious children, where is Sapphire? Topaz, do you know?"

"I don't," Topaz answered, again truthfully.

"That boy." Dahlia shook her head. "Incorrigible."

"Well, my dear." Frederick smiled at his wife across the table. "At least we have four of our brood safely settled. Topaz, you need a good night's rest. Settle your energies. The weather is vile, and it's best for you to stay in."

"Yes, Father," Topaz said, glad he didn't know she had her night all planned.

****

The key felt cold in Topaz's hand, preternaturally chilled as if it had been iced. She'd had to wait hours for the house to settle into silence, and now her nerves leaped at the slightest sound.

The kitchen stood full of gloom and mechanicals on shutdown. Her parents had long since retired to their respective rooms; that didn't mean her father would

150

stay in his. As she had learned last time, he could move almost soundlessly when he chose.

She leaned against the cellar door and listened before she inserted the key in the lock. She had dressed for this task in a black silk shirt and black trousers, with the stiletto thrust through her belt, and had tied her hair back out of the way. She could move as silently as her father. But Frederick might track her movements with a sense more acute than hearing.

Heart beating double time, she turned the key and opened the door.

The stairs fell away before her, and beyond that the corridor, lined with closed doors, stretched away in gloom. Steam lights, well turned down, burned at intervals, barely enough to chase the shadows. Was Romney here behind one of those doors, rather than back at Grayson? She had to know.

Shivering, Topaz stepped through, closed the door behind her, and found herself wrapped in silence.

She hadn't realized how greatly the spirits always crowding around her father intruded on her consciousness. How did he ever sleep? Here, most of that clamor fell away. She could still catch it, but only from a distance.

This felt quiet as the grave—almost.

She tiptoed down the stairs with uneasiness—and something more—nibbling at her mind. A soul lived in the cellar.

A single soul.

Chapter Twenty-Two

Topaz pressed her palm against each door as she passed it, employing her inner sense to search with ever-increasing ease. No one there. No one there.

Romney had said corpses lay somewhere down here—perhaps they'd now been taken away. Corpses had a short shelf life; these might have outlasted theirs. But nothing lived beyond the closed doors.

She supposed she should open them anyway. She needed evidence to share with Patrick Kelly, but now, sensing that single glimmer of life, she could do nothing but locate it.

Halfway down the hallway, her inner sense quickened almost unbearably. She looked hard at the door in question: not locked but barred from the corridor side.

Someone wanted to keep something in there.

All the hairs on the back of Topaz's neck rose as she laid her hands to the bar and lifted.

She had been in the cellar before, of course. But not recently, not since Danson Clifford came to work in the house.

Danson Clifford, the undertaker.

She drew a deep breath and opened the door. Inside, a single steam lamp burned.

One of the larger rooms, it had been fitted out with equipment: tables, tools of dubious purpose, a deep sink, and a decent-sized steam plant. It smelled of cleaning fluid and disinfectant, with another underlying odor even less pleasant.

On two of the tables lay forms shrouded in sheets—corpses? The hairs on Topaz's arms rose in sympathy with those on her neck.

She hadn't sensed corpses.

On the third table something stirred. Rom? But no, she didn't sense him. Topaz's hand flew to her stiletto. Against every instinct, she stepped farther into the chamber.

A woman slid from the table onto the floor and stood facing her.

Tall and strongly made, she had light brown hair worn loose down her back and pale skin that showed livid marks at wrists and temples. Her face, a plain oval, looked unremarkable save for the eyes, which burned with desperation. She wore only a nightdress, which seemed inadequate against the chill, and she certainly appeared alive.

"Who are you?" she asked. Her voice creaked like that of a very old woman, though she couldn't possibly be more than twenty-five.

Topaz had to draw a long breath before she could speak. "My name is Topaz Hathor. Who are you?"

"Get me out of here. Get me out, get me out—" The woman's voice rose dangerously.

"Hush! Do you want someone to hear? How did you get here?"

"I want out. Away." The woman glared at the two shrouded forms on the other tables and then down at herself. "This isn't my body."

Topaz's heart clenched and dropped; her stomach

twisted. "Whose is it?"

"I don't know. Not mine. I think I died. Yes, I'm sure of it. I remember he beat me. I fell and cracked my head. I died."

"Shhh," Topaz cautioned again, sure her father must surely sense this encounter and come, which only added to her horror. She could feel this woman's spirit—strong, burgeoning, fighting the flesh as she might the bars of a cage.

She sucked in a breath. "If you died, how did you come to be—in that body?"

"He called me. The other one forced me in. He's the Devil."

"He—?"

"The man with the dark eyes called me. I was almost free—I didn't want to come back, but he's powerful, so powerful. He held me, and the Devil forced me in here. It hurt."

She held out her hands and showed Topaz her wrists. "Hurt."

Topaz nearly recoiled in horror. The woman's wrists showed not only bruises to match those on her face but livid burns, as well. She swallowed convulsively. "Do you have a name? Do you remember it?" Topaz could feel the spirit's confusion. "I can report your name to a friend who may be able to investigate."

Not precisely what Topaz wanted to do; whatever unsavory thing went on here, Topaz's father had to be in it up to his ears. Was she truly prepared to incriminate him?

"I'm not sure about my name."

Carefully Topaz said, "Let me understand.

Following your death you were called here?"

"Netted. Trapped."

"Caught and forced into another body, into that body?"

"I think it's a corpse. Like those." The woman nodded at the shrouded forms, and a long, slow shudder convulsed her. "I don't want this. Let me go!"

"I've no idea how." Aside from committing murder. If Topaz used the stiletto at her side, would the spirit then be freed? But that raised all sorts of ethical questions. Could one murder a spirit already dead?

The woman waved her hands wildly. "Reverse the process."

"I don't know how to do that either. What about them?" She too nodded at the tables. "Are they alive?"

"Failed attempts. I heard the Devil and the enchanter talking. They're not the first. I'm not sure why it worked with me—but I'm not the first that's succeeded, either."

"This Devil—describe him."

"Sheer evil. I could see it from the other side. His aura is dark. You have a powerful aura—not unlike the enchanter's. Do you also possess magic?"

"It's not magic." And at this point it turned Topaz sick to think she shared any of Frederick Hathor's abilities. "Did you hear any names, the name 'Danson Clifford,' perhaps?"

"No. Look, get me out of here."

"I wish I could, but I don't dare. I promise I'll get you help. It may take some time."

The woman stepped toward Topaz. "No. I refuse to let you shut me back in this terrible place. Let me out."

"Quiet, or he'll come. My father will come." Topaz

could now see the woman had brown eyes that burned with fervor. Only they weren't her eyes, were they? She tried to imagine how it would feel to be trapped in someone else's flesh.

"All you have to do is step aside. I'll leave on my own."

"And do what?" Topaz's thoughts raced. "Go where?"

"I don't care. Anywhere but here."

"How much do you know about what's been going on in this place? What else did you hear?"

"Enough."

Abruptly, Topaz made up her mind. "Then yes, come with me. But you have to be absolutely silent and tone down the anxiety. He will pick up on it."

"I'll try."

"Come up to my room; we'll find you some clothes. And I have one more stop to make."

****

Creeping past her father's door with a reanimated corpse on her heels proved one of the most terrifying things Topaz had ever done. Once they gained the safety of her room, she eyed the woman critically.

"Find something to wear. I'll be back shortly."

"Wait." The woman seized her wrist with fingers chilly as ice—or death. "You promise to take me away from this place?"

"Yes, but we need to bring someone else with us."

The third floor lay still and very nearly dark. Topaz could sense the spirits of those who slept the sleep of the exhausted. She found if she listened hard she could identify Carlotta's spirit among the others. But she shared a room with two other girls. How to get her away?

After some inner debate, she moved into the room soundlessly, laid her hand across Carlotta's mouth and bent to whisper in her ear. "Be silent. Get up, gather your clothes and belongings. You can dress in my room. Bring your coat." She added, for the sake of gaining the girl's compliance, "We'll go find Sapphire."

She crept back out, not giving Carlotta a chance to argue. Soon the girl slipped through the door, clothing in her arms and her hair loose around her shoulders.

"Miss, what—"

"Hush! Just come."

She half expected the strange woman to have fled for freedom. But she and Carlotta entered the room to find her standing clad in some of Topaz's best clothing, working at her hair with those scorched hands.

Carlotta balked. "Who's that?"

"Someone I'm helping."

"One of your streetwalkers? Sapphire says you help a lot of them."

"Yes."

The woman drew herself up indignantly, but voiced no objection to the label.

"Get dressed quickly, please. We need to leave at once."

"You're taking me to Sapphire?"

"Yes." Eventually.

Carlotta climbed into her clothes and turned to don a ragged coat.

"Here," Topaz said, "that's not warm enough. Wear this."

She had a heavy jacket, now too small for her, that

she thrust at the girl. She could still hear sleet ticking against the window, and wind rattled the glass.

"Now come, both of you. Absolute silence."

"What about the steamie in the front hall?" Carlotta objected.

"We're going out the back."

"Through the kitchen? But they're all—"

"On shutdown. Let me go in first; I'll deactivate them. Now, not another word."

Topaz realized she had begun listening with all her senses, the facility to use the sixth increasing as she went on. They passed through the throng of spirits outside her father's door, and she listened within. The bright power of Frederick's spirit lay banked, dormant. He slept.

She could feel the emotions of the two women who accompanied her—Carlotta quivering with anxiety and the other woman seething. Anger? Fear? Violence? Topaz couldn't quite decide.

She left them at the kitchen door and went on into the cavernous room, where she flipped the switches on all the units. Only one roused before she reached it; she heard the tick as its boiler reignited, and it stared at her even as she thumbed its button.

Damn. It had seen her and would be able to tell her father. Not that he wouldn't figure it out as soon as he discovered both Topaz and the woman from the cellar missing. As a last thought, she locked the cellar door and pocketed the key before collecting her charges and herding them out through the kitchen exit.

Chapter Twenty-Three

Outside, the weather met them, a foul, black night full of driving wind and stinging sleet. Underfoot, treacherous ice caused Carlotta to slip almost at once. Topaz caught her arm before she went down.

Where to go? She could think of only one place, and they would never make it so far on foot.

"Come." She took one of their hands in each of hers. Together they battled their way around the side of the mansion, keeping close to the privet hedge. If her father had a steam unit on patrol, it might not find them amid this melee.

Out on the parkway she paused. It must be all of four in the morning by now, and given the weather she despaired of finding a steamcab. But just then she saw one drop a fare down the street. When it approached, she let go of Carlotta's hand long enough to flag it down.

"In with you." She thrust both women ahead of her and told the driver, "To West Ferry Street as quickly as you dare."

"Can't drive very fast on this," the cabbie objected. "It's sheer ice."

Topaz glanced over her shoulder at the house in time to see a single light come on in the front second-floor window—her father's room. Her heart leaped sickeningly. "I don't care." She climbed into the cab.

"Drive."

The cabbie grumbled, but he put his foot down and the cab vibrated as the boiler flared. A gush of steam obliterated the view out back. Sleet prohibited much visibility in front. Wiper blades clattered against the windscreen, but ice had built on the glass so they mostly rode atop it.

"Where are we going?" Carlotta asked piteously.

"To the home of a friend." Topaz just hoped to find him there.

"Who is she?" Carlotta stared at the other woman, who had taken the seat opposite her. In the close air of the cab a strange scent arose from her—not decay so much as a chemical overlay.

"You never did tell me your name."

"Rose. I believe it's Rose." Flickering light from the street lamps beneath which they passed, distilled by the ice on the cab windows, threw her oval face into light and then shadow.

The cabbie turned his head. "I think we're being followed."

"By a vehicle?" Already? Topaz pressed her cheek against the glass and peered back. "I don't see anyone."

"Not a vehicle, a steam unit. A fast one."

Topaz's heart fell again, sickeningly. One of her father's runners—that would be one of the two superior steam units he allowed into the cellar.

"What do you want me to do?" the cabbie asked.

"Can you outrun it? Or lose it?"

"Don't know. The streets are pretty slick."

"Try, please. Maybe you can make it crash."

"Hang on."

The cabbie turned right off the parkway onto a

darker, narrower street. The cab slid dangerously before gaining traction. Carlotta pressed her face against the opposite window.

"I see it. Oh, God, miss! It's keeping up with us and puffing like a train."

"Faster," Topaz called to the driver.

"Miss, this is as fast as I can safely go."

"Go unsafely, then."

The cab took two more corners at perilous speed and skidded sideways for some distance on the second. Carlotta swore, using a word she could only have learned from Sapphire, because it was one of his favorites.

Topaz, her fingernails embedded in the upholstery, shot a look at Rose. The woman sat with her eyes closed in an attitude of deep serenity.

Well, Topaz reflected, when one had already died once perhaps the prospect lost some of its menace.

Carlotta screamed. The steamie had caught up with the cab and now hung by all its fingers from the left rear door handle. Its visage—bright silver and set in an emotionless mask—seemed more terrible than a grimace, and tiny points of flame reflected from its eyes.

Carlotta threw herself into Topaz's arms.

"Don't let it get in!"

Topaz drew not her stiletto but the small side cannon she'd shoved into her coat before leaving her room. She didn't want to blow the window out, but would if she had to.

"Faster!" she called to the driver. "Shake it off!"

He grappled with the wheel, throwing it from side to side as they barreled down East Ferry. The steamie pulled itself up and placed one foot against the window, preparing to kick in the glass.

Several things happened then, all at the same time: Carlotta screamed again, Topaz fired up the cannon, and the driver swerved, hit a patch of icy road, and lost control of the cab.

Topaz distinctly felt the wheels break traction. The cab sped up and the steamie flew off, its arms spreading out like the wings of a large bug.

Topaz dropped the cannon and grabbed hold of Carlotta, her one thought for the vulnerable life of her niece- or nephew-to-be. The driver hollered, the cab hit something, slewed sharply, and began to roll over sideways.

Topaz saw Rose fly from her seat and drew Carlotta closer. Then they were tumbling, tossed weightless, arms and legs tangling. Topaz saw the glass of the side window come at her an instant before everything turned black.

****

Floating in the depths of dark oblivion, the man calling himself Romney Marsh saw the single star to which he clung so desperately wink out.

He screamed into the void.

****

"Miss? Miss, can you hear me?"

Apparently Topaz could. The disembodied male voice descended from above her while she sprawled on her back, staring upward. Cold sleet pricked her face like repeated stabs from tiny blades, and from somewhere came the dirty light of a street lamp.

She gasped and tried to exert control over her limbs.

"No—don't move," the man said. "You've been in a bad accident. Your steamcab slid on the icy street. The ambulance is just arriving."

"The girl who was with me…" Oh, God, Carlotta and her baby! Sapphire would never forgive her.

The voice made no reply. Topaz thrashed and tried to sit up. Hands pushed her back firmly.

"You may be concussed."

"Get your hands off me." She scrambled up and nearly went down again as she lost her footing. "Icy" didn't begin to describe the street.

Desperately, she looked around. Her rescuer had stepped away as the ambulance with its strobe light inched up. The steam cab, nearly on top of her, lay on its side, all the windows shattered. She couldn't see the driver, but Carlotta lay flung against the curb with another man bending over her. She didn't see Rose's form anywhere.

"Carlotta!" she called and felt as if her head would burst.

"Miss," someone called, "don't move."

"There was another woman with us, in a blue coat."

"We're taking you all to the hospital."

"All? Where is she?"

Misunderstanding, the man indicated Carlotta, whom the second fellow had covered with a blanket. Topaz's heart stood still in her chest. Was she dead?

She hurried to bend over the swathed form, and it moved. "Carlotta, are you all right?"

Huge, panicked eyes sought hers. "I don't think so, miss. My baby—"

"They'll take you to the hospital. I'll look for

Sapphire. I can't come with you—I have to find Rose and get her away." If the police or the doctors saw those burns on Rose's skin, there would be no way to explain.

"Yes, miss. Just so long as you send Sapphire." Carlotta's eyes filled with tears. "Before it's too late. Is Rose all right? She flew…"

"I must go and see. Be brave."

Carlotta nodded. Topaz straightened and walked around to the other side of the cab, where its overturned bulk cast deep shadow. Breath gusted in her chest when she saw Rose huddled against one wheel. Had none of the rescuers seen her yet?

Topaz nearly stumbled over a pile of twisted metal and recognized it, belatedly, as the steam unit that had pursued them. It lay barely an arm's length from Rose.

As she knelt down, she reflected it might almost be best for the woman to be dead. But Rose's eyes, full of wild light, flew open when Topaz touched her.

"How badly are you hurt?" Topaz asked.

"I don't know. What happened?"

"The steamcab crashed. Do you think you can stand? We'd better not let them find you here."

"Them?"

"Rescuers—on the other side of the cab." Topaz could hear the voices now. In another minute they would round the cab and see Rose.

"There was another passenger," a voice called. "Where did she go?"

"Give me your arm." Topaz took Rose's elbow and, both of them groaning, levered her to her feet.

"Can you walk?"

"Not sure."

"Try. Here—between these two houses."

"The steamie?"

"Over there. It's dead."

"I don't want to go back to that house."

"We won't."

"I hate this body. I want it to die, but I don't know if I want that to happen here on the street."

"Then come."

A nightmare ensued, composed of cold, dark yards, darker alleys, and block after block of icy, glistening streets. Sleet dashed into Topaz's face, and Rose grew ever heavier on her arm.

"Do you know where we're going?" Rose gasped at one point.

"I hope so."

At last, on a dim corner, Rose sank to her knees. "Can't keep going."

"Where are you hurt? Are you bleeding?" Topaz asked.

Rose laughed darkly. "Can I bleed?"

"Of course."

"But what am I?" Rose stared up into Topaz's face. "A reanimated corpse. I was like those two others, wasn't I, before that Devil did whatever he did?"

"And a spirit," Topaz told her. "Don't forget, that's the part that's *you*."

"Trapped in rewarmed flesh." Rose gasped. "I'm in pain. I think something's broken."

"Listen, you can't be found here. I don't think we have to go much farther."

"All right."

By the time they crossed Richmond, Rose's weight nearly had Topaz defeated. She looked at the slick faces of the houses, trying desperately to remember which was Patrick's.

"There."

She dragged Rose up the walk, her exhaustion almost lost in pain. Both her palms were skinned, and she felt blood dripping down one leg.

Please, she thought as she pounded on the door. Let him be home. Don't let him be on duty this night.

The door opened.

"Pat!" She nearly wept. "Oh, thank God."

Chapter Twenty-Four

"We need to call a doctor," Patrick Kelly said.

"No—no doctors." Topaz reached out from the chair where he had put her—his big armchair—and seized his hand. They had placed Rose on the narrow settee, where she lay as if once more dead. "No doctors and no hospital."

He hunkered down beside the chair, and she stared into his green eyes. She fancied she saw concern there. "Your friend is badly hurt, Topaz, as are you. You say your steamcab crashed?"

"Yes." To Topaz's dismay, she had to blink back tears. "My brother's friend Carlotta was with us; they've taken her away in an ambulance. I couldn't let them find—her." She nodded at Rose. "She's from my father's cellar. Patrick, she's..."

How to explain it to a man who wore his own dead skin? Perhaps he'd understand better than anyone.

She struggled up in the chair on a wave of pain. "She's the result of an experiment, Pat—a successful one. Most of the others didn't work."

"You have discovered what is going on there?"

"Bits of it. I believe, when we're able to talk to her, she will have more answers. You must see I can't let her be taken by the authorities. Not before we learn what she knows."

Patrick glanced at Rose's motionless form. "Or at

167

all. I do see that. But she needs care." He hesitated. "Tell me again what happened."

Topaz had blurted it all out, not very coherently, when they came through the door. Now, with her fingers still gripping his, she went through it all again, striving for calm she couldn't quite achieve.

"We were pursued by one of my father's steam units," she concluded. "It caught hold of the cab. I think that helped trigger the wreck. But no," she added wretchedly, "it was all my fault. I told the cabbie to lose the steamie. If anything terrible happens to Carlotta or her baby, Sapphire will never forgive me."

"Are you saying this Carlotta carries your brother's child?"

"Yes. He's gone to procure them lodging and look for a job. Pat, we have to try and find him, tell him what's happened. I promised Carlotta."

"I can make queries, yes. But Miss Topaz, you must also let me summon medical care. Your companion is badly hurt—I think she may have broken bones. From my observation, you have some broken ribs, as well."

"No..." Topaz began again.

He forestalled her. "The doctor I have in mind is nearby and discreet. I have used him before, when the girls—the streetwalkers—needed help and proved reluctant to get it elsewhere."

"But how will we explain Rose?"

"He will require no explanations."

"How can you be sure we can trust him?"

"He is not fully accredited and will not wish to be reported for practicing medicine."

"A hack, then."

"He is a good doctor who has not been given a fair chance. May I summon him?"

"If you believe it necessary."

"I do. Trust me, Miss Topaz." Patrick got to his feet. "Do you think you were followed here? If so, I will also summon the lads."

"The lads?"

He made a soft grinding noise—a laugh. "Many members of the Irish Squad reside here in this house, remember, or nearby. I will send one of them for Dr. Rasmussen. I can ask the others to form a perimeter."

"The steam unit was destroyed in the wreck, but there may be others."

"One or two of the lads on patrol, then. You rest while I take care of it."

Topaz subsided into a well of pain.

****

Pain. It remained always with him now, his sole companion other than the smothering darkness. The darkness would be the thing to unravel his mind—not the electrodes or the water or the fear of what else might be brought into play. Not even the disintegration he felt happening within himself. It would be the disorientation and the lack of air.

He shivered where he lay. The temperature in the cell had dropped as time passed, and he wore only his smalls. How long had he been alone? When would they come again?

Dread cramped his guts, and to distract himself he tried to remember. All those questions the evil rabbit had asked him: his name, his profession, his objective in leaving England.

England. He tried to picture it and won only an

image of a great, trackless green marsh, sky of soft gray lowering over it all, and the sea beyond. He tried to convince himself he now floated on that sea, and failed. The darkness stole any such illusions.

He must think of something else—he must. Something besides the dark and the fact that he couldn't breathe. Think of...

Topaz. She blazed across his inner vision the way fire might rake the night sky. He saw her in motion, turning to speak to him, her golden eyes glowing like the jewels after which she'd been named, black hair swinging about her. She moved like a dancer, or an assassin.

Her beauty lay not so much in her features as in her movement, in the fierce spirit that, from the very first, had drawn him.

But she'd disappeared from his awareness. Or had she?

Need, raw and hot, blossomed inside him. He didn't care who she was or what she was—he needed to be with her, to feel the steady vibration of her soul, the comfort of her presence.

He fought back the wild desire and found his miracle. For in his debilitating darkness, full and golden, her flame once more burned.

****

Dr. Rasmussen proved to be tall, thin, and not above thirty, with a thick accent. He arrived carrying a battered leather satchel and after exchanging words with Patrick went at once to Rose.

Topaz, who now hurt all over with an intensity that prevented her from discriminating among her injuries, hauled herself up from Patrick's chair and went to watch.

Rasmussen gave her one glance from pale blue eyes before he set to work, divesting Rose of most of her clothing while the woman lay senseless.

Or dead.

But no—Topaz marked how her chest rose and fell. She still breathed, and blood trickled from a small cut on her forehead.

The burn marks on her wrists and neck stood out lividly. Rasmussen examined them with careful hands and looked at Patrick.

"These marks, how did they happen?"

"I don't know, Doctor." After returning to the room, Patrick had poured himself a glass of the ubiquitous whiskey. Topaz wondered fleetingly if he needed it to steady his nerves and then dismissed the idea as absurd.

"They are quite recent." Rasmussen's gentle hands moved over Rose with care. "She has concussion. Broken right arm. Contusions to the hip and knee. Must have been thrown onto her right side."

"Chance of recovery?" Patrick asked.

"Good. I can set the arm. Once I do so, we will have to try and rouse her."

He set about the task, and Topaz, restless, started for the window. Patrick caught her back.

"No. I have lads on watch. They will tell us if anyone comes. I have sent two others to bring your brother if they can find him. They may have no luck until morning."

"Patrick," she whispered so the doctor could not hear, "what's going on in that cellar is a terrible thing. Rose was dead. I believe my father and his new partner trapped her spirit and forced it into another body, that of a cadaver."

Patrick didn't so much as blink.

"My father has long been involved with experiments, implanting the spirits of those deceased into steam units—a bit like you, actually. Or into the bodies of animals, though he plays that down. Why not into reanimated corpses?"

"Aye, why not? Yet to reanimate a copse is no easy matter."

She leaned still closer. "I believe that's where my father's new partner comes in. In Britain his people have been undertakers for generations. What if he brought some knowledge with him from England?"

"I do not think it can be a coincidence that this man and your soul mate, whom you seek, are both from England."

Her soul mate. That froze Topaz where she stood. Two weeks ago she would have sneered at any such notion. Now her entire being leaped toward it.

"No coincidence, Pat. The last time Romney—my lover—contacted me, my spirit followed him back to where he's being confined. I believe he must be in Grayson, since he's not in the cellar of my father's mansion. But here's the thing—the man holding him captive and torturing him is none other than Danson Clifford. He is the connection. He's evil, and his spirit terrifies me."

Patrick tipped his head. Topaz could virtually hear the clicks as his artificial intelligence assimilated the information. "I see. An interesting development, and one that may ultimately help us. I will treat this man with respect, for you are not a woman easily terrified."

"I didn't used to be." It suddenly seemed to Topaz she had been bold and unafraid mainly because she felt careless. Easy enough to take risks when she had little to lose. Now, though, the desires piled up on her: to find Romney by whatever name; to protect Carlotta and, yes, Rose; to discover the horrors taking place at Clifford's orchestration and keep them from happening again.

"What should we do next?" she asked Kelly.

"Leave it to me. You and your companion will stay here—safe—while I set things in motion. Once your brother is found, he will need to be apprised of what has happened and taken to Carlotta at the hospital."

"And then?"

"And then we will attempt to free your Mr. Romney."

Topaz's heart leaped, but she fought back the tangled desire and desperation. "You will act through the police? But apart from my suspicions and Clifford's identity, we have very little actual proof."

Patrick lifted a brow. "You assume I will act through the police because I am an officer."

"Well, yes."

He leaned so close she could feel the warmth from the boiler in his thorax. "But, Miss Topaz, I am a couple of other things even before a police officer: I am an Irishman. And I am your Friend."

She stared at him, and he raised the glass of whiskey to her. "Trust me."

Chapter Twenty-Five

The bright lights of the steel room once again, blinding him. He struggled against his bonds even though he knew by now that struggling did no good. He feared if he quit struggling he'd be worse than dead.

He cursed in his mind and clung hard to the spark of light inside, the one that represented Topaz. The pounding brightness of the steel room all but blotted her out, another physical pain.

"String him up."

That voice—that hated voice, soft and relentless... he didn't even have to look into the man's face to know him. His gorge rose, and had he anything in his stomach, he would have lost it.

"Clifford, I must protest." The man with the black beard.

"I have told you not to use my name in front of him."

"He is barely conscious—certainly not competent to face questioning. I must protest in the strongest terms. I feel you have crossed a line from professional curiosity to—something else."

The two steam units in the room, ever obedient, ignored the bearded man's protests and went ahead, lifting and stringing up their victim. Every muscle in his body screamed, and he sealed his lips against a groan.

"This is my project," the hated voice responded.

Clifford? He should know that name, but his fractured mind refused to make the vital connection. "You are involved only peripherally."

"But I will be culpable if something goes wrong."

"Then I should think you would be in favor of assuring he cannot implicate us."

"Yes, but in my opinion this is no longer medicine; it's torture."

"I did not ask for your opinion."

"Then I will not stay for it. You are on your own."

The bearded man crashed out of the room, leaving the air reverberating.

"Bring the water," the hated voice instructed the steamies, and he tried to close his mind to what must come.

How long did the torment go on? He lost all capacity to tell. After a while, time ceased to matter. He heard the evil rabbit's questions for a span, before even they faded into pain, pain, pain.

Let me go, he begged his body. Let me go to her.

From somewhere—from everywhere—came the knowledge: if you leave your body now, it will mean death.

"—agent of the Queen?" The words came to him from a great distance. "Sent to apprehend me?"

Speech beyond him, he could not reply. *I don't know you, do I? Except through this bond of hate.*

The electrodes, applied once more, barely roused him. His flesh flopped and flailed; his mind remained numb.

Dimly he became aware of a great ruckus. Like the voice, it seemed quite distant and consisted of pounding and men's raised voices. The rabbit swore and dropped the electrodes, but he, the prisoner, lacked the strength to open his eyes.

"Right, lads." A new voice echoed in the steel room. "Do not let him get away."

There came a blast that stunned the senses in the confined space. Something threw itself against him where he hung, causing him to swing violently. He felt heat before a second blast came, still louder.

"Bastard has a steam cannon. Riley's down!"

The man who had hold of him said, "All right, lad, I've got you. Somebody help me cut him down." And more softly, into his ear, "I'm taking you to Miss Topaz."

****

Breathless, Topaz gazed into the face of the man who sprawled across Patrick Kelly's bed—asleep or unconscious, she couldn't tell which. Like a woman in a trance she examined his every feature, marked each wound, and traced every hair. She had seen him before, or more precisely seen *through* him, but never in the flesh.

Oh, how she'd craved his flesh! And now, now...despite his injuries and clearly debilitated state, he surpassed all her imaginings. Sapphire claimed she had a type; Topaz didn't know if that was true, but if so, this man must personify it.

Fair hair the color of ripe corn and with a decided wave—now streaked with dirt, sweat, and blood— tumbled over a wide brow, the nobility of which found its match in a high-bridged nose with a decided hook. Lean cheeks, also marked by dirt, bruises, and golden beard, tapered to a square jaw. And his lips...

Topaz longed so strongly to feel them with her own

she felt dizzy. But the thick brown lashes lay closed, and his spirit felt far from her. She hadn't yet seen the color of his eyes.

Patrick Kelly came up beside her, and she tipped her head to look at him. "Pat, what can I say? Thank you." To her dismay, tears clogged her throat.

Patrick squeezed her shoulder with one hand. "I would have taken him in any case, even if you didn't want him, once I saw what was happening in that room. I am only sorry the miscreant got away. He shot two of our men and used the distraction to slip out a hidden doorway. By the time we got outside, we could locate him nowhere."

"Your men—will they be all right?"

"They already are. We can take a hit, Miss Topaz. It knocks us down but rarely kills us."

"I'm glad." She covered his hand with hers. "You made this raid in an unofficial capacity?"

"Quite unofficial. We were all masked and can't be identified. Of course that means I cannot go to the authorities with what we discovered." Patrick nodded at Romney. "When we found him, he was still hanging in the chamber where the culprit and his steam units had him, and he was unable to talk to us. Hopefully once he comes to he will give us more tactile evidence I can then take to my superiors."

"I hope this doesn't strain your integrity to an unbearable degree."

"You are my Friend, Miss Topaz. As I have said, I would do far more to assist you."

"You are a good friend, Pat. A good man."

"I am not a man at all." He glanced over his shoulder at Rose who, much recovered, sat in a straight chair situated behind the draperies that allowed her to see out the window without being seen. "Like your new acquaintance, I am not sure I fit any definitions."

"Has she told you what she remembers?"

"Not in detail. I hope to sit down with her now while you strive to awaken your love."

"I only hope I may. I can feel his spirit, but it's very far from me."

"Shall I summon the doctor once more?"

"Perhaps. Let me see if I can awaken him first. You go speak with Rose."

Patrick moved off, and Topaz returned her gaze to Romney. He lay with his head turned slightly on the pillow, one cheek uppermost. Patrick had brought him in just before dawn, covered only by a soft shirt the automaton had lent that certainly did not hide his injuries.

How had he endured the infliction of such wounds? The severity of the pain had driven him from his flesh once. What if he had now retreated beyond her reach?

She cursed herself for her refusal to pursue those lessons her father had offered to impart. Not because she wanted to be like Frederick Hathor—never that— but because she felt completely unequipped to recall this man to her, even though her very heartbeat seemed to rely on his presence in her life.

Behind her she could hear Patrick and Rose speaking together, their voices low and even as if they discussed the weather rather than atrocities too terrible to contemplate. They sounded like two ordinary humans.

And what constituted true humanity? Surely something beyond the mere possession of a human body. Who could claim the larger share of humanity, Patrick Kelly or Danson Clifford?

She took Romney's hand in both of hers and closed her eyes, sensing for him. *Come to me.*

She could feel him, but barely, so distant. Could she drag him to her by sheer will?

Did she want to? Far better he came to her freely, by choice.

Closing her eyes, she reached for him, not with her mind but her spirit. And it proved easy, far easier than she'd dared hope. Gladness flared when they made contact—his gladness or hers, she couldn't tell.

Ours.

Come to me, she begged. *Be with me.*

Kiss me.

Without hesitation she bent and laid her lips on his. Light flared still brighter as his spirit streamed to hers and stretched full into his body once more. Their collision made such a cataclysm, she couldn't believe neither Pat nor Rose heard, yet they went on talking.

She took her lips from his and opened her eyes. His eyes, now open, were all she could see—quite possibly all that existed in her world.

They were blue, the exact color of a clear Buffalo sky in May, quizzical and full of intelligence. Air filled her lungs and with it momentous relief.

"You're back," she whispered. "You returned to me."

"I believe I will always return to you."

He lifted a hand, livid with electrical burns, to touch her face, and she saw as well as felt delight flood him.

"I can touch you."

"And I can touch you." Tenderly she laid her palm against his cheek.

"Makes all the pain worth it, if I've come to this."

"Don't say that," she begged.

"It's true. You kept me sane, Topaz Hathor— you're all that did. I would suffer far worse to be with you." Light filled his eyes. "Now kiss me again. And don't stop."

Chapter Twenty-Six

"With what Miss Topaz has told me and Miss Rose's help, I believe I have formed a working premise of what has been taking place at the home of Miss Topaz's father," Patrick Kelly announced, "and possibly at the place you call Grayson, as well."

Romney—he supposed for want of a better appellation he'd better continue calling himself that—eyed the big automaton. He then turned his gaze on Rose, scarcely able to accept what he'd been told.

The four of them sat around the small table in Kelly's parlor, Topaz holding Romney's hand. He still felt as if he'd been run over by an ale lorry, weak beyond expressing, but better when she touched him. It seemed as if her strength flooded into him whenever they made contact. And as he knew, Topaz Hathor possessed formidable strength.

They looked like a band of wounded warriors holding a war conference—which perhaps they were. Rose wore a cast on her right arm, bandages around her ribs, and a host of scrapes in addition to dark singe marks confined to her wrists and neck. She also wore an air of calm like a suit of mail, but her eyes held a lost, desperate expression.

Kelly had apparently taken a glancing hit from one of the blasts fired during Romney's rescue. It had burned away the skin on his cheekbone and at his temple, revealing steel beneath. One of his fingers had also been torn and now hung by a knuckle, a state to which he paid no attention.

Topaz—Romney turned his gaze on her and felt the gladness—the rightness—flood him again. She too bore a number of scrapes to hands and face, and she limped when she walked. He'd heard Kelly ask how her ribs felt, which she'd answered with a mere shake of her head. Her black hair, loose on her shoulders, made him ache to touch it.

As if she felt his regard, she turned those golden eyes on him. Her fingers tightened.

"Help me make sense of it," he bade Kelly. "From what the evil rabbit said, I was sent here as an agent of the Queen, apparently to hunt him down. He's called the Undertaker in my country. But most of it's lost to me."

"Queen Victoria?" Rose looked momentarily distracted from her deep unhappiness.

"Yes. At least, I think so."

Topaz said, "The first thing you need to remember is that the Undertaker, after whom the Queen sent you, and Danson Clifford—my father's assistant—are one and the same."

"Ah." Rom considered it, the missing piece falling into place. This explained, perhaps, why he'd streamed to the house on Humboldt Parkway in spiritual form, following his assignment even then. And it explained in part why he'd turned to Topaz for assistance. "I should have tumbled to that, shouldn't I?"

Topaz tightened her fingers on his hand. "You were in no condition to tumble to—or remember—much."

Rose gave a tight smile. "You recall too little, sir, and I far more than I wish. For I remember it all—every separate detail."

Topaz leaned forward. "I know you've been over all of it with Patrick, but will you please tell us?"

Rose twisted her fingers into a knot. "It began with my husband—a man I never wanted to marry, a brute who insisted on controlling me in words, deeds, everything from whom I saw to what I ate. When I rebelled, he raised his hand to me. When I went to the police"—she glanced at Kelly—"he paid them off. He is a very wealthy man."

"Here in this city?" Topaz asked.

"No. We lived in Philadelphia, but he is here now. He came for the express purpose of consulting with Frederick Hathor, who I understand is your father."

"He is." Topaz drew a breath Romney could feel. "And you came with him?"

"No. By then I was dead—killed when he pushed me down a flight of stairs and I struck my head. My husband, Louis Dennison, had heard there were two men in Buffalo who could entrap spirits and force them into new bodies."

Topaz faltered out, "Mechanicals, you mean."

"No." Rose shook her head. "Into corpses—reanimated through a process designed by the man called the Undertaker."

"Danson Clifford," Topaz said quietly and with loathing. Romney twitched in response.

He spoke out of horror and wonder. "Is that what you are, Mrs. Dennison?"

Her smile turned bitter. "I am. But please don't call me by that name. I want no connection with the man and consider our marriage ties were severed when I died."

"Of course." But Romney couldn't keep his gaze from wandering over her. "You say you remember everything. Do you recall the process?"

"Vividly. It happened in the cellar of the house from which Miss Hathor helped me escape yesterday evening. Frederick Hathor called me from the ether where I lingered after my death. I wanted to move on, but I could not. There is a time when we hover and reexamine the events that occurred during the life just passed. I was with many other spirits, but he snared me, captured me." A delicate shudder passed through her. "He is very powerful."

Topaz said nothing, but again Romney felt her dismay.

"You understand"—Rose laid a hand flat on the table—"I did not wish to return, especially when I sensed the presence of Dennison. I fought without success. When once captured and I realized what was intended for me, my horror became complete."

Romney asked gently, "From whence did they procure this body you now wear?"

Rose looked at him, her gaze that of a tortured animal. "She was killed there in the lab located in that cellar."

"What?" Topaz half rose. Romney pulled her down again.

"Yes, Miss Hathor. I believe she was a poor woman lured with the promise of employment. I have no access to her memories, but I heard the two who did this to me speak of it—of her."

"My father party to murder?" Topaz shook her

head. "I know he is unscrupulous in his dealings with his clients, but for him to dismiss one spirit from a body only to replace it with another... What would prompt him to such an act?"

Patrick Kelly replied, "Money. Miss Rose says a fearful amount of money was to change hands when she was returned to her husband in this new flesh."

Rose nodded. "One million dollars."

"What!" Topaz uttered the word again and fell silent, though Romney could feel her thinking furiously.

Rose leaned toward her. "Your father's name, Miss Hathor, is most apt. Mr. Kelly tells me one of the duties of the Egyptian goddess Hathor was to conduct the souls of the dead to a new life. Though he never said she made a profit from it."

Patrick Kelly looked at Romney. "I believe, Mr. Marsh, you must indeed be an agent of the British government sent to follow Clifford here and perhaps try to halt his activities. If so, you and I are now working on the same side. We make an odd team of four, do we not?" He emitted the grinding sound that for him represented laughter. "A man who is not, in fact, a man; another who does not recall his past; a fledgling spiritualist; and a woman with no desire to be alive. A curious situation."

"Indeed." Rose's gaze fell to the table. "I intend to tell Mr. Kelly, here, all the details I possess so he may apprehend these monsters. And then I will decide whether to end my life."

****

Much later, Topaz and Romney lay together in Patrick Kelly's narrow bed. As soon as evening fell,

Patrick had demonstrated exquisite tact by vacating the place and taking Rose with him, leaving Topaz exactly where she wanted to be. But with the dark came Romney's agitation. He began to pace and glanced repeatedly toward the windows even after she drew the drapes. Despite his exhaustion and obvious pain, he refused to settle.

She lit every lamp in the room and wondered how best to comfort him. Through their spiritual connection she'd experienced the edges of the darkness that had confined him and could now feel him fighting against the terror. Perhaps distraction would serve.

She led him to the cot, pressed him down upon it, and joined him there, trying unsuccessfully to make herself small. Immediately, she felt some of the tension leave his body.

Like a woman in a trance, she gazed into his eyes.

"Do you know how much I've wanted this?" she breathed. "To touch you, I mean."

Wryly he said, "That was quite a buildup between us. I hope I'm not a disappointment, given this poor, battered body."

"No disappointment on my part. Better, in fact, than I ever imagined."

"Really?" He quirked a brow. "I'll admit my imagination has run wild."

"As has mine. But now—bless Pat Kelly—I have the chance to satisfy it. That is, if you wouldn't rather wait till you're recovered—"

"I think we've waited long enough, don't you?"

"Yes. Any more anticipation and I just might not survive. You just lie there. How about if I begin by removing your clothing?"

"That won't take long. I'm not wearing much."

"Good." She kissed him, and it felt like the first breath of air after an age-long suffocation. The sweetness of it flowed through her blood, and she sensed it laid claim to him as well, despite his weakness. His desire flared, inevitable desire that had existed from the moment they'd first encountered one another in her room. They were the two halves of one whole: stiletto and foil, question and answer, body and heartbeat.

"Topaz." He lifted his hands and cradled her face; the connection between them intensified unbearably. He laced his fingers through her hair, and she shuddered with desire. "I must have you."

"Take me." She unfastened the shirt she wore. No room here for insignificant things like modesty. He'd already seen all of her, and anyway, she belonged to him without reservation.

"But despite how much I want you, there's a darkness in me."

"Then," she said a moment before she kissed him again, "let me see if I can burn it away."

Chapter Twenty-Seven

A man could quite happily die with Topaz Hathor in his arms, Romney thought. But he discovered, sharp as pain, how much he wanted to keep on living, stay right here in the flesh where he could touch her, taste her, and indulge each fantasy that had haunted him these many days past.

Every light in the room now blazed. Topaz knew he feared the darkness just as she knew everything else about him—where he wanted her to put her hands and her mouth. She must feel his weakness also—bone deep—but she ignored it as if he were whole again.

Complete.

The mad idea flitted through his mind: He would only ever be complete when this woman touched him, when he touched her.

And oh, she'd been made for touching, for his hands, and for his pleasure. Her generous curves molded to his fingers as he caressed her, and her tongue claimed him wherever it touched—the inside of his mouth, his throat, his chest, his belly. Her hair slid over his skin like a curtain of black silk, quickening every nerve, and when she took him in her mouth he forgot the darkness in a blaze of inner light.

Weakness? What weakness? It fled from him, chased by the magic of her tongue, the heat of it like the touch of flame.

"Topaz." He spoke her name for the sheer joy of it even as she worked her lips and tongue up and down him—now miraculously upstanding—in an avid dance. She was magic, an enchantress, a part of him so primitive it underlay all else, even identity. "I want—"

"No need to tell me. I know." She slid back up his body and gazed at him with bright, golden eyes, and he promptly lost all the breath in his body.

Beautiful. Her lips blood red and her flesh, atop his, one caress.

"If I love you now," she told him, "there's no going back from it. You know that, don't you? We will be bonded beyond severing."

"We already are."

She smiled, glorious as the sun, and he felt her strength uplift him. "Yes, spiritually. But if I take you inside me it will be forever—beyond even the point when death may part us."

"You don't even know my name."

Her gaze held his. "I don't care about your name. I want you—your intelligence, your light."

"Sorely diminished—"

"Let me reignite it."

She began to move atop him, a goddess made of strength and vigor. His heartbeat and energy rose to meet her in a crest of glorious passion.

This made up for the hours in the dark. This made all the pain worthwhile. This, he thought at the moment he arched up into her, when she tossed her black hair and rode him with consuming pleasure, made even losing himself worthwhile. For at least he'd found her—and himself in her—forevermore.

With each flex of her muscles, her body called to

189

his, with each brush of softness overlying her strength. He could see now that bruises covered her white body, including a dark area across her ribs and a livid scrape down one of the legs that straddled him. She disregarded those hurts even as he disregarded his own, fixed her gaze on his, and did not waver. And when he strove to be gentle and spare her, she demanded his fire and summoned his strength from a place so deep he never knew it existed.

"Come to me. Come in me," she seduced.

And she'd been right; he felt the connections between them flare irrevocably at the moment they climaxed together. She collapsed against him and, still inside her, he wrapped her in his arms.

"Beautiful Topaz. You are so beautiful."

She went still in his arms. "I'm glad you think so."

"Let me drink of you again."

She opened her lips to him readily, and he drank deep with eyes closed on a wave of bliss. Still inside her, he grew hard once more.

She broke the kiss and laughed softly, one of the most arousing sounds he'd ever heard.

"What?" he asked and palmed the delectable mound of one breast.

"It seems your strength returns swiftly."

"So it does." In one glorious movement he flipped her on her back. "I suggest you lie there and allow me to show you just how swiftly."

"Show me. Oh, show me," she begged.

****

He awoke to the enduring bliss, warmth, and yet more desire. It didn't hurt, he reflected, to wake with his cheek pillowed on Topaz Hathor's breast, his lips but a breath from one luscious nipple. Had he fallen asleep while suckling her? Quite possibly. He tried to remember the details of the night just past and found only a jumble of mind-searing images. They had roused—quite literally—several times during the night desperate for one another. Once he had fallen into a pit of darkness, dreams too terrible to contemplate now. Her touch had pulled him from that place and saved him. Each time she loved him, he grew stronger.

In fact, he now felt surprisingly restored—far better than he could have imagined this time yesterday when every nerve end had seemed blasted by pain. He flexed his body surreptitiously, unwilling to wake Topaz. His muscles protested, but not unbearably.

He pushed up and looked at the miracle in his arms. What made her so beautiful, besides that wickedly seductive hair, those curves he found so irresistible, and those enchanting eyes, now closed? The strong, exotic planes of her face spoke of far-off places, wild music, and firelight. Her ruby lips had been all over him last night, whispering, caressing.

Even now, when she slept, her strength burned steady as a flame. How could he ever hope to express what she meant to him? And how would the future ever sort itself?

As if she felt his regard, her black lashes twitched and she opened her eyes. He promptly lost all his worries on a rush of joy.

"Good morning," he told her.

"Morning." She examined him minutely, measuring the width of his brow, tracing his nose, and lingering on his mouth. "It wasn't a dream—you're really here."

"There were dreams. You saved me from them."

She lifted a hand and placed it against his face. A new expression flooded her eyes, grave and mysterious. He'd seen many things there before: anger, courage, defiance, desire. But this stole his breath.

"How do you feel?"

"I'll do, Miss Hathor. And you?" He caressed her with his gaze. "You took quite a beating in that crash. You should have reminded me."

"Yes?" She quirked an eyebrow. "And what would you have done differently?"

"Been gentler with you."

"You were gentle with me." Heat kindled in her eyes. "I trust you will be again."

"Oh?" He teased in an effort to hide his emotion. "Are we going to make love once more?"

She tipped her head on the pillow. "Is it 'love'?"

"I believe so," he answered steadily.

She drew a breath that did amazing things to her bosom. "Ah, but I have no experience with that emotion. Like Patrick Kelly, I can't begin to fathom it. I never believed it would find me."

He brushed his lips across hers lightly. "Just proves even the matchless Topaz Hathor can be wrong."

Beneath his hand, her heartbeat accelerated. "I must warn you, I'm not sure I can do love."

"I'm certain."

"You will need to help me through, Romney."

"Place your trust in me. I will give you my certainty; you give me your strength."

"It seems an equable arrangement, give and take. But fair warning—when I'm this close to you, I lose all perspective. I don't know what this day will bring. I shudder to think. All I know is, before it begins, I want you."

"I need you," he returned.

And there in the bright light of morning they deepened their bonds still further. What matter, he thought again, if he'd lost his identity? In her, he found himself anew.

****

If Topaz didn't know better, she'd say Patrick Kelly looked curious when he returned to his room. He'd arrived soon after she and Romney rose—at last—from bed and now stood just inside the door, examining the place with interested, green eyes.

Did he wonder what had taken place here during the night? Would he be so bold as to ask?

Topaz, bundling her hair into a knot at the back of her head, also wondered just exactly what had taken place last night, beyond the obvious. Romney had barely been able to stand when he arrived here. Now he looked pale but steady, and she could personally attest to the return of his strength.

She'd never been one to shirk battles, verbal ones with Sapphire, mental ones with her father, bouts on the waterfront. She prided herself on her fearlessness. But this bonding with Romney both thrilled and terrified her because, miraculous though it was, as her need for him deepened so did her vulnerability.

"Good morning, Officer Kelly." Romney still buttoned his borrowed shirt. Just thinking about what lay beneath his clothing raised Topaz's temperature several degrees. "Thank you for your kind hospitality last night."

"Please call me Patrick, or Pat. We are friends, are

we not?"

"I do hope so."

"Being a friend of Pat Kelly is most enviable." Topaz crossed the room and took Kelly's hands. "He has proved a true friend to me, and I'm grateful."

Kelly squeezed her hands gently. "I trust you spent a pleasant night."

Topaz fought the sudden desire to grin. "Most pleasant."

"Good. I come with news. Your brother, Sapphire, has been located and is on his way to the hospital where your injured companion was taken."

"Where was he found?"

"At a house on Pennsylvania Street, where he has taken rooms for himself and his fiancée. Apparently he intended to collect her from your father's house later today."

"He called her that? His fiancée?"

"He did."

Topaz sobered. "Any word from the hospital about how Carlotta's doing?"

"No. I imagine you would like to join your brother at her bedside."

"I would."

"Unfortunately, I do not consider that a safe option. Nor do I believe it safe for you to stay here. I have located a house where you may, as they say, 'go to ground' for a time."

"Oh." Topaz glanced at Romney, who said nothing. "Together?"

Patrick Kelly replied, "I wouldn't dare to suggest anything else."

Chapter Twenty-Eight

The building to which Patrick Kelly conducted them belonged to another of his friends. The automaton, Romney reflected, possessed more close ties than might be expected. But then, Kelly had a strong and generous spirit.

And could an automaton—a machine built of skin laid over steel that didn't breathe and had no actual heart—possess a spirit? It seemed abundantly evident Kelly did.

And Romney had already begun to learn it was all about the spirit, not the flesh at all. He'd met Topaz first in spirit; he knew for a fact that during duress the spirit might vacate the flesh. But it did endure.

And now his spirit had bonded to Topaz Hathor's, and his flesh craved her, like a fire burning.

Kelly shuttled them by horse and buggy, well-swathed against the cold, down Niagara Street to the warehouse that had been adapted into a dwelling. A sign out front read, *Buffalo Animal Refuge*, and Kelly's knock was answered by a diminutive woman, visibly pregnant, who promptly threw herself into his arms.

"Pat, come in out of the cold. Jamie's just in the yard and will be here directly."

"How are you, Miss Cat?"

She smiled infectiously and gestured at herself. "Blooming, as you can see."

"These are your guests." Patrick turned to Romney and Topaz. "Names, I fear, are not in order—for your own safety, you understand."

The woman fixed Topaz with a level, hazel stare. "Well I can certainly give you my name. Catherine Kilter and—oh, here's my husband, James."

A man had entered through a door at the back of the building, silhouetted by the bright morning light. Romney had time only to note his height, which nearly matched Kelly's, and the powerful way he moved before he reached them.

Romney still held Topaz's hand and felt her twitch when she saw the man's face. Or should Romney say his half face? Dark auburn hair sprouted from the left side of his head—on the right, scar tissue prohibited any hair growth. The damage, no doubt the result of severe burns, extended down the right side of his face in a livid mask. But his blue eyes held a kind expression, and Catherine looked at him as if he illuminated her world.

"Welcome," he said, and his lips twisted in a half smile. "I'm Kilter—James."

Romney stuck out his hand. "Thank you, Mr. Kilter, for offering us a bolt-hole."

"Any friends of Patrick are welcome here."

"I thought since it is a refuge," Kelly put in, "two more would not hurt."

"Certainly not. I prepared our spare room after I got Pat's message this morning." Cat shot another adoring look at her husband. "Not so long ago we were shuttled hither and yon from one safe house to another. Remember, my love?"

She doesn't even see his scars, Romney thought,

and his heart bounded.

Topaz turned to Kelly. "What about your other guest?"

"She was able to impart the rest of her story to me last night. I will share it with you when we have more time. For now, I think it best to house her elsewhere." His face did not change expression, but Romney felt his caution. "The miscreants will come after her. They cannot do otherwise."

Topaz nodded unhappily. "And my brother?"

"One of the Squad will bring him here as soon as he's finished at the hospital. Meanwhile, I urge you to keep your heads down."

Romney placed his arm around Topaz and drew her against his side. Keeping her acquiescent would be a challenge. But he said, "We will, and thank you for all you've done."

Kelly left after shaking hands with James Kilter.

"Have you had breakfast?" Cat asked. "Our quarters are upstairs. Would you like me to show you around first?" She smiled impishly. "Only I'm always hungry these days."

"She can eat prodigious amounts, for such a tiny thing," Kilter put in, his voice a caress.

Cat leaned toward Topaz confidingly. "It's the baby. I think it's going to be a boy, a big one."

Together they toured the large building, which had a reception room in front, a small area that served as a surgery, and a number of indoor cages, all immaculately clean. The cages were occupied—one by a mother cat and her kittens, another by a nearly bald rat. Out back in the sunshine, feeling miles from the bustle of the city, sprawled a yard filled with kennels, many occupied by dogs, and a small paddock area holding two horses.

"I never would have guessed all this was here," Topaz said in wonder.

Cat laid a hand on her husband's arm. "All James's doing."

"With Pat's help," Kilter put in. The clear, outdoor light revealed the worst of his disfigurement, but the animals, who all pressed forward eagerly at the sight of him, did not seem to care any more than did his little wife.

"The dogs come to us as found," Kilter said. "The horses were both taken in cruelty cases. Bobby there—the white horse—was far too old to be working when we found him. Jenny—well, you can see the scars from the whip, if you look."

"What will happen to them?" Romney asked.

"We doctor and rehabilitate those that need it and search for good homes." Kilter slanted a look at them. "I hope you don't mind dogs, for there are some upstairs who seem to have become permanent residents."

"Come on," Cat invited. "I'll show you."

The quarters upstairs, bright and sunny, had been extensively remodeled. New windows, floors, and wall coverings made the rooms feel homey. A small horde of dogs came to meet them, everything from a tiny ball of white fur to a large yellow lurcher that held back standoffishly.

"That's Greta," Cat explained. "She's looking for James." Kilter had stayed below in the yard.

"How long have you lived here?" Topaz asked curiously.

"Since we married last June. I'm due in March."
Cat blushed charmingly. "We didn't wait, you see."

Love fills this place, Romney thought, rooted like a
primrose blooming on a stony street. A lesson, perhaps?
For the love here clearly went beyond the physical—
and even the barriers of species—to spirit.

But surely Kelly, an automaton, couldn't have
brought them here merely to show them that?

****

He hung in the darkness again with the voice—that
hated voice—once more in his ears. Pain flicked
through his body like the bite of a whip, and he
shuddered.

"Remember. What do you remember? Where were
you born?"

Writhing where he hung, dreading the next touch
from the electrodes, he strove for the information. They
had been over and over this: his questioner knew he
could not retrieve the answers to his questions. Why
continue to torture him?

But suddenly strength flooded through him, beating
back the darkness, burgeoning, and uplifting him.
Knowledge streamed into his mind, whole.

South Sussex, Romney Marsh—the great green
wastes of his childhood, unchanging and serene, that
yet this monster who now tormented him would taint
with his unnatural practices.

But he could not, he would not tell his tormentor
that. Nor that he'd been sent to stop the Undertaker at
any cost, even if that cost included his life.

"It's all right, hush. Hush. You're safe here with
me."

A second voice intruded on his panic. This one

curled through him like an extension of his own being—like comfort, hard won. He breathed again.

"Topaz?"

"Yes. I'm here."

The pieces of reality fell into place and he suddenly knew where he was: the small room to which little Mrs. Kilter had shown them, the one that overlooked the big yard with all its refugees. He lay in the bed. More importantly, he lay in Topaz Hathor's arms.

That knowledge allowed him to draw still more air into his lungs. He could not see her, but he could feel her—arms, naked breasts, spirit.

She moved in the bed and began to sit up.

"No," he said.

"I am just going to light the lamp." She spoke as one might to a child.

She swore as she fumbled with the lamp on the bedside table. She struck a flame which seared Romney's eyes. By its radiance he saw her leaning above him, black hair raining down and eyes full of concern. His world abruptly steadied.

"I'm sorry. I left the lamp by the door burning—I didn't want the dark to find you. It must have gone out while we slept."

"It doesn't matter. I dreamed—but that doesn't matter either." He caught hold of her, seeking to impart the magnitude of what he had to tell. "Topaz, I've begun to remember."

"You have?"

"Yes—not all of it, but enough. Bits and pieces. I know the rest of it will come." He gazed into her eyes. "And it's because of you. You're the answer, the connection. Topaz, I do believe I was meant to come to you—you, not your father—that first night. There's some meaning in it. Every time I love you, I grow stronger. You make sense of everything."

"Just by loving you?"

"By joining with me. Don't you see? It's the two of us together that makes the magic."

"I need no persuasion to share myself with you. But," she sobered, "if we fight my father and Danson Clifford, we face an uphill battle indeed. My father is a spiritual master and fully invested in finding Rose. If he employs all his power to search for us—"

He cupped her cheek in his hand. "You have power also—I've felt it. It's grounded me, pulled me back from the brink. Maybe you can use it to shield us now."

She shook her head. "Against my father?"

He told her with absolute conviction, "I believe in you."

Her eyes filled with tears. "And I would sooner die than fail you. Yet I'm but a fledgling. I never applied myself to the lessons my father tried to teach me. And now it's too late."

"You're the only one who can challenge or thwart him."

Wildly now, she shook her head again. "I'm not strong enough."

"We will strengthen each other." And he pulled her into his arms.

Chapter Twenty-Nine

Topaz rose from the bed with a parting glance and caress for the man she left behind. As always when she looked at Romney, her heart stuttered in her breast. Of all the emotions she'd experienced in her life—daring, confidence, anger, loathing, or even fear—she found this tenderness the hardest to bear. Softness did not come easily to her, or this love that she felt, fierce as it might be.

He didn't stir, still exhausted by what had befallen him at Grayson as well as their activities during the night. She knew just how deep his debility reached—she'd felt it on the most intimate of levels. By rights they shouldn't be making love until he healed.

Yet he would have her believe lying with her restored his strength, along with his memories.

She hoped so, for she didn't think she could give him up now if she tried.

Quietly she finished dressing, twisted her hair into a braid, and tiptoed from the room. In the dining room she found Mrs. Kilter along with a circle of dogs, several of which greeted her.

"Good morning." Cat Kilter waved the toast in her hand. "Where's your companion?"

"Still sleeping."

"Come and have some breakfast. James has gone to do a job for his friend Tate Murphy. It's just me and the animals."

Topaz, nothing loath, pulled out a chair and sat down. Her inner sense—which once limbered now seemed to operate on its own—sensed only light and a great deal of joy filling this woman's spirit.

"Help yourself." Cat gestured at the generous selection of dishes on the table. "Tell me about yourself, at least what you can. I gather from what Pat said you shouldn't give away much."

"Better not." Topaz eyed her hostess cautiously. She'd never been close with her older sisters and had very few female friends apart from the streetwalkers she helped train.

"Maybe," Cat suggested, "just enough to satisfy my curiosity. How did you and your lover meet?" She dimpled. "That's what he is, right? Your lover?"

"Yes." Admitting it made it more real. Topaz helped herself to toast and sausage. "As for how we met—you wouldn't believe it."

"Try me."

The small white dog jumped up onto Cat's knee. The two of them—animal and woman—watched Topaz with identical hazel eyes.

Cautiously, Topaz asked, "Did Pat give you any idea who I am?"

"Said it wasn't safe to tell me. But he didn't have to. I recognize you—and I know who your father is. Most people in this city must."

"Then you're aware of his reputation, his…abilities? I inherited some of them. When I first met my lover, it was not in the flesh."

"Oh." Cat contemplated that and shrugged. "Not so inconceivable. As you may imagine, my attraction to

Jamie didn't begin with the physical, either." Blithely she added, "Though I adore every inch of him now."

Obviously.

"Some more than others. But I do believe I fell in love with his spirit almost immediately—strong, kind, and so beautiful."

"He's a lucky man that you saw all that in him."

"I assure you, I'm the lucky one."

Ruefully, Topaz said, "From the very beginning this has seemed like some mad dream, all of it. And I confess I can't see our way clear of all the difficulties."

Cat leaned forward and covered Topaz's hand with hers. "I know how that feels, to despair over anything ever coming right. I was where you are once. But just look at me now."

Topaz nodded gravely. The biggest of the dogs, the short-haired yellow lurcher Cat called Greta, sidled up to Topaz and fixed her with an enigmatic stare.

"Just look at that," Cat remarked. "You must be special; Greta rarely responds to anyone."

Topaz put out a hand, and the big dog placed her head under it. Fur like warm velvet met Topaz's fingers.

"James will never believe that. He rescued her from a pit back before I met him."

"A fighting pit, you mean?"

"Yes. If you look under the fur you can see her scars. She has a warrior's heart." Cat fixed Topaz with another enigmatic look. "Maybe she senses a kindred spirit in you."

Before Topaz could answer, a knock sounded from downstairs. Barking immediately broke out, and Cat jumped up, the white dog caught in her arms.

"Somebody's here."

She went off and returned in a few moments followed by Patrick Kelly and Sapphire. Topaz leaped up and immediately froze, arrested by the expression in her brother's eyes.

"Carlotta?" she questioned even as Greta pressed against her side.

Usually bold and careless, Sapphire's face now wore a pinched look and grief filled his eyes.

"Oh, no," Topaz lamented.

"We lost the child," he blurted. "Carly—she'll survive. But the little one is gone."

Grief and remorse crashed over Topaz in equal parts. She barely saw Cat and Patrick Kelly leave the room. Most of the animals followed; only Greta remained at Topaz's side.

"I'm so sorry."

Sapphire looked at her accusingly. "Why don't you tell me exactly what happened?"

"I…" How best to explain? "I used the key you got for me and searched the cellar. Sapph, I made a terrible discovery." She knew Sapphire's feelings toward Frederick were as complicated as her own, but she doubted he would easily accept the ramifications of this thing in which his father was now involved. "I couldn't leave her there—Carly, I mean. I thought you'd want me to take her to safety."

"You thought!" he exclaimed bitterly, his pain a weapon. "And you always know best, don't you?"

"Me? I know nothing." Topaz stated it with complete veracity.

"She was safe there."

"I didn't think so."

"I meant to fetch her away the next day."

"I know that now. But I wasn't sure where you were and, Sapph, listen to me—that new partner of Father's…"

"I don't care about that! All I know is if you'd left her where she was, our child would still be alive." Disconcerting tears filled Sapphire's eyes. Topaz couldn't remember ever seeing him cry, not even as a small boy. "Alive," he emphasized, "instead of just a spirit released back into the ether—gone forever."

"No," Topaz breathed, appalled. "You'll have other children."

"Carly says no. She insists she'll not marry me now, insists the only reason I asked her was because of the baby. She says she wants to go away; she sent me from the hospital, and—"

"Oh, Sapph! She'll come round. She loves you. That's just shock and reaction talking—and grief. But she'll want to see you later."

"You know that too, I suppose. Just like you knew it must be a good idea to take a fragile, pregnant girl out in a steamcab on icy streets."

"I did what I thought best."

"Yes, well," he said savagely, "now you can live with the consequences. The steamcab driver died at the hospital. Did you know that?"

"No."

"His wife was there. They have two teenaged children. Alone now, thanks to you."

"Sapphire, please—" Instinctively, she reached for him, but he drew away. "Don't touch me. And stay away from Carly, understand? Don't try to find either of us. We don't want to see you again."

Topaz withdrew from the heat of his anger and the hatred in his eyes. Her brother might be many things but he had never been hateful—at least not toward her.

She flinched even as did Greta, who slunk away from the confrontation, her tail between her legs. Sapphire spun on his heel and stalked out, leaving Topaz's heart bleeding.

****

"He'll forgive you." Romney drew Topaz closer in his arms, in their bed. Night had come; Topaz wished she could crawl into it like a black sack and hide from everything. Everything, that was, except this man who held her.

She could feel so many things about him: his pain that flickered through his body like the remnants of lightning; his bone-deep weariness; and the steady light that burned like a flame deep inside him. She nestled her head in the hollow of his shoulder.

"That was his grief talking," Romney went on. "His fear."

"I know." Topaz bit her lip. "But you don't understand—we were always so close. He was the only one in my family I could turn to. Now he hates me."

"He doesn't."

"And, damn it, he has a right to hate me. Why didn't I leave Carly at the house?"

"You had no way of knowing he meant to collect her so soon."

"I just couldn't bring myself to leave her in the same house as...*him*." Horror crawled up from Topaz's belly to her throat. "Not once I realized what he's been doing—trapping spirits... Well, I always knew he did that. But to force them into other bodies—*dead* bodies reanimated by that fiend, Clifford. Getting Carly out of there was a gut reaction. Sapphire will never see it that way."

Romney kissed her temple. His concern flooded through in a wave of comfort.

"Frederick Hathor's my father," she went on, revulsion sounding in her voice. "I always found it unbearable that he interfered with the spirits that were on their way to—well, to wherever they're meant to go. I could feel their bewilderment, their fear, and their longing for their past and their future, both. But this is so much worse. What's happened to Rose, that's spiritual slavery. How could he do such things? He, above all others, who knows what it is to bond with those who come to him."

"There must be a fortune in it, and greed is a powerful motivator."

"But he already has all he needs. You've seen that house." She slid her palm across the skin of his chest, naked beneath the shirt he wore. "Enough—more than enough for anyone."

Before he could reply, she drew a breath and went on. "And it's not as if he doesn't understand the depth of the harm he does. He must have been able to feel Rose's distress. I could feel it! My God, Rom, she's thinking of killing this new body in which she's trapped rather than endure living in it."

He turned her face gently till her eyes met his. "I don't think you have to worry about that. I doubt Patrick Kelly will permit her to do any such thing."

"Pat?"

"He seems to have taken her under his metaphorical wing—which is not a bad place to be.

When you think about it, he might prove her perfect protector. He understands her quandary, and there are only so many demands he can make on her."

"Pat? And Rose?"

Romney smiled. "Rather, I think, their equally troubled spirits. If we've learned one thing from all this, Topaz, it's that spirit bonds with spirit. Everything else is pure window dressing."

He brushed her lips with his. "Though I have to admit I'm intensely attracted to your window dressing."

"And I to yours."

"Will you make love with me?" he asked simply.

She gazed into his eyes and saw there, in equal measures, her strength and her weakness.

"Only try to stop me."

Chapter Thirty

"Mr. Gideon, I need not tell you this is a matter of utmost confidence. Here in England we have hatched a monster of distressing proportions. And now that he has fled our shores, we have a responsibility to recall that which we have unleashed upon the world."

Romney looked at the diminutive figure who sat before him, clad all in black with a white lace cap on her head. Repugnance twisted her rather plain features, and horror filled her eyes.

"Yes, your majesty." He inclined his head.

Impulsively, Victoria leaned toward him. "We know we can rely upon your discretion, Mr. Gideon, even as we have in the past. The Hyde Park Strangler springs to mind, and the situation with the Parliament atrocities. You have proved yourself the foremost of my agents."

"Thank you, ma'am."

"And this time," the Queen went on, "I must send you forth like a hawk after a crow—all the way across the ocean."

"Our information places Clifford in New York, ma'am," Gideon agreed. "Not the big city of New York but a smaller one on the Niagara Frontier—Buffalo."

"Why there, do you suppose, Mr. Gideon?"

"Your majesty, it's a border city adjacent to your dominion of Canada. I suppose he thought that would give him easy entry and possibly a bolt-hole back to the dominion if things should go wrong for him there. Also, our intelligence puts him in touch with a man who lives there—a spiritualist named Frederick Hathor."

Victoria lifted her brows. "Spiritualist, you say, Mr. Gideon?"

"Yes, ma'am, by all reports one world-renowned and far more powerful than any with whom he worked here in England."

"Ah." The Queen's hands fluttered in distress. "That does not bode well for us."

"No, ma'am."

"Mr. Gideon, I charge you: this man's appalling activities cannot be permitted to continue. What will come of it, I ask you, if the dead are brought back to life indiscriminately? What of the respect owed those whose bodies have been laid to rest only to have this monster raise them for his own purposes? How long before he begins choosing host bodies that are less than perfect or, worse, contracts the deaths of those whose living bodies meet his clients' criteria?"

"Aye, ma'am. That is what I fear also."

She said, "I, above all others, my dear Mr. Gideon, know what it is to love—and to grieve. The loss of my dear Albert drove me to the greatest depths of mourning. But, even to experience again the presence of his spirit, I trust I would never engage in such a dire abomination!"

She widened her eyes. "Go to America, Mr. Gideon. Apprehend him for us—at any cost."

****

Romney awoke abruptly and sucked a great, painful breath into his lungs. Yes, Romney actually was his given name. But his surname was…

Gideon.

How strange that amid all the pain, distress, and disconnection he'd managed to retain the name Romney while connecting it to the marshes where he'd been born. A place he loved most in the world—even now he had only to close his eyes to see the vast green expanses with the gray sea beyond. The same place, as Victoria had reminded him in his dream, that had spawned the unnatural creature who had seized, confined, and tortured him.

At any cost, Victoria had said. And he had already paid a high cost—and failed. Danson Clifford could not allow him to live, at least not sane and with his memory intact. Just as he could not give up his mission now and allow Danson Clifford to succeed. A classic battle.

And what weapons did he, Romney Gideon, possess? The sanction of his Queen—a holy writ—and the memories even now returning to him in pieces. The strength of this woman in his arms.

He drew Topaz still closer, reveling in the feeling of her naked flesh meeting his. Before falling asleep they'd made intense, deliberate love; she had given herself to him fully and generously. Did she realize what she meant to him: his strength, his desire, and quite possibly his sanity? Did she know when she looked at him with those amber-colored eyes or even touched him in passing he lost the capacity to resist her?

He hadn't bargained for this when he went to serve at Victoria's bidding. He'd had no place in his life for love. As for this need that staggered him every time he so much as looked at Topaz…

Yet he now knew he would have to sacrifice even his love for her, if asked, in pursuit of Clifford.

But not this night.

That thought curled through his mind as he placed his hand on Topaz's breast, marveling at her warmth and softness. She stirred in her sleep but slept on.

In a wordless pledge of devotion, he bent his head and placed his lips on hers, which even in her sleep she parted for him. He explored the inside of her warm mouth with long, leisurely strokes of his tongue, remembering how it felt when he entered her on a strong current of passion. Before the kiss ended, she awakened and began to participate with unbridled enthusiasm.

She tasted wild and sweet, of musk and bright delectable desire and the fire that lit the world.

Take her now, his soul whispered. *Tomorrow may never come.*

"Umm." She made the sound in her throat as she invited his tongue in deeper. She shifted and slid beneath him so the weight and heft of him pillowed on her thighs.

He stopped kissing her to say, "You truly are a goddess, Topaz Hathor."

She laughed huskily. "I do not mind hearing you say so. But is that the best use to which you can put those talented lips of yours? I can think of better."

So could he. The rosy, erect buds at the tips of her breasts awaited his pleasure and hers. If this be the last time we lie together, he thought, even as he ran his mouth down the swell of her breast and caressed her with his tongue before latching on, only let it last. Let morning never come.

"Shall I show you?" he whispered across her damp nipple. "Shall I worship you as you deserve?"

She shivered with delight. "I know not what I deserve. I want whatever you will give me."

He laughed and trailed kisses across her belly downward, moving ever more slowly. When he reached the nest of black curls between her legs, she arched her back and opened for him.

Paradise! The heady scent of her spurred still sharper desire, the need to plunder her so thoroughly and completely with his mouth she would never, never forget this night.

A purely physical act, but he could feel the strength of her soul burgeoning, holding and uplifting him even as he urged her thighs farther apart with gentle hands, as he entered her with his tongue. He felt the fusing of their spirits when she tangled her fingers in his hair, and his passion rose with hers as he wooed and opened her more and more to him. And when the waves of pleasure came, he drank her passion and made it his own.

Only after she lay in pieces, shattered beneath his hands and tongue, did he kiss his way back up her body, rear over and enter her, watching her face in the faint, ambient light that sifted through the window. To his amazement, she quickened once more for him, and they came together in a joining so complete he experienced both her emotions and her physical pleasure.

Ah, so this was what it meant to be joined at the soul level. He eased down on top of her with his face at her throat, inhaled her scent, and felt her tremble.

For one priceless instant his existence became complete—no past, no future, no impossible task to perform. Only this woman bonded to him as indelibly as his own flesh.

She turned her face and sought his mouth with hers, poured words and kisses upon him.

"I love you. I don't know how it happened. I guarded my heart so well! But I'm not so foolish as to deny it now. I love you, and I'm yours for good— forever. If it be a year, a day—an hour."

"I love you, Topaz Hathor," he told her with equal fervor. "There can be no truer, stronger bonding than this."

"I'm utterly yours," she breathed, "as you are mine. No—don't you dare." As he moved, intending to withdraw from her, she wrapped her arms about him fiercely. "Stay where you are. Give me my completeness."

So she felt it too, the exclusiveness of the emotions between them. Giving himself up to the joy humming through him, he whispered in her ear, "Call me Romney."

"Eh?"

"I want to hear you say it again now that I know it for my true name. May I introduce myself, Topaz Hathor? I'm Romney Gideon."

"You've remembered?"

"I dreamed it and know, now, I was called after the wild marshes where I was born."

"Romney," she whispered it. "Rom." She laughed. "There's irony for you: a Rom for the descendant of the Rom. That's what I am, you know."

"My wild gypsy."

"But things are truly coming back to you?"

"Yes, and all because of you. I was shattered when

I found you, Topaz, splintered body from soul, sheared off into madness. You've healed me, and every time we're together like this my strength grows." He sobered. "But I'm on a dangerous mission, charged by Queen Victoria. That means I cannot spare myself. I cannot worry about whether or not I will have a future."

"Well, my fine Romney, since we don't know what approaches or if we will ever have the chance to lie together again, I suggest we make the most of this night."

"Just what I thought before I woke you."

"This night will last as long as we let it." She shifted in his arms. "Romney Gideon, look into my eyes."

He did. Despite the dim light, they glowed with golden fire.

"I make this vow," she pledged solemnly. "I may not be much more than a gypsy, and a warrior gypsy, at that. But I will fight for you however I may and with everything I have."

And from his heart he answered, "I never doubted it."

Chapter Thirty-One

"We're in for a real fight," Patrick Kelly said gravely, somehow managing to convey his vehemence without changing expression. "I want you to know, Miss Topaz, I will stand with you—I and whatever members of the Irish Squad are willing. But despite Mr. Romney's involvement, it cannot be in an official capacity. I am unable to go to the authorities without exposing Miss Rose, and that I refuse to do."

Topaz glanced at Rose, who occupied one of the chairs in the Kilters' parlor, looking very much as if she didn't want to be there. She'd been given a new set of clothes, a warm coat, and a hat that she wore pulled down to her eyebrows, but she appeared no happier than when Topaz had last seen her.

She raised her eyes to Patrick and spoke in her old woman's voice, "I told you, let me murder this body in which I'm trapped and you will no longer need to concern yourself with me."

Pat turned toward her. "And I have told you I cannot allow that. I will protect you, Miss Rose, even if it is against your wishes."

Distress flared in her eyes. "Officer Kelly, would you truly force my spirit to remain trapped in this body I abhor?"

Pat made the grinding sound that, for him, represented laughter. With a fine show of Irish sarcasm, he replied, "Aye, lass—for I would not know, at all, how that feels."

Topaz looked at Rom Gideon, who stood beside her. He raised his eyebrows and quirked his lips; at this point she could almost hear his thoughts. He'd been right; a deep and curious relationship had developed between these two.

At Topaz's other hip stood Greta. The big yellow mongrel had been lying outside the guest room door when Topaz opened it this morning and had since refused to budge from her side.

Pat resumed, "Miss Topaz, I have spoken at length with your brother in an effort to persuade him to our cause. I feel he would make a valuable ally, and we will need all the help we can get."

"Let me guess—he refuses to have anything to do with any plan that includes me." Topaz could hear the pain in her own voice.

Pat didn't prevaricate. "Yes. And you, Miss Topaz, are our most valuable asset of all."

"How is that?"

"Panic has gripped your father's household. Your father and the man who has been working with him—"

"The Undertaker," Rose said in a spectral voice that made Topaz jump. "That's what the other man, the one who trapped me, called him." She shivered in response to her own words.

Pat went on, "They do not know where Miss Rose is at present, and they cannot have her loose in the city—in the world. Already your father searches." He looked at Topaz. "With every skill at his command."

A spear of disquiet pierced Topaz. "You mean he searches spiritually? For her soul?" As she knew all too well, every spirit had a signature. She would now be able to identify Romney's spirit among a seething throng of others. "But how can we possibly conceal her from his mind?"

"That," said Pat, "is where you come in. I have in the past done some reading on the subject and know there is such a thing as psychic shielding."

"Possibly." Topaz stared at Rose and the automaton at her side, ruing not for the first time her past refusal to learn the lessons her father had sought to impart, knowledge that now might be used against him. "But you can't expect me to turn away my father's mind. He's far too powerful."

"Miss Topaz," Pat said determinedly, "you are my friend. I feel I know you well enough to say that above all else you are a warrior. What difference if you fight with your stiletto or your mind?"

"It is different. My father is a master spiritualist. How can I hope to go up against him?"

Pat leaned toward her. "Not to differ with you, Miss Topaz, but how could you, a mere woman, as society might insist, and in need of a protector, hope to defeat men in hand-to-hand combat? How fend off potential abductors and would-be assassins? How organize other women in this city, the most vulnerable of them, to defend themselves?"

"That's muscle and determination, not—" She stopped speaking because her throat closed. Rom took her hand, and she felt immediate strength flood through her. Greta pressed closer against her hip.

Pat said, "Quite obviously you will not stand alone." He gestured almost gracefully at Rose. "The decision, of course, is yours. But I thought you might want to hear the details of Miss Rose's story before you make up your mind."

Topaz nodded. Reluctantly, Rose got to her feet and drew a breath. Topaz wondered what it would be like to breathe through someone else's lungs, see through someone else's eyes. The bruises and burns on Rose's skin had faded only slightly. She looked at once robust and strangely unwell.

"I will tell this swiftly, since Patrick says we have little time. As I've already related, I was in an abusive marriage. You cannot imagine—and I will spare you—all I suffered at the hands of my husband, a wealthy man with dark perversions. Suffice it to say that the night he killed me I found release and took it with great joy. Joy and relief. There is a world beyond this one that I cannot hope to describe, filled with light and peace.

"Upon death we review the life we have just lived—examine and catalog what we learned and failed to learn during that time. I had a sense this can take very little or a considerable amount of time." She paused and swallowed with difficulty. "I'd barely engaged in this process when I felt a psychic net fall into place around me. It's the only way I can describe the sensation. I fought against it. But you are right, Miss Hathor. Your father is strong."

Topaz hissed, "There's no question that he did this to you?"

Rose inclined her head. "No question. He ensnared me and then hauled me to that house of his—to a room in the cellar. There the true horror began."

Topaz shifted uneasily and glanced at Romney. His face had become almost as unreadable as Pat's.

Slowly Rose resumed. "Others had been trapped just like me. I could feel them, though your father was careful to keep us separated, in psychic cages. I continued to fight against mine, to no effect. Meanwhile I became aware of what was intended for me.

"I could hear them talking, you see. Through the bars of your father's mind, I could. There were four entities that worked over us: your father, the monster called the Undertaker, and two highly sophisticated steam units. Those are all I saw before you found me, Miss Hathor. One of those mechanicals was destroyed in the steamcab crash. Three remain who know the truth about me."

"Yes," Topaz agreed. At the name "Undertaker" Romney had twitched, but he didn't speak.

"They had corpses in the cellar—a number of them. I never learned from whence they were procured." Rose glanced at Pat again. "But Patrick has a theory."

Pat stirred, with a very faint pop from the boiler in his thorax. "Money can accomplish much, and, Miss Topaz, your father has a great deal of money. I believe there are agencies in this city that can be bribed—back-street clinics, those that care for the indigent, even the agents over at Potter's Field."

"The cemetery?" Topaz couldn't help but question.

"I suspect some of the corpses, excluding that Miss Rose currently inhabits, which met its end by murder there in the cellar, were procured just before they were supposed to go into the ground."

"But," Topaz objected, "she would be known, if she lived in Buffalo. She can hardly be expected to walk around this city without risk of her next of kin seeing her."

"I was never intended to 'walk around this city,' Miss Hathor. The procedure merely took place here because this is Frederick Hathor's location, as well as where the Undertaker has set up shop. My late husband, who purchased the service from them, would have taken me back to Philadelphia." She lifted her chin. "Where he would have continued to abuse me."

"What about the others?" Topaz questioned.

"The procedure has only been successful three times before my transfer, according to what I was able to overhear. Those three survivors were sent out of the area. Your father charges an enormous amount of money—enough, I believe, to let him procure corpses both locally and from farther afield—including across the river in Canada."

"How?" Romney spoke unexpectedly. "How does the procedure work? Do you remember that, Miss Rose?"

She gave him a bitter smile. "I told you, I recall everything. I only wish I didn't. Frederick Hathor traps the spirit, and the Undertaker prepares the flesh host—that's what he calls it." She looked down at herself. "A flesh host."

She lifted her gaze back to Romney. "He has an English accent, like yours."

"I was sent after him from England in an effort to forestall his activities. I'm beginning to remember it all now."

"He used electrodes," Rose said, and Romney flinched again. "Powered by a steam plant there in the cellar. The current has to be just right—failure to adjust it properly accounted for all his spoiled experiments, from what he said. He applies the electrodes to the pulse points and 'jump starts' the body. When it achieves animation, Hathor forces the spirit inside."

Again she looked at Topaz. "I fought, and fought hard—you cannot imagine how hard. As I say, your father is a brutal man. He gave me no quarter. Once he had me imprisoned here, other laws came into effect. There is a tenacity between spirit and flesh—even foreign flesh, so it seems."

"I know how merciless Clifford can be," Romney said softly. "Those burns and bruises I see on you—they're the effect of the procedure?"

"Yes." She paled visibly. "As I say, it was incredibly painful, excruciating. But, unfortunately, successful."

Pat said, "If he thinks he has the formula right, he will use the procedure again. We cannot allow that."

"And," Romney put in, "he will stop at nothing to find Rose before the wrong person sees her or she tells someone who she is."

"Like us." Pat grimaced—his version of a smile. "As you might expect, members of the Irish Squad are interested in this, and they can be discreet. They are also skilled at the art of investigation. I have set certain members to making inquiries around the city. The house on Humboldt Parkway will be watched, as well as the place where you were confined, Mr. Marsh."

"Gideon. The name is actually Romney Gideon."

Pat inclined his head. "Glad to meet you."

"Happy to be working with you," Romney returned.

Topaz drew a breath. "Do you think we can defeat them?"

"I do," Pat said. "But in order to spare Miss Rose, we will have to get them dead to rights, so to say. And you, Miss Topaz, will need to prove a brave defender. Because even now your father is busy searching this city—with the power of his mind."

Chapter Thirty-Two

The house to which Pat Kelly led them on Connecticut Street looked no different from its neighbors—tall, narrow, and nondescript. But Pat said it was owned by a member of the Irish Squad, one of his fellow automatons, and it made as safe a berth as he could currently find. He dared no longer leave them at the Kilters' for fear of bringing danger to those he loved.

Could an automaton love? Romney asked himself that question even as he eyed the man who answered Kelly's knock, and followed him inside. It seemed evident Kelly could experience friendship, loyalty, and protectiveness. Was love so impossible?

Their host ushered them into a sparsely furnished parlor and turned to face them. Romney examined him closely, looking for signs that he was not, in fact, human.

He had to search hard. The two mad geniuses who created the units that had eventually become the Irish Squad had done their work well and chosen only prime stock with which to work.

This specimen, whom Pat introduced as Michael O'Riley, possessed a strapping frame constructed, as Rom very well knew, of steel overlaid with a skin and scalp that had once belonged to an Irishman. In this case the skin bore a profusion of freckles. The hair—

sandy blond—curled, and the eyes were blue.

"Pleased to meet you, Officer O'Riley." Rom put out his hand. "Thank you for offering us your hospitality."

O'Riley accepted his palm and shook it almost gingerly. He fixed his gaze on Greta, posed at Topaz's side. Little Mrs. Kilter had insisted Topaz take the hound with her, and when she'd consulted her husband, James, he'd agreed.

"She's chosen you," he told Topaz. "For once in her life she should have the right to choose."

Now O'Riley's eyes brightened, though his expression did not change. "You have a dog."

Rom said, "I hope that's not a problem."

"Not at all. I like dogs."

"Is Sapphire here?" Topaz interrupted, not very politely. Rom could tell how tightly she was wound, could feel her fear and self-doubt—all in a woman who did not suffer uncertainty easily.

"Yes," Pat answered. "I persuaded your brother to move lodgings over here from Pennsylvania Street, a location I did not believe safe."

O'Riley looked at him. "From what you say, Pat, no location is safe. But this will do for the time. Miss Hathor, your brother is upstairs. His mate remains in hospital but is due to be released this afternoon."

Topaz nodded. "Thank you. I appreciate all you're doing for us."

"I consider what your father and this 'Undertaker' are attempting to be an abomination," O'Riley said. "They must be stopped."

Rom looked at Kelly. "What about Rose?"

"I shall house her elsewhere." Pat gestured at

O'Riley. "We debated the wisdom of keeping you all together and decided it would make it too easy for Hathor to home in. It is risky enough now, but I knew, Miss Topaz, you would wish to speak with your brother. And I would not presume"—he paused and emitted his grinding laugh—"to separate you from Mr. Gideon."

"Quite right." Rom drew Topaz closer to him. Greta shot him a look from her yellow-hazel eyes but tolerated the contact.

"What happens next?" Topaz asked.

"You try to persuade your brother to join us in our fight."

"I'm the last person he'll want to see."

"And the only one who can persuade him. You say that, like you, he inherited some of your father's talent?"

"Yes."

"I believe you will need to join forces if we are to succeed. Your father even now scours the city for Rose and for you. He uses both his inner sense and the automatons from his household. Before he finds you or Rose, we must procure enough evidence to warrant an arrest. Another clandestine raid will be launched on the place you call Grayson, where Mr. Gideon was imprisoned. Getting into your father's cellar will be far more difficult, but we are hoping while his minions are otherwise engaged, and your father is occupied by you, we can seize an opportunity."

"Occupied by me," Topaz repeated, stunned.

"Aye," O'Riley rejoined. "It's our only option."

Rom looked at Kelly. "How do you intend to protect Rose?"

Kelly grimaced. "I have a method in mind. A pure figure of speech, you understand, as in fact I have no mind."

Both automatons laughed softly in appreciation of this dark humor.

Kelly went on. "Best you do not know my intentions—that way the knowledge cannot be wrested from you."

Topaz exchanged incredulous looks with Romney. "How am I to shield her if I don't know where she is?"

"Concentrate on shielding your brother, Mr. Gideon, and yourself, if you can spare the energy."

"Very well, Pat. Officer O'Riley, I'd appreciate it if you'd take me to my brother now."

Romney caught her hands. "Best go without me. I'm the last person he'll want to see."

"No." She swallowed convulsively. "I am."

"Upstairs," O'Riley told her, and crooked a sandy brow.

"Take Greta," Rom said. "I don't think you'll get away without her."

****

The narrow staircase creaked as Topaz followed the big automaton to the second floor. Her heart seemed to thud in time with their footsteps.

This is what you get, my girl, for your arrogance. For priding yourself on being fearless, for thinking you could take on all comers.

She should have stipulated that "all comers" did not include fellow Hathors. Persuading Sapphire—an angry Sapphire, no less—to work with her was one thing. It paled beside the prospect of facing her father down.

I can't do this, she thought, even as they paused in front of a door and O'Riley knocked. But for Rom's sake, I must.

The door swung open, and Sapphire's emotions came out in a psychic blast. Greta cowered against Topaz's side.

Sapphire looked like a wild man. His dark eyes burned, his hair—for once—was messy, and he had completely lost his usual *savoir faire*. When his gaze found Topaz, its heat increased by several degrees.

"What are you doing here? I was told this was a safe house."

O'Riley answered, "Mr. Hathor, your sister wishes to speak with you. I will leave you alone."

He beat a hasty retreat. Topaz wished she could follow.

"I don't want to talk to you," Sapphire snapped, and tried to shut the door.

Greta whimpered, and Sapphire's gaze flew to her. "Since when do you have a dog?"

"She belongs to a friend of Pat's, but she's attached herself to me. I can't imagine why."

"Neither can I. But if the animal likes you, I suppose you can't be completely unredeemable. Come in."

The room, like the parlor below, had been furnished with only the most basic necessities. Dim afternoon light bled through the window, promising more snow. It made a grim refuge—or prison.

"Sapph," Topaz attempted to apologize once again, "I'm so sorry about the baby—"

The corners of his mouth quivered and turned down. He began to pace the limited space between the bed and the window, his expression distracted.

"I think I'm going mad. I never expected any of this, never thought I'd fall in love, didn't imagine I'd be capable of it. We shouldn't be able to love, Topaz—not given the way we've been raised. But here I am, sick with love over a little maid, of all people. One who shouldn't mean a thing to me."

Topaz sucked in a breath and perched on the edge of the bed, out of Sapphire's way. Greta made herself small and pressed to Topaz's knees.

"You knew her before, so Carly said—in a past life."

Sapphire shot her a close look. "I don't suppose you believe in that kind of thing."

"Who am I to believe or disbelieve? I've been forced to accept a lot these past days."

He stopped pacing long enough to glare at her. "All I know is, I need to be with her—need, more than want."

That, Topaz did understand. "Yes," she murmured.

He tossed his hands in the air. "As for the child—" His throat spasmed, and he fought past the emotion. "I never wanted children. Holy hell! The very notion of me, of anyone in our household, raising a child! Now I'm breaking my heart over the loss of this one."

"Sapph, I did what I thought best by getting Carlotta out of there. Once I discovered what's going on—you have no idea."

"Oh, but I have." He thrust his fingers through his dark hair, mussing it further. "I knew something was afoot even before I procured that key for you. I should have taken Carly away then. I knew what would happen once Father discovered the key had gone missing." He shot Topaz another desperate look. "And I had a long talk with our host after I got here. He's an automaton, did you know that? Just like your friend Kelly. At first I couldn't even tell. Know why?"

"Why?" Topaz returned.

Sapphire leaned toward her. "Because I could feel his spirit. He has a spirit, Sis—just like you and I. It's different, maybe, but it's there."

Gravely, Topaz said, "I'm beginning to learn everything has spirit—everything alive, that is. In fact, it's not so much that people have spirits as that spirits have bodies, like houses. And"—she lowered her voice—"as Father must long have known, those houses can be changed."

Sapphire blinked at her. Greta whined, an eerie sound in the quiet room.

"And when the house is changed without permission of the resident spirit," she concluded, "that's a frightful sin. I won't ask you to forgive me, Sapph— only help us stop Father and Clifford. Please."

Doubt flickered in his dark eyes. "You think even the two of us together can defeat Frederick Hathor?"

"I don't know. But I'm willing to fight—to try."

For a moment more he contemplated her. She felt his spirit reach out and touch hers—a force full of his restless energy, his undulating darkness, much more powerful than she could have imagined.

"Very well, then," he said at last. "But I warn you—if it comes down to it, I'll protect Carly above all others."

Just as Topaz would protect Rom. "I understand," she told him. "Do we have a deal?"

"Yes, and may all the gods have mercy on us."

Chapter Thirty-Three

"I hope Pat Kelly knows what he's doing," Topaz fretted. She shivered and pressed closer to Rom in the dark. Greta, as Rom well knew, already lay sprawled across Topaz's lap. At least the big animal gave off some warmth. "I mean," Topaz breathed in Rom's ear, "a cemetery—really?"

"Pat Kelly has very decided notions," Rom agreed. Admittedly the scheme would be more comfortable accomplished in July rather than January. "He seems to feel hiding us here at Forest Lawn amid a horde of other spirits will confound your father." He hesitated and added, "Can you feel them?"

"Yes." She shifted still more uneasily. "And I can feel Sapphire, all the way from the other side of the graveyard. The spirits—those that aren't acquiescent— seem to be flocking to him."

"Acquiescent?" Rom repeated, though he didn't actually want to know what she meant.

"Most of the bodies here are empty, the spirits long flown. The newer graves have spirits hanging around them—some quiet and content with the state of things, some confused and searching. Those are the ones heading for Sapphire."

"None for you?"

"Some for me too." She shivered again, a bone-deep shudder this time. "I hate all this. Talk to me, distract me. Tell me what you've remembered about yourself."

He drew her closer and wrapped his arms around her, to lend warmth. "What do you want to know?"

"Everything."

"Well, then, I'll tell you all I remember so far. I was born in Romney Marsh, East Sussex. My family extends back to the first settlers who came from Denmark in ancient times."

She turned her head in an effort to see his face. "Beowulf-ancient?"

"Yes. Fancy you knowing about Beowulf."

"My father procured tutors for us. So—perhaps pursuing monsters is in your blood."

He laughed almost silently. "Perhaps."

"Go on."

"Since early days, those of my blood have been involved somehow with the Crown—stewards to the reigning monarch or some such thing. When the time came I took service with Victoria and got assigned to the most difficult and nebulous cases. The Undertaker's vile operations came to our attention, and I was told to investigate."

"So Clifford has always known who you are, that you were after him."

"Yes. When he took flight from England, I followed him across the Atlantic to New York City and then to the Niagara Frontier. That's where things became murky. I don't remember how he captured me. I do remember a bit of being taken to Grayson. I fought and struggled, ultimately to no avail."

"His henchmen—how many were there? Who were they?"

"Now I think on it, I believe they were all mechanicals except for Cecil Crittendon, the man who runs Grayson. Hard to tell how many, given my state of mind."

"I wonder if they were my father's mechanicals—if he's been involved from the first."

"Oh, he's been involved." Rom's voice became distant even to his ears. "Now that I think on it, I believe he was there at times during my questioning, though he was careful not to let me see him."

Topaz moved in violent protest. "During the torture, you mean." When Rom didn't speak, she went on, "I felt some of what was done to you there at the end. It was terrible, obviously enough to fracture you, split body from spirit."

"And I came to you."

"Did you? Or did you just come looking for my father the way any good hunter would?"

He caressed her cheek. "I felt drawn to something at that house, and it wasn't Frederick Hathor."

He bent his head and let his lips follow his fingers across the velvet of her cheek. When he found her lips, time seemed to stand still. Warmth lay in her kiss, and passion and belonging.

But she ended it much too soon and whispered, "I have another question, a most important one."

"Yes?" He lifted his brows.

"In this other life of yours in England—is there a wife?"

"No wife. No desire for one. Just a wild lad running the fens, refusing to grow up, and playing at monster-hunter, thinking it quite the lark to be in service to the Queen."

"So it is, quite a lark." She bestowed another little kiss; this one parted his lips. He felt her tongue slip inside. "But no desire for a wife?"

"Not till now."

She caught her breath. Connected to her as he was, spirit to spirit, he felt her hesitant delight. "But now?"

"I would ascribe to the state of wedded union in an instant, but I am fairly sure the woman I have in mind is not the marrying sort."

"Is she not?"

"I wouldn't have said so." Again he skipped his lips across hers softly. "Even wilder of spirit than I am, she is—fiercely independent."

"Perhaps so. But then, she'd never met a man like you." She sampled him. He felt the sweetness flare, and along with it desire.

"Well, now," he murmured. "Surely she hasn't reconsidered the marital state?"

"I think she has. If you might ask her to marry you—"

"In a graveyard? At midnight?" He could not help but chuckle.

"Even so. Seems fitting, don't you think, for two people who first met in spirit?"

He captured her face between his cold hands and gazed into her eyes. "Will you marry me, Topaz Hathor—in the event we survive?"

"I will, Romney Gideon—in the event we survive."

They sealed the pledge with a long kiss before she said, "Sapphire insists he knew Carly in a past life. I don't think I ever knew you before, though your spirit attracts me like," she struggled for expression, "a missing piece of my own."

"You might have been a wild gypsy queen and I lord of the marshes."

At their side, Greta growled softly. Topaz froze in Romney's arms.

"What?" he breathed.

"He's here. My father is here."

"Where?" Rom peered out into the darkness. "I see no one."

"I'm not at all sure he's brought his body."

****

Topaz quailed inwardly as she felt the force of her father's consciousness overspread the graveyard. No mistaking that presence—she had been aware of his spiritual signature, at least peripherally, all her life. Greta must have picked up on her subconscious awareness and reacted. And if she needed further confirmation, she felt Sapphire's awareness spike also, across the expanse of graves. But she didn't really need the confirmation.

Instinctively, she got to her feet, the dog trembling beside her. A warrior faced battle on her feet, and this would be a battle of the first water.

Hastily, Rom pulled her back down into his arms. "No, don't draw attention to yourself."

She could feel everything about Rom—his spirit, his heartbeat, and the love for her that burgeoned inside him. She could also feel Frederick Hathor's power close around the graveyard like a fist around a dove.

"No need to draw attention," she whispered. "Rom, I want you to leave me here—go now, while he's at least partially distracted by me and Sapphire. Save yourself."

"Like hell I will." He spoke the words without

emphasis, but she felt his intent, unbending as iron. He possessed strength, this man she loved—enough to survive the separation of flesh from spirit.

But she looked at him and said, "Please. He's after me, not you. He knows I fled his house with Rose." She drew a quick breath. "I can risk anything but your safety."

"If you suppose I'll walk away from here not knowing what might happen to you—"

"They'll kill you if they find you. But I'm his daughter." He couldn't kill her, could he? Desperately she contemplated the question even as her father's power flared like unseen light. "Let me fight him, Rom, without worrying for you."

At that moment, Greta lunged forward into the darkness. Topaz narrowed her eyes. The undulating expanse of the cemetery lay lit by only a few steam lamps; one burned at the entrance near the statue of Redjacket, another across the way where she thought Sapphire had secreted himself, near Main Street. But she and Rom had chosen a nest of darkness.

Now, though, she thought she caught a hint of movement in bright silver—a mechanical moving toward them silently.

Just one? Breath gusted between her lips. Her father had possessed but the two advanced units that he'd trusted in the cellar, and one had been destroyed in the steamcab crash. Did her father now send the other searching for them, guided by his spirit?

Horror clawed its way up her spine. For suddenly the graveyard felt alive with spirits, as aware of Frederick's presence as she. They arose from every side and began flocking to him, like iron filings to a magnet.

She felt several brush past her from behind and caught back a curse. This had been Pat Kelly's intention, to stymie her father when he came looking, inflict psychic overload on him and make this place into a trap. But Frederick may not have come in person. How far did his power extend? Still, the flocking of the spirits argued he might be here in the flesh, as well.

And what of Danson Clifford, who needed to recapture Rom at any cost?

Oh, why had she ever brought Rom here with her? For the comfort of his company? All at once it seemed the height of foolishness.

She didn't know if all the strength she and Sapphire together could muster might defend against the power her father had now unleashed.

Chapter Thirty-Four

Greta had run into the darkness and did not return. Topaz stumbled once more to her feet and stood with her eyes closed and her hands clenched. She felt for her father's consciousness and tried desperately to wield a sense she'd sought all too seldom to employ.

In truth, she'd fought just this all her life, had hidden from it, preferring to rely on muscle, quickness, even a length of steel in her hand. This power she'd inherited from her father could twist her awareness, warp her life—even steal her will if she let it.

Now, though, she reached for it greedily, seeking to fashion a shield that might, among all these seething spirits, make the man beside her invisible. She cared little for herself and all for him.

With her eyes closed, everything turned to light. The graveyard became a velvet expanse and the spirits all around her moving points of brightness. Most of them streamed toward Frederick where he—or his consciousness—hovered near the main entrance. It looked like the air around the house on the Parkway. Others moved aimlessly near what must be their graves. Still others gravitated toward where she knew Sapphire hid.

Would all this activity, as Pat believed, camouflage her and Sapphire from their father? Would it obscure Rom? She wondered suddenly just how much faith Pat had in his plan, given he'd secreted Rose elsewhere.

Carefully, tentatively, she sent her senses out searching—rather one particular sense, the one she so seldom employed. She'd used it to make contact with Rom when he suffered at Grayson. Now she did not want to draw attention to herself or him. But she wanted to locate her father in truth.

At first the presence of the other spirits confounded her. But she'd grown up surrounded by such psychic background clutter and must have learned more than she suspected during that time, for she was able to filter at least some of it away.

Her blood began to pound in her veins—gypsy blood that had traveled from North Africa across Europe and jumped an ocean to reach this place. She needed to trust that blood.

Upon the thought, everything snapped into place. She could "see" Sapphire on the other side of the cemetery. His shield did little to hide him from her and that made her heart skip a beat because it meant Frederick Hathor would eventually find both of them.

She touched briefly, spirit to spirit, with her brother and felt a surge of reassurance. Sapphire possessed more power than she'd ever guessed. Could the two of them together overwhelm Frederick?

Greta had disappeared. Where? Topaz reached farther and picked up the spark of the dog's consciousness—headed straight for Frederick.

"Come." She caught Rom's hand and towed him into motion. If he wouldn't leave her, she had to protect him as best she could, and that meant joining forces with Sapphire.

But her brother, when they reached him, looked

pale and tense with strain. He rolled his eyes at Topaz like an unbroken horse feeling the harness for the first time.

"I hate this," he greeted her, and bared his teeth. Topaz saw how he sweated. "I'll have you know I've resisted using this accursed ability all my life."

"As have I. I don't think he's here in the flesh. Do you?" No need to specify which *he*. Both of them now knew only one.

"It isn't his flesh that worries me." Sapphire gasped the words. "I hope your friend the automaton's plan is sound. If they take the opportunity to go after Carly while we're trapped here..."

"Why should he go after Carly?"

"Because you took her with you and Rose; because that will make him think she knows too much. He didn't get where he is by being less than perceptive."

"He's after Rose. Or Rom." That last thought terrified Topaz beyond measure. She tightened her grip on Rom's arm. Did her father, or more importantly Clifford, suspect all of what Rom had begun to remember?

Sapphire grunted, all his attention focused elsewhere.

"He's brought his pet automaton," Topaz said. "The last remaining one. I saw it."

"He's brought at least five or six." Again Sapphire rolled his eyes at her. "Must be household units pressed into service."

"Is Pat here?" Rom asked in Topaz's ear. "Can you tell?"

She shook her head violently. The hybrid's spiritual signature was, at best, hard to pick up.

"Well, then," Rom breathed, "I suggest I set about taking out your father's steam units; you two see to the psychic defense."

"We are not splitting up!" she told him.

Sapphire grunted again. "Quiet, for God's sake. And don't be a fool—we have to use him any way we can."

Rom caught Topaz's shoulders between his hands. "I'm an agent of the British government, love. You can't keep me tethered to your side."

"But—" Terror rose in a dark wave.

He kissed her, a brief, hard kiss. "Be strong, strong as you really are." And he disappeared into the night.

Topaz wanted to scream, wail out her despair and protest. For an instant she couldn't breathe. Then she caught a hint of the light that was Rom's spirit moving away from her, pausing, moving, before it mingled with the other lights and became lost to her.

"Push against him," Sapphire said suddenly, startling her.

"Against Rom?" But, no—of course Sapphire meant against Frederick.

"See if we're strong enough together to trap him, or at least confound him."

"He'll know we're here."

"He already knows, fool! We must keep him occupied till your friend arrives. It's the best way to protect your lover."

Her lover. The other half of her soul. But Topaz refused to think about Rom somewhere in the dark ahead of her, for fear that would draw Frederick's attention to him.

A spirit passed by her, so close she jumped back.

Others still streamed toward the blaze of light and intelligence that represented Frederick Hathor, near the cemetery entrance.

Sapphire reached out and clasped Topaz's hand. Immediately her senses focused and strengthened.

"Envision a net. Throw it around him. Let's see what we can do."

****

In daylight, Romney reflected, this must be a pleasant place, with its broad roadways and undulating lawn, punctuated with looming forms of funereal statuary. Only the finest of Buffalo's residents would be buried here—the departed elite. Unlike Topaz, he couldn't sense their spirits, yet the mood of the place lying beneath its blanket of white snow gripped him. And he could still feel his connection to Topaz, now well behind him, like a cord stretching tight.

Fear gripped his belly at the thought of her going up against her ruthless father. Would he be more likely to spare his children than any of the others whose spirits he'd forced into what amounted to slavery? Perhaps, perhaps not. Who knew what motivated such a man?

As a partner of the vile Undertaker, he must be stopped. Rom reminded himself he had crossed an ocean for just that purpose and couldn't let himself falter now merely because the better part of his heart, his sanity, no longer rested inside his own body but with Topaz.

He ducked around a white marble plinth twice his height and saw something moving on the roadway ahead of him—a steam unit, but not one of those that had done Clifford's bidding at Grayson and strung him up like so much meat.

Don't think about that, he bade himself. In those thoughts lay madness. And he couldn't afford a mistake.

This looked like a common household steam unit made intimidating by the presence of the side-cannon it carried, a big model that breathed faint wisps of vapor, betraying itself as fully charged. Death, as he well knew, lay in the mouth of that weapon.

He looked around for a weapon of his own. The lawn, immaculately cared for and groomed even in winter, offered little. But he did see a broken limb hanging from the lower branches of a nearby tree. Moving with all the stealth he could muster, he leaped for it, swung like a monkey, and pulled it down with a loud *crack*.

The steam unit turned. Above the reaching branches of the tree, the wind drove the clouds apart. Wan moonlight filtered down and glinted off the unit's metal skin.

It saw Rom, and he charged forward even as it raised the cannon.

Would it aim to kill? What were its orders—to maim, capture? The last thing Rom wanted was a return to the echoing cell at Grayson and the smell of his own seared skin in his nostrils.

Upon that thought, he leaped into the center of the road and faced the unit. The sidearm fired and Rom leaped again, swinging his wooden weapon even as the steam blast roared by him, so close he felt the heat on his leg.

The unit spun to face him. But this—no advanced model—floundered and flailed as it moved. Rom's first blow took it where its head met its metal shoulders. The second, with all his strength behind it, separated the two components but broke his branch in the process.

The headless unit floundered some more before trundling away from him—to report his whereabouts, perhaps? Rom chased after it, knocked it down, and kicked it to pieces, burning his foot when its boiler erupted.

Somewhere a dog barked—Greta. His eye caught the glint of yet another steam unit moving his way. He spared a thought for Topaz somewhere behind him and told himself he had no cause—and no time—to worry about her.

A warrior, she could take care of herself. As he jogged to meet the next unit, the steam cannon now in hand, he remembered the night he'd watched her take on her two would-be abductors—the same night they'd met.

Strong and beautiful, that was his Topaz. Would she prove strong enough?

Greta barked again, closer this time. He bet the dog would circle around and rejoin Topaz, where she wanted to be.

Rom charged on into the darkness.

Chapter Thirty-Five

Far off across the broad lawn sewn with graves, Topaz heard Greta bark. The sound raised her anxiety another notch. She could again feel the dog's consciousness, faint but frenetic. She could feel so many things, all those she'd striven to deny most of her life.

It all came upon her now, for the love of a man.

Who would have thought she could be tripped up by such feelings? But she could no more deny Rom's importance to her than declare herself free of Hathor blood and this gift or curse that resided within her. She adored everything about him, from his sense of humor—dark as her own—to the way he tasted on her tongue. But if she wanted a life with him, she would have to face that which terrified her most.

She closed her eyes again and sent her consciousness out in a wave. Every spirit in the graveyard once more transformed into light. Sapphire, beside her, burned like blue fire—how had he ever concealed all that power? The spirits of the dead still streamed to her father, whose consciousness made it difficult to see anything else, like trying to see stars in daylight. But she did glimpse fainter points that must be members of the Irish Squad surrounding the perimeter.

Pat Kelly would be pleased to know he did in fact possess a visible spirit—provided she survived and had a chance to tell him.

She hoped Pat's trap would work. Frederick might not even be here; someone, likely the Undertaker—would be directing the steamies. If the Irish Squad could capture him…

At her side, Sapphire groaned. "He's increasing his concentration. Can't you feel it?"

Topaz could. She stood rigid as Sapphire grasped her hand, his fingers hot.

And at that instant her father's voice burst into her mind.

Daughter, why have you turned against me? Why do you stand in defiance? Where is the one we seek?

The one they sought: Rose. Wise of Pat Kelly not to let her and Sapphire know where he'd secreted her. For even beneath this unbearable demand, she couldn't break and tell.

"Raise a barrier," Sapphire gasped, and his fingers tightened on hers. "Shove him out of our heads."

"How?"

"Call up the power." With the words, knowledge flooded into Topaz's mind from Sapphire's. She called up all her ability and joined it with his in a wall of psychic stone.

For an instant their father's power wavered. Then he seemed to gather himself and in a tremendous show of might pushed through their defenses like a fist through a plank.

Sapphire cursed. Topaz swayed with the impact and would have fallen but for her brother's grip. Dimly she heard Greta barking, barking, and felt Sapphire struggle as Frederick's grasp tightened around their minds.

Where is she?

I do not know! Topaz shouted in victorious defiance. She felt a blinding pain as her father rifled her mind, let her go, and pounced on Sapphire.

Topaz fell to the ground, suffused by pain and weakness. Beside her she felt Sapphire struggle, throw back his head, and roar like an animal in agony. A violent burst of light exploded, shattering Sapphire's defenses, and ended in fathomless darkness.

****

Rom, more than halfway across the lawn and stalking his third steam unit, heard Topaz's voice in his mind, calling his name. He spun like a dancer, his new weapon raised in his hands. All his awareness leaped to hers, searching, searching, and found—

Fear and distress!

His heart jumped into his throat sickeningly. Topaz almost never gave in to fear. What, then?

Without warning, Greta rushed out of the darkness past him and ran in Topaz's direction. Rom, about to follow, instead halted at the sound of a voice behind him—one he knew full well.

"So there you are."

Rom spun again to see the Undertaker flanked by not one but four steam units. Only one of the units worried him; he recognized it from the questioning room at Grayson. The others were common household steamies such as those he'd already destroyed.

He fixed his gaze on Clifford. The man fairly oozed confidence, and a dim corona of light surrounded him, visible even to Rom's eyes. Lent by Hathor? Protection?

"How dare you run from me," Clifford said. "No

one runs from me. But," he added with satisfaction, "I have you now."

"No." Rom raised his weapon. He could take the premier steam unit out first and then Clifford himself—clean up the others after.

"Take him," Clifford told the units. "But don't injure him too badly. I may need his body."

Cold horror washed over Rom. Did that make one of the reasons Clifford had tortured but not killed him? The Undertaker had decided he'd end up like Rose.

After he broke, his mind too devastated to report the details of the procedure or anything else he knew.

The steam units came at him in unison. Rom fired on the largest of them even as it flipped up the steam cannon it carried. He needed to seize the offensive, but once his cannon fired it would take time to recharge. How much?

He blasted the leading unit even as the other three closed in around him, and hit the arm that held the cannon. Arm and weapon both exploded, taking out the wheels on a second steamie, which tipped over, flailing its arms.

Rom smiled grimly, now in his element. As soon as the cannon recharged he would take out the units and then face Clifford fairly, man to man, without bonds and electrodes.

No sooner had that thought blossomed in his mind than a blinding flash of light burst through the graveyard, rolling like a tidal wave from the direction of the entrance and over the rolling lawn. He saw the other units go dark as it reached them, felt it sear his own consciousness, and heard a scream in his mind—one of agony.

Topaz!

His blunted consciousness reached for her, searching, before the light went out.

****

Topaz came to slowly, in agonized pieces, the way one might put together a puzzle bit by bit. Pain found her first, most of it centralized in her head and radiating out through every limb, then distress, then terror. She couldn't seem to open her eyes. She didn't know where she was.

Rom.

The idea of him blazed across her mind, almost as bright as the wave of light that had seared all her senses. Yes, that was what had felled her. She remembered...

Rom.

She pried her eyelids open one at a time, at a great cost in pain. It did her little good, for she still couldn't tell where she lay: on a cold surface, the sensation coming up through her back told her that, and in a dim room.

Rom.

With the blunted ends of her consciousness she searched for him, used now to her awareness of their connection. More pieces clicked into place. She recalled...

Forest Lawn. Sapphire. Her father.

Her heart leaped into her throat, and she struggled to draw breath past her pain. Not a woman to suffer terror gladly, she felt it now, and not on her own behalf.

"Daughter, I am sorely disappointed in you."

The voice sounded so close beside her, she started. Desperately, she focused on the form beside her and saw...

Her father looked much as he did when prepared to receive clients: immaculately clad in a black suit with brocade jacket lapels and a silk shirt, his red tie a cascade of brightness on his chest and his black hair elaborately dressed. As soon as her gaze met his she felt the impact of his will. The rest of the pieces fell into place.

Somehow she freed her gaze from his and cast it about the room. She knew this place—the very chamber from which she'd freed Rose. Her horror deepened. The corpses were gone; in fact, she lay on one of the metal tables where they'd once rested. Sapphire lay on another; he looked dead. The Undertaker, wearing a black doctor's coat, stood with his back to her and hanging from a metal pipe overhead—

Her mind winked out and in again, the way sunlight winks through the windows of a moving train.

Rom. He dangled from metal fetters locked around his wrists, feet just shy of the floor. He too looked unconscious, or dead.

No.

She sat up so quickly she nearly butted Frederick on the chin. He took a measured step back and told her, "Careful, Topaz. Do not force me to overwhelm you again. Such violence could do permanent damage."

Topaz did not look at him; she couldn't take her gaze off the man hanging from the pipe.

"What are you doing?" she croaked. "Let him go."

Clifford turned around. He wore a smirk of satisfaction on his face and leather gloves on his hands. Each hand held what Topaz recognized as an electrode. And somewhere close at hand a steam plant chugged and throbbed.

They were going to…

Her mind blinked out on the thought.

"We need to have a serious talk, Daughter, about loyalty."

"Loyalty?" she spat. "What about madness? You cannot possibly expect me to join you in this—this scheme."

"Why not?" Frederick's dark eyes, almost hypnotic, recaptured her gaze. "Do you not owe me that much?"

"Owe you?"

"Oh, yes." He spread his hands. "Did I not provide you with a good life? I gave you every comfort, this grand house in which to live, the finest food, luxurious clothing, freedom from want. Everything I've done, I've done for my precious children—my jewels, as I call you. And how do you repay me—you, and him?"

He switched his gaze abruptly to Sapphire on the next table, who promptly stirred as if he felt the touch of his father's mind.

"You did this for money and power," Topaz corrected. She felt Sapphire's awareness rouse, as sluggish as her own.

"What do those things buy but a good life for my family?" Frederick returned, and frowned. "But what to do with you now? That is the question."

Clifford, who peered at them over his shoulder, giggled. The sound chased itself over Topaz's skin like a shudder of horror.

"Kill them," Clifford suggested. "They're powerful enough to be dangerous."

"Yes," Frederick returned almost conversationally,

"that's the thing. My children are powerful. I always knew, Topaz, you had inherited a measure of my ability. I will admit Sapphire surprised me. He hid his light so very well."

When Frederick spoke his name, Sapphire opened his eyes, and Topaz felt his spirit leap and flare with fear, loathing, determination. Had Sapphire the strength left to help her fight? They'd not had much success standing against Frederick at the graveyard, even before taking that frightful psychic hit.

She spared a fleeting thought for Pat Kelly, wondering what the blast in Forest Lawn had done to him and the other members of his squad.

Then, unpreventably, she focused on Rom. "What are you going to do to him?"

Clifford giggled again. He, not Frederick, answered her with what sounded like glee.

"Oh, just wait and see. You're going to like this."

Chapter Thirty-Six

Echoes. Pain and the dim return of memory. He knew this place, or one very much like it. Fear, dread, and loathing twisted through him with devastating violence.

No, not that. Not again.

Combating the terror, a voice curled through him, precisely like a rush of adrenaline.

Topaz's voice.

The connection between them flared, and he opened his eyes.

He was in time to see her move, slide herself off a metal table, and come to stand between him, where he hung, and—

Two men occupied the room, along with a number of steamies, one of them heavily damaged. He'd done that.

Memory rushed at him like a train. Forest Lawn. Greta. Topaz.

Topaz faced one of the men, her father, poised on the balls of her feet like a dancer, or a warrior. The other man, Rom saw with sinking dismay, was Danson Clifford, a set of electrodes already in his hands. But this wasn't the room at Grayson. Where?

And did Topaz truly believe she could defend him? He felt her protectiveness, her determination; he virtually tasted her love. He saw the black curtain of her hair, now loosened, twitch as she set her powerful shoulders. But in the graveyard Frederick had overwhelmed her. Could he not do so again?

"Move aside, Daughter. You have no weapons you may use against me."

"I have my hands—my heart—my will. You'll not touch him."

Frederick tipped his head. "What is this poor specimen to you? I told you, if you wish to marry—a state in which you've never expressed an interest—I will procure a suitable husband, as I did for your sisters. Someone worthy."

"I'll choose my own husband, thank you."

She already had. Rom remembered the promises given in the graveyard, and strength flooded through him, battling the dread.

"The heart makes a poor weapon," Frederick said scornfully. "It can so easily be turned against you. Do you truly care for him?"

Topaz hesitated, and Rom felt her dilemma: reveal her vulnerability? Make a bid for mercy? But no mercy would be forthcoming.

Steel entered her voice as she said, "A miracle I'm capable of loving anyone, given the way I was raised and the examples before me."

Frederick actually managed to look injured. "Whatever do you mean? Everything I did, as I have said, I did for love of my family."

"Don't say that!" Topaz exclaimed, and her voice cracked, revealing her emotional fragility. "Do you claim to love Ruby and Pearl, auctioning them off to the highest bidders?"

"To men with the ability to look after them

lifelong. My children shall never want for anything."

"Except affection. Or is that what you are supposed to feel for Mother, with your separate bedrooms?"

"You know nothing about my relationship with your mother. The presence of the spirits disturbs her sleep. That is why I spare her."

"Enough of this," Clifford cried. "You can play emotional games with your children later, Frederick. Now we have a paying customer, and a spirit waiting for *his* flesh."

"No." Slowly, almost gracefully, Topaz drew the stiletto from the pouch on her belt.

Frederick raised his eyebrows. "Would you use a blade on your own father?"

"Only if I have to. Cut him down and let us go."

"Can't," Clifford replied. "He knows too much. All three of you do." He stepped toward Topaz and slanted a look at Frederick. "You do realize we can't release any of them."

Frederick did not speak.

Clifford edged around him. "Move aside, girlie, unless you want to feel the bite of these electrodes."

Topaz snarled, sounding like a maddened dog.

Rom lifted his head and croaked, "Topaz, love, do as he says." Anything—even his own death—would be better than seeing her tortured.

Topaz and Clifford leaped at the same moment, she with her stiletto flashing. Clifford dodged her, giving a yelp as he did so, and the electrodes found the flesh of Rom's bare chest. Agony arced through him, and he hollered as it ran along pathways already set during past sessions, knocking down his flimsy resistance.

A bright line of red sprang forth across Clifford's

cheek—he had not dodged quickly enough, and Topaz's blade had achieved a glancing strike.

He paused, breathing hard and snarling at Topaz. He no longer looked like a mild rabbit but a ferret half mad with excitement.

"I can kill him, you know," he told Topaz, once more waving the electrodes in Rom's direction. "There's such a fine line between torment and death, and it would not take much to break his mind. Then my good friend, your father, will banish his spirit and replace it with another."

Topaz turned her head and looked at her father. "Would you do such a thing? Use your talents to banish a spirit from its holy dwelling place for money?"

Frederick did not reply. He stood as if frozen, his dark eyes glittering, and regarded his daughter.

Clifford once more emitted his disturbing, high-pitched giggle. "Do you expect him to have scruples? He's a gypsy. Beneath all the trappings, the fine clothes, and the grand home, he's no better than the filthy tinkers who roamed the fens back where I was born."

Still Frederick did not react. Rom, fighting his way through the aftermath of pain, swaying where he hung, blinked at him.

Clifford, electrodes still in gloved hands, turned to face Frederick. Blood dripped down his cheek and spattered on the floor.

"You know we have to finish it. Things have gone too far now. It's perhaps unfortunate your children became involved, but their loyalties are obviously engaged and those loyalties do not belong to you. We have a paying customer for the agent's body, and it's the perfect solution." He flicked his gaze at Rom. "A very wealthy woman described in some detail the new body she wants for her husband's spirit. You fit the bill almost perfectly."

Vomit rose into the back of Rom's throat. And did Hathor have the power to tear his spirit away from Topaz?

"No," Topaz said and backed up so she stood directly in front of Rom, so close he could feel the heat of her body. "You will have to go through me."

Clifford sneered. "Remove her, Hathor."

Topaz looked at her father, and Rom, through their connection, felt her defenses rise. Could she withstand Hathor? He'd been able to overwhelm both her and Sapphire at Forest Lawn. Upon that thought, Rom looked at Sapphire who lay—supposedly still insensate—on a second metal table. Sapphire's eyes were open and full of caution.

Frederick extended a hand to Topaz. "Do not make me harm you, Daughter. Give me the weapon."

She shook her head, and her black hair brushed the new burns on Rom's chest. He felt her spirit rise still more fiercely and knew at that moment she would fight to the death for him.

"If you do not want to kill them outright," Clifford insinuated, "then we will keep their bodies alive. You can deal with their troublesome spirits." He flicked Topaz with his gaze. "She's a robust specimen, if lacking in refinement. I am sure such a flesh host would fetch a fine price."

Frederick stirred at last and turned toward his associate. "You're asking me to cast my own children into the outer darkness?"

"They have proved disloyal to you and—as I have pointed out—know too much. If you do not wish to do the job, have the unit strap them to the tables and I will do what's needed with these." He raised the electrodes, still live and sparking.

"Father," Topaz said. Only that one word, but it caught all of Frederick's attention.

Rom wondered suddenly what lay between them. From the moment he'd met Topaz she'd displayed dissatisfaction with her father. Yet, as Rom well knew, blood ties ran deep.

For an instant longer Frederick hesitated, his glittering gaze fixed on the floor rather than on his daughter. Then, with a sudden movement, he turned away and spoke to the steam unit that stood by.

"Take her. Subdue her. Let it be done."

Chapter Thirty-Seven

Breathing hard, air scorching her lungs even as she fought her bonds, Topaz writhed on the table. Her ears still rang with the percussion of the steam blast fired in the confined space. The steam unit, taking her father's orders literally, had caught her a glancing blow with it. Part of her right side, from her breast down, had been seared by superheated steam.

Some of her writhing came of pain, some from rage. Her feelings for her father rose in such a fierce wave they nearly choked her. Their relationship had always been complicated, but deep inside she'd believed that in his twisted way he did love her.

She found that impossible to believe now. Bitterness joined the anger that choked her. Frederick Hathor—the great spirit master—had chosen wealth over decency and traded his conscience to this madman with the graveyard skills. And now—now he chose his own welfare and survival over that of his own child.

It is all about survival, Daughter.

How many times had he said those words to her over the years? Enough that she now seemed to hear them in her mind.

The steamie had relentlessly closed on her, wrested away her stiletto, and strapped her down to the table—the same where Rose had been brought back to life. And would her father truly let Clifford keep her body alive, replace her spirit with another? Would he banish Rom's spirit, as well?

Upon that thought she turned her eyes on him. Obviously in agony, his wrists strained white, he hung from the iron pipe, his feet reaching desperately for the floor. New, livid burns marked the skin of his chest, but his blue gaze reached for Topaz, vital as a touch.

She drew a deeper, easier breath. She could endure so long as she felt him, as she first had when he appeared in her room.

And when the Undertaker's work was done, would her spirit and Rom's join together? That alone might make her fate bearable. But, ah, she would have liked to love that body of his one more time.

The steam plant, still chugging away, drummed in her ears in time with her heartbeat. The sound blotted out the words her father and the Undertaker exchanged. That they planned the event of her death, and Rom's, she did not doubt.

But what was death? What life? Did it end with the flesh? If Clifford could be believed, her flesh would live on, sold to the highest bidder, taken away to some far place where no one would recognize her. Her spirit, she knew, would live on also—but not a life she could easily comprehend. No sting of sleet on her cheek, no hunger or thirst, no desire. She looked again at the man who hung from the pipe. No tasting the enticing tang of his flesh or feeling him plunge into her, bringing unimaginable completeness. She wanted that—oh, how she did!

The argument, for such it was, between Frederick and Clifford grew louder. Did her father still resist after all? But maybe they argued only over methods. She pressed her eyes closed and prayed to she knew not what. She did not wish to watch Rom die. Call her cowardly, but she couldn't bear it. *Please let them kill— or banish—me first.*

"Topaz."

At first her ears barely caught the hiss that came from the direction of Sapphire's table. When he had remained still for so long, she'd believed him unconscious. Now she turned her head to find his dark gaze, narrowed between black lashes, fixed upon her.

Her heart leaped again, this time with hope. Like her, Clifford and Frederick must have supposed Sapphire sufficiently incapacitated that they'd failed to strap him down. She didn't know what had happened to him during that terrible psychic flash at Forest Lawn, but he had clearly regained his senses.

He mouthed something, the words making barely a sound. With the boiler hammering in the background Topaz couldn't hear. She shook her head and stole a look at her father. Abruptly, Sapphire's voice invaded her mind.

Join with me.

She started, and Frederick twitched his shoulder almost as if he heard. Not daring to turn her gaze back on her brother, she thought instead, *How?*

Mind.

That hadn't worked in the graveyard; even together they had insufficient power to defeat Frederick. Yet what options did she have? She contemplated it as ruthlessly as she ever had a physical opponent and decided, as she always would, to fight.

She gave Sapphire one nod. *When?*

Now, he told her and leaped from the table.

He made not for the steamie—still armed—or for his father, but for the Undertaker. Before Topaz could blink he had the frail man in his clutches, one arm hard across his throat, the other around his rib cage, making of him a shield.

Frederick, shocked for once, stepped back. The armed steamie raised its cannon but could not shoot without hitting Clifford.

"It's over, Father," Sapphire said in a voice that bore no relation to his usual smooth tones. "All done. Release Topaz and her companion or I'll crush his windpipe."

Sapphire, who had taught Topaz to fight, knew how to make good on the threat. A man's windpipe, so he had once told her, was nothing but a thin tube and easily collapsed—a vulnerable point, were she ever attacked.

Now he looked like nothing so much as an assassin, dark hair mussed, eyes glittering, and face intent. Frederick must believe him, yet he made no assent. Instead he attempted to speak.

"Son—you must not betray me."

Sapphire howled a cry of pain. "Why not? Tell me, Father." He made of the last word an epithet. "What have you ever given me?"

"Security, a strong roof over your head. Good food in your belly. A superior education, and every advantage in choosing a career," Frederick retorted. "Far more than your forefathers ever had."

"We are not our forefathers!"

"We are, though, son. We are the ones who were hounded and chased across Europe, whose children slept on the cold ground, who were exterminated like foxes. The ability we carry comes from them. Would you betray the memory of all they endured and what they fought to pass on?"

Sapphire bared his teeth. "You are the one guilty of betrayal! You're selling their sacred talent to the highest bidders."

"An easy mark is an easy mark, Sapphire—wherever he may be found."

"So," Sapphire sneered, "you are no more than a schemer, a user, a dirty gypsy."

"Don't say that." Topaz rarely heard her father angry. He seldom had cause to raise his voice, but he did so now, and his will flared up to clash with that of his son. Topaz distinctly felt them mesh and battle, and raised her own strength to support her brother, eyes riveted to her father's face. It flushed with rage and then drained white.

"We are the sum of our ancestors," Frederick insisted, "but so much more. We have achieved more than they dreamed. I cannot let you toss all that away, Sapphire. You must see I cannot."

With that, Frederick unleashed his power, hurled it like a whip, striking Sapphire in a burning lash of pain. Topaz, who caught the mere edge of it, did not know how Sapphire kept his knees from buckling.

"You think you can defeat me, Sapphire?" Frederick roared. "I, who gave you life?"

Sapphire swayed where he stood. The steamie, wholly flummoxed, posed with the steam cannon pointed at Sapphire's head, awaiting orders.

But Sapphire and his father were locked in a battle of wills, one perhaps many years overdue. Topaz, immobile yet linked in spirit with both her brother and

Rom, felt Sapphire draw strength from her, strength with which to fight.

Still with his fingers clamped around Clifford's throat, he stared into his father's eyes—and squeezed.

"Cut them loose," he grated, "or by all the gods, I will kill him."

"Go ahead," Frederick told him. "I've already learned his methods and no longer need him. And I don't think you have the balls for it."

"Do it," Rom urged suddenly, hoarse with agony. "Remove the blight from the world."

At the sound of his voice, Topaz arched her body, fighting for freedom. But she could not break the bonds that fixed her to the table.

Sapphire, never looking away from his father or so much as blinking, tightened his fingers and twisted brutally. Clifford made a strangled sound and sagged to Sapphire's feet.

"Shoot him," Frederick commanded, and the steamie fired.

Chapter Thirty-Eight

The second steam blast in the confined space almost blew out Rom's eardrums. He felt the various spirits that always flocked around Frederick Hathor flee, even as he ducked instinctively away from the scorching blast.

They must have heard that—and the last impact—upstairs, he thought, even as his eyes sought Sapphire. Hurt? Dead? No, though he had landed on the floor when he ducked and rolled away beneath another of the tables. Was he trying to get behind his father? Trying to reach Topaz where she lay?

Frederick whirled, and the steamie with him. Rom—utterly vulnerable where he hung—knew the steamie's side cannon would take many seconds to recharge. Sapphire must know it also, for he leaped upon his father even as the automaton raised the weapon again.

As soon as Sapphire's fingers closed on Frederick a terrible power rose in the room, the full fury of Frederick's outrage at being attacked by his son.

Momentarily forgotten, Rom drew himself up and examined his situation. He cared far less for himself than for Topaz—freeing her and getting her away out of this madness.

He eyed the chains from which he hung, which ended in the manacles on his wrists. They'd been slung over the pipe that ran beneath the ceiling joists, not affixed permanently as in the torture room at Grayson. He sucked in a breath, tensed all his muscles, and almost unconsciously drew on the connection between him and Topaz for the required strength.

She turned her head and looked at him. He could feel her deliberately lend her will as he began to slowly draw himself up, climbing the chains, reaching for the pipe which clattered and flexed beneath his weight.

He slipped and felt Topaz buoy him. His grasping, half-numb fingers reached for the metal pipe, gripped it securely. He hauled himself up even as the room shuddered with the impact of Frederick's ire.

The pipe over which his chain had been slung did not reach the ceiling. Not till he had hauled himself up could he be sure he'd fit between the joists and be able to squeeze over it. A tight fit, for sure, but he plunged forward, wriggling like an eel, and forced his way through, losing half the skin on his back.

He leaped down, and the steamie saw him. It whirled and fired the weapon, missing Rom with all but a sizzling frisson of air. Rom ducked and, the heavy chains dragging from his wrists, crept to Topaz's table and popped up beside her.

Golden eyes, half maddened, stared into his. "He's going to kill Sapphire. I can feel it."

Rom could feel a lot of things—far too many: Topaz's fear and love for him, her love for both men who thrashed together on the floor. He did not even pause to ask which *he* she meant. Her bonds fastened with stiff buckles; he began working on the first of them frantically.

"No," she begged. "Not me. Stop them. Stop

them."

He could feel what she felt, it filled him also, a backwash of what she collected through her connections with both men. He ignored her; he cared little for anything beyond her safety.

"Rom, please!"

He ducked instinctively as the steamie, now completely adrift and without direction, fired again. He gasped, feeling Topaz's pain as the beam passed directly above her body. The blast struck the boiler, and the room exploded.

Topaz screamed, a sound Rom felt even more than heard. Steam, fire, and boiling water erupted from the breached boiler on the far side of the room. Had Rom still been hanging from his beam, he would have been cooked alive.

"Sapphire!" Topaz cried. Or did she only think it? Rom could no longer see the two men. Clouds of steam and a flood of hot water began to fill the space. A jet of water struck the automaton and took it down; the cannon fell from its grip.

Rom dragged himself back up and set to work on the buckles again. All the while Topaz's will beat at him, demanding he go to Sapphire's aid. But he could hear flames from the generator crackling up the wall behind him, and if she thought he would do anything before he got her out of here, she was mad indeed.

The first buckle came undone and he moved to the second. Topaz's free hand clutched him with dire strength.

"Help him."

The battle on the floor—more spiritual than physical—continued. Rom spared one look for the two men locked together before he returned all his attention to his task. The hot water flooding the floor had not reached them yet, though it had now engulfed the fallen steamie and fast approached the rest of them.

The second buckle came free and Topaz popped upright. She screamed at her brother, "Sapphire!"

At that instant, unbearable pain invaded Rom's skull. It took him a moment to realize it stemmed from Frederick Hathor and came to him from Sapphire—its recipient—through Topaz.

Sapphire went still. Rom, working on the last of Topaz's buckles at her right ankle, actually felt his consciousness leave the room. Dead? He didn't know and had no intention of waiting to see. He gathered Topaz into his arms and, turning his back on the terrible scene, went through the door.

The barren corridor met his gaze. To the left lay more doors and a blank wall, to the right the flight of stairs that led up.

He could now hear flames crackling in the room behind him. Topaz seized his arm.

"Fire! We can't leave him there. We have to go back for him."

"Which of them?" Rom asked.

"Sapphire."

"I'll come back for him. I'm getting you out of here first."

"There's no time!"

He started for the stairs and heard a roar behind him. He whirled at the foot of the steps, Topaz clutched against his chest, and beheld...

It must be Frederick Hathor, but it didn't look like him. This figure, misshapen, appeared as nothing so much as a dark form surrounded by a corona of light. Power, Rom thought, even as his spirit shrank from the aspect.

"Stop," Hathor cried.

Topaz wriggled in Rom's arms and slid to her feet. Rom felt the strength within her stir. She raised it even as she might the stiletto, a purely defensive action.

"Where's Sapphire?" she asked, her voice broken. "Have you killed him? Did you kill your own son?"

Frederick shook his head slowly. Regretfully he said, "Daughter, I cannot let you go, lest you betray me."

Topaz's head came up. "You can rely on it."

"Then I must overwhelm you, as I did your brother. I am sorry. It is not what I ever wanted to do."

"Father, it doesn't have to be this way. We can—"

Topaz got no further. Frederick unleashed his full power at Topaz, and Rom felt the snap of it through her consciousness, enough to rattle his teeth. Topaz stiffened and, dredging strength from somewhere, withstood the onslaught. For half a dozen heartbeats the two of them stood facing one another, father and daughter, before he heard Topaz's voice in his mind.

Go.

"No." He said it out loud, every part of him rejecting the prospect. They were truly joined; he would stand with her even if it cost his life.

"Get help. Get Pat."

"I won't leave you."

The crackle of flames had grown louder. The glow from the other room made a ghastly backdrop for what Frederick Hathor had become—a figure of darkness, unredeemable, lost. Topaz seemed to realize that at the same instant as Rom. She tossed back her hair, screamed, and called up her full power.

Rom felt it come—not easily—clawing and scratching, fighting its way up through her to get out. Dazzlingly bright, golden as the sun, it streamed forth into the corridor to battle the darkness. ·

For one blessed, glorious moment Rom thought she must win. He saw Frederick's knees buckle before the man caught himself and stumbled backward. Of course, Rom thought—because darkness couldn't stand against true light.

But Frederick regained himself and bared his teeth at his daughter. The spirits of the place, so recently driven away, streamed back, poured into him, and augmented his strength, which he thrust into a gout of power.

It caught Topaz in a net woven of darkness, cast by her father's mind. Rom felt her stiffen, experienced her terror and pain, and his heart fell. He caught her in his arms before she could sag, and bore her upward.

Frederick Hathor, caught in his daughter's defeat, did not notice the figure that dragged itself up by the frame of the doorway behind him. He never looked around to see the ghastly look on Sapphire's face, or to notice the weapon in his hand.

Topaz's stiletto.

The blade took Frederick Hathor just beneath the left shoulder blade in a perfect position to pierce his heart.

Frederick fell, and a cloud of what looked like multicolored steam arose from his flesh. Vast it was, deeply dyed in red like rubies, green like emeralds, sapphire blue, and the bright glow of topaz. It gathered all the other spirits into it and ascended through the ceiling of the cellar, into the house, and out of sight.

"Sapphire!" Topaz cried. Rom turned in time to catch Sapphire as he went down. A glance into the room from which he had emerged showed it engulfed in flame, with Clifford—not dead after all but boiling in water and steam—moving feebly.

"Leave him," Sapphire croaked when Rom would have ducked back in. His eyes met Rom's. "Let the evil burn—let all of it burn."

Chapter Thirty-Nine

The fire followed them as they struggled up the stairs, both Topaz and Rom supporting Sapphire between them. As Topaz told herself with every step, if the door at the top proved locked, they would all die down here together.

It wasn't till she touched the door she realized something besides the fire followed them. A glance behind showed her Clifford, scalded by boiling water, his face and hands red and blotched, had dragged himself from the inner room and pushed past Frederick's body and up the hallway.

Without conscious thought, she turned the doorknob. The door opened, and she thrust both Rom and her brother through.

"Take him, Rom. I'll handle this."

"No—" Rom began, and she felt his protest arc through her.

She slammed the door on him, whirled, and drew a breath. No weapon, save her body. It would have to be enough. Her gaze skimmed the blackened, lifeless form that had once been her father before fastening on Clifford.

His eyes, bloodshot and set in a face now mottled and barely recognizable, held no mercy. How many poor souls had looked into those eyes, searching for humanity that didn't exist?

He had already lost his soul; she had only to finish his flesh.

She flew down the stairs on eager feet. If she were to die here, lost to the now-roaring flames, it would not be too high a price so long as she took this monster with her.

The power of that thought sent her feet first into Clifford, heedless of all else. Her boots took him in the chest and knocked him over. She landed on top of him, face to face, her eyes staring into the darkness that possessed him.

"Be gone," she told him.

"Not unless I take you with me."

His hands closed around her throat. Pain blossomed as he found the pressure points there, and darkness rushed at her, composed of hate and greed and all the emotions that made him the abomination he was.

"I think I will appropriate your body," he said. "You see, mine is ruined. But yours—strong and supple. Only imagine what I might accomplish with it."

"Never." She bared her teeth and fought back, breaking his grip and smashing his head against the stone floor. But his fury, that of a maddened creature, had him reaching for her again. This time his fingers tightened till she saw dark spots dance against the bright flames roaring down the hallway.

Topaz! Rom's voice screamed in her mind. He could feel her peril through their connection. Would he be forced to feel her die?

No. Instead her spirit rose up in a wall of brightness to confront Clifford's intense darkness. Like a golden shield, she raised and battered him with it, bright and savage, finding at last the might that had always dwelt within.

His eyes widened and his fingers slackened. His head struck the stone floor one last time before his spirit—dark as foul smoke—left his body and hovered above it.

Topaz, still gasping, recoiled as from the stench of decay. On her feet, she backed toward the stairs even as his foul spirit reached for her with tendrils like fingers. Her mind, working now without her intent, caught up her own brightness and made of it armor—that not of a flesh-and-blood warrior but a spiritual one. Clifford's darkness rebounded from it, arose like a hive of bees, and streamed away through the ceiling.

Topaz drew a breath—hot from the encroaching flames and scampered for the stairs. The flames would take Clifford's body even as they must consume her father's. She felt a twinge of loss but dismissed it even as she dragged herself up the stairs and ducked through the door into the kitchen. Time later to sort out her complicated feelings for her father. Not now.

Abovestairs she found chaos and a great deal of smoke. Steamies stood everywhere in various states of shutdown. In the grand foyer she found Rom ushering out the last of the human servants while Sapphire, much recovered, held their mother caught in his arms.

"Topaz!" Dahlia called. "What's happening? Where's your father?"

Where, indeed? Topaz fancied she could feel his spirit all around her, just as she felt Rom's relief when he turned and saw her. Impossible to imagine the spirit master could be destroyed.

"Get outside," she told her mother and cast a look at Rom. "The house is going to come down. Is that everyone?"

He nodded, reached out, and threaded his fingers through hers. They exited together with Sapphire carrying Dahlia, to find confusion in the street, as well.

The first person she saw—Patrick Kelly—gave orders to the fire wagon that had just arrived. Two more steamed up the Parkway. Sleet fell from an ink-black sky like needles, pelting everyone. Neighbors and their servants poured from other houses to observe the spectacle.

Topaz, with Rom's arm now wrapped around her, turned to look also.

The house, flames soaring upward from the cellar, looked like a candle-lit jack-o-lantern, the windows ghostly carved orifices. Topaz watched the last of the spirits—those always attracted to Frederick Hathor—stream away as might bats from a cave, into the deeper darkness of the sky.

Did that mean he was gone, his spirit also driven away? Did they follow him even yet?

"Frederick!" Dahlia screamed desperately as the flames leaped higher, into the second and third floors. She fought against Sapphire, who still held her. "Let me go to him."

"Mother, no." Sapphire wrapped his arms around her more tightly, and she dissolved into sobs against his chest.

Patrick Kelly approached, clad in his police uniform, his face expressionless.

"Miss Topaz, I am glad to see you safe. Do you know if anyone remains inside? I would not wish to risk members of my squad needlessly, but will send them in if there is a chance of saving human life."

"Steam units," she replied. "My father—dead. Clifford—dead."

"Dead?" Rom repeated in wonder.

"I finished him myself." She looked at Pat. "Self-defense."

He nodded.

She asked, "Has this become an official investigation?"

"Indeed. I will need to take statements from everyone involved. But that can wait." He looked at the building, already well beyond salvage. The fire wagons concentrated on keeping the neighboring homes dampened down. "Meanwhile, let it burn. There is, I believe, such a thing as cleansing fire."

Topaz reached out and clasped Pat's hand. He looked startled and even more so when tears came to her eyes.

"Thank you, Pat. You are an extraordinary friend, and it's an honor to know you."

He smiled, pure Irish. "Likewise. I can only say you are a woman of great courage."

"*My* woman of great courage." Rom's arms tightened. He inquired of Pat, "Is Rose safe?"

"I left her under the protection of some friends."

Topaz looked at Pat seriously. "Now that this is over, she won't do anything…dangerous to herself, will she?"

"I assure you, Miss Topaz, I will not allow that." Pat exhaled steam into the hot air. "I believe if anyone can persuade her to exist in a body she finds repugnant, it is I."

He walked away before Topaz could speak the words that sprang to mind: *Rose is a lucky woman.* She relaxed back against Rom. *But not so lucky as me.* "Is it over?" she murmured. "Please tell me it's over."

"I believe so," Rom whispered in her ear, and sent a frisson of delight through her weary body. "Just the pieces left to pick up."

A terrible, great number of pieces, Topaz acknowledged. But for now she could only stand and watch her family home burn.

Chapter Forty

"You'll be anxious to get back to England," Topaz said, gazing into the bottomless blue depths of Romney Gideon's eyes. She could feel the longing for home simmering inside him just as she could feel everything else: the healing of his body and spirit and his love for her, steady and bright. "To your marshes, your ancient fens—that place you love so well."

Rom's only reply came as he pressed his mouth to hers in a warm, languorous kiss. They'd spent the last two days and nights in bed, back at the Kilters', with only brief intervals otherwise, to make statements to Pat Kelly and various members of the Buffalo police force. Topaz didn't even need to eat, not food anyway. All her cravings centered upon this man within her reach.

But now restlessness stirred inside her. Things between them needed to be settled, questions answered.

"That always was the plan, to solve the Undertaker problem and go home." He stretched his naked body beneath hers and palmed one breast. "Come with me, Topaz. Embrace the roving gypsy you are inside."

"Is that what I am?" She tossed her hair over her back. She'd lost track of how many times she'd ridden Rom in the last two days—tasted him, given herself to him so completely she barely knew who or what she was anymore. Her identity hadn't mattered much because every time they made love she could feel him grow stronger, and that in turn restored her strength. One thing seemed evident: it would not be healthy for them to part.

"Kiss me again," he requested, and she did, open-mouthed, even as his fingers, still at her breast, coaxed a maximum response. "My wild gypsy." His eyes smiled into hers. Did her future lie in that smile?

"I'm not sure I can face making any plans just yet," she confessed. "I can't imagine what the Kilters must think of us, shut away here together all this time."

"I can." The smile in his eyes deepened. "Haven't you noticed the way they look at each other? Just what do you suppose goes on in their room, eh?"

Topaz laughed softly, and some of her tension eased.

Rom kissed one corner of her mouth and then the other. "I should return to England, love, if only to accept my commendation from the Queen. She wishes to congratulate me on my success in defeating the dread Undertaker who threatened to besmirch her nation's reputation. You really should come along, if only because you're the one who actually defeated him."

"We did it together, everything together."

"Then what's this doubt I see in your eyes?"

Topaz didn't know; she couldn't understand why she felt so torn. She lifted herself from atop him and sat on the edge of the bed. His spirit protested for an instant before it became acquiescent. Was this how it had been for her father—living in essence two lives, one in the physical world and one parallel to it, always seeing and sensing? No wonder he'd lost all perspective.

She'd worked hard all her life to keep her barriers raised, to build a protective shell around herself made of equal parts terror and confidence. But the barriers between her and Rom had long since fallen, and she knew he could feel her emotions just as she could feel his. Lucky for her he was sensitive and decent enough to allow her space when she required it—like now.

She experienced his desire to touch her, to tangle his fingers in her hair and smooth his palm down her naked back. This shared experience made the sex outrageously good. It also put a dent in her long-standing and hard-earned autonomy.

"Perhaps," she said slowly, testing the waters, "you should go on your own, give us a chance to see if we can manage to exist apart."

He drew a breath that she felt, but he said nothing.

"Perhaps," she pressed, "we need that before we make the decisions we must."

He said, sounding very casual for all the turmoil she felt inside him, "Decisions are easy enough to make."

"Are they?"

"People make them right and left. Your brother and Carly have decided to get married as soon as possible and try for another child."

"So they have."

"Your mother has decided to go live with her sister in Boston."

"Yes."

"Rose has decided to choose life—and to share it with Pat."

Foolish tears rose to clog Topaz's throat. She had never seen Pat Kelly so happy. As for Rose, she'd found love without strings, belonging without demand.

"James and Cat," Rom went on softly, "have

decided to have the first of what will no doubt be a brood of happy children, affirming their faith in the future. And Greta," he indicated the big dog now lying at Topaz's feet, "has decided to trust again."

Tears—which Topaz so seldom shed—began trickling down her cheeks.

Rom laid his palm against her back. "Go ahead, love—weep for him. He was your father."

She turned in a rush to face him and saw only loving sympathy in his eyes. "He's not gone, you know. Oh, his spirit is—I felt it go, stream away. But he lives here in me—in my heart and my head." She clasped her hands to her breasts. "That's the awful thing."

"The wonderful thing," he corrected gently. "It makes you the woman you are, the spirit you are. I fell in love with that spirit first—with its strength, its recklessness, its beauty, many-faceted like a jewel. Your father was right. You are his gems, the things of beauty he created."

"I should want to run away, to go with you to England and escape all the memories. I should jump at the chance. But this city is part of me—the light and the dark of it, the place where I grew. Maybe this gypsy has put down roots after all."

"Then," he said affectionately, "far be it from me to pull them up."

"You'll go without me and accept your commendation from the Queen?"

"If I did, I imagine I'd still be able to feel you in spirit. Just as Sapphire feels Carly and recalls a past they shared, as Rose feels the humanity trapped in Pat's steel shell. We can't really part, can we?"

Topaz closed her eyes, trying to imagine what it

would mean to send him away from her, to feel the cord forged that first night in her bedroom stretch all the way across an ocean. To reach for him and not feel him there beneath her fingers.

She asked, trying mightily to hide her dread, "When does the Queen expect you?"

"The ceremony's set for February second."

She opened her eyes, startled. "But that means you'd have to leave almost at once."

"I don't *have* to do anything." He caught her fingers and raised them to his lips. "Tell me, Topaz Hathor, what you want from your future."

Her answer surprised her. "To use this new ability that's come alive inside me—but not as my father did. I want to help not harm, to call upon the spirit that inhabits everyone from streetwalkers to automatons."

"A noble intention."

"Is it? Because I'm thinking it could be a battle fought down and dirty. Speaking of streetwalkers—I'd like to do more to help those girls and provide them with choices. I could open a refuge, a safe house like this place, only for women."

The smile in Rom's eyes intensified, reaching to Topaz's heart. "That's my girl. You should have the money to accomplish it, when all's said and done and your father's estate is settled."

"I suppose I will. I'll be a woman of independent means at last."

As if he couldn't help himself, he ran his fingers through her hair. "And I should let you be just that."

Topaz protested, "I didn't mean—"

"I know, but our bonding came swift and hard. You may need some time on your own."

"No." Tears filled her eyes, but she lifted her chin. "Is that how it seemed when I gave myself to you there in Forest Lawn? When we pledged our lives to each other? In truth, we need no marriage ceremony, Romney Gideon. And I need no time away from you."

"Your decision to make, my love." He raised her fingers once more to his lips. "But, at the very least, you need someone to put you first for a while." His gaze kindled. "Let that be me."

"What about England?"

"Forget England." He drew her down upon him, full body contact.

"What about the Queen?"

"Let her wait. She can postpone the ceremony or hold it without me. If and when we go to England, it will be together. Together, love. Do you understand?"

"I do," she agreed, as her body eased onto his and their spirits mingled with a delicious sense of belonging.

"Because parting from you," he whispered a moment before he kissed her, "would be sheer madness."

A word about the author...

Born in Buffalo and raised on the Niagara Frontier, Laura Strickland has been an avid reader and writer since childhood. She believes the spunky, tenacious, undefeatable ethnic mix that is Buffalo spells the perfect setting for a little Steampunk, so she created her own Victorian world there. She knows the people of Buffalo are stronger, tougher, and smarter than those who haven't survived the muggy summers and blizzard blasts found on the shores of the mighty Niagara. Tough enough to survive a squad of automatons? Well, just maybe.